BOOKS BY NIKKI RAE

FANGIRL SERIES
REBLOGS & HEARTS
SUMMER TOURS & HEARTS
HOMERUNS & HEARTS
BOOKMARKS & HEARTS

BOOKMARKS & Hearts

NIKKI RAE

ISBN-13: 9798991474160

Cover design made using Canva (canva.com) by: Nikki Rae
Graphics designs by: Nikki Rae

Library of Congress Control Number:
Printed in the United States of America

DEDICATION

For all the book lovers, writers, artists and creatives. Don't let anyone or anything dim your shining light. The world needs your stories, your art, your creativity.

DELANEY

The crowd was going wild for the three ladies on stage with extraordinary love stories. The fanfiction writer who fell in love with her inspiration. The best friend stuck in between her two best friends the wild rockstar and the quiet, responsible one. The baseball loving girl who met her hero then faked dated him until falling in love for real. All were the stories you would find in books and that is why Delaney Bishop was up on stage with them in front of thousands of fans. Their love stories were now a series of books taking the literary world by storm.

Emerson Holbrook leaned forward, "So Delaney, who are you a fan of that you could potentially fall in love with?"

"Oh, I don't know…" Delaney's cheeks burned, "Probably the closest person I would be considered a fan of would be Graham A. Jacob."

Laurel Adler brought her mic up, "That name sounds familiar."

Delaney smiled, "He's a New York Times Bestseller for his thriller series, *The Lost and Abandoned.* He is famously known for never doing press or promotion tours for his books. No one has seen him in public and if they did they wouldn't have known it. He never has an author photo, and a lot of people think he's a pen name for some other famous author."

"Ohhh, intrigue and mystery." Emerson said then her eyes widened, "Wait… is this the author who is coming to your bookshop?"

Raelyn Burton-Jameson piped in, "Oh yeah, if you guys didn't already know. Delaney has an amazing indie bookshop that everyone should support. It's the cutest bookshop I've ever been to. Tell us a little more about it as well."

"Thank you, I really appreciate that," Delaney smiled proudly, "My best friend, Quinn and I, opened the Scattered Pages five years ago after I had ended a very toxic relationship. Since then, we've been voted the number one indie bookshop in Chicago two years in row. We carry a lot of local Midwestern authors including these amazing ladies on stage."

The audience clapped and cheered as Laurel patted Emerson's knee, "Well some of us aren't truly from the Midwest but we accept her anyway."

"Hey! I still come back to Chicago to visit, and I'll be tagging along with Delaney when the convention is over." The crowd booed, "We still have plenty of convention time left. I mean, have you seen the main event panel?"

There was another round of deafening cheers, "I mean those guys are pretty hot and funny. Hopefully, you'll give them hell."

"Back to Delaney…" Raelyn redirected the conversation to Delaney's dismay, "Tell us about your book and more about the elusive Graham Jacob coming to your shop on his book tour."

She remembered her and Quinn jumping like crazy fangirls meeting their favorite boyband after receiving the news that Graham Jacob was coming to their shop. It was the first time he had ever done a public press tour for any of his books. He kept his life private, and Delaney had a certain respect for that. She also happened to be one of his biggest fans and owned every book he had ever written.

"We're extremely excited to be hosting Graham Jacob during his book tour. Much like you ladies are fans of actors, musicians, athletes. I'm a huge fan of his books and can't wait to read the last book in his epic mystery series." Delaney felt her cheeks suddenly burning, "It's no secret that his books had a great influence on me and my writing. I chose to write romantic thrillers combining my two favorite genres."

Laurel reached into her bag beside her chair, "I just happen to have an advance reader's copy of Delaney's book right here. I have to say not only did the thriller aspects keep me on the edge of my seat, but the slow burn romance was…" She gave a chef's kiss.

Delaney's stomach tightened uncomfortably from the praise, and she forced her lips into a wide smile.

"I really appreciate that, Laurel. I'm excited for the world to read Hope and Alex's story."

She looked over to Leigh who was giving her the wrap it up signal.

Emerson reached over, patting her hand, "So, from everything I've heard there's still a chance to live out your own fangirl love story."

"We'll see, but for now I would love for everyone to give a round of applause for Raelyn Burton-Jameson, Laurel Adler and Emerson Holbrook!"

Delaney followed the others off stage, watching as they each went to their significant other. A dull ache began to radiate over her chest seeing the happy couples talking with one another. She spotted Emerson looking her way and Delaney averted her eyes to her bag. She focused on putting her things away when she heard Emerson called out her name.

"Delaney, get your ass over here." Emerson waved her over.

She was terribly awkward in social interactions especially with couples. She tended to be stand-offish when it came to being around men. Even though she knew Austin, Zeppelin, Pacey and Thomas were all great guys. Past experiences had hardened her towards men in general.

"Hey, we're all going to have dinner tonight after the convention. We were hoping you would join us." Emerson said as her boyfriend Pacey Tucker wrapped his arms around her.

Raelyn slipped her arm around Delaney's shoulders, "Don't let Emerson pressure you into going. We'd love for you to come if you feel up to it. I know from personal experience that conventions can be draining on your social battery."

"Thanks, maybe I'll go back to my room and rest for a little while then meet you all for dinner. Text me where you guys decide to go." She was thankful for Raelyn being able to pick up on her social panic and giving her an out.

"Sounds good." Emerson said as the group started to head back towards the green room, "I'm sorry if it sounded like I was trying to pressure you. I just want everyone to get to know you like I have these last couple of months."

Delaney gave Emerson a one arm hug, "I know and I really want to get to know you all. I'm just not good with social gatherings."

Emerson pulled her into a tight hug, "That's perfectly okay. We're all here for you whenever you're ready. No pressure or expectations. Also know that we'll spam your text messages every chance we get."

"Oh, I know." Delaney laughed, "I appreciate it though, truly. I'll try really hard to come out but I'll let you know if I'm not up to it."

Emerson nodded then headed off in the direction of the others giving Delaney her first opportunity to breathe comfortably for the first time all day. She made her way back to her hotel room on the upper levels of the convention hotel. The mix of fans at the convention was mind blowing. The majority of them were Red Moon fans followed closely by Heartstrings fans with brightly colored hair wearing all black and fishnets. Finally, there were quite a few baseball fans who had braved the convention to meet their favorite player. As she rode the elevator up, a couple of girls wearing Red Moon shirts with Explorer jerseys got into the car with her.

She loved moments like this where no one knew who she was. She was just a lucky girl who happened to get to moderate a panel at the convention. The girls got off on the floor below hers and once again, Delaney was alone. Walking into her room, she headed straight for her bed and flopped down on top of it. Her tense body finally relaxing and nearly melting into the mattress. That's when her phone started to buzz. Looking at the screen she smiled.

"Hi Quinn."

"About damn time you answered the phone. How did it go? Tell me everything? Did you meet the guys? Are they as hot in person as they are on screen? Don't leave me hanging." Quinn Larson, spoke at lightning speed which only Delaney could understand after twenty plus years of friendship.

Delaney had to remind herself that she loved her outgoing, extroverted best friend, "Slow down my brain is running, at best, at thirty-five percent. Everything went fine. The girls were great during the panel, and I didn't fuck up anything. I met the guys, yes they're hot. Now I'm hiding in my hotel room trying to convince myself to be a normal human being and go to dinner with them in a few hours."

There was a long moment of silence before Quinn spoke. Her voice soft and nurturing as if she were approaching a wounded animal on the side of the road. Delaney was used to this by Quinn, her parents and even her twin brother. Sometimes it pissed her off and other times, like now, she appreciated their care.

"I'm sorry. I was just excited to hear about your first convention experience. I'm glad it went well."

"It's fine. I'm sorry my temper is short." She sighed as the guilt pressed down on her chest, "I promise I'll tell you everything when I get home tomorrow. You're still able to pick me and Emerson up from the airport?"

"Yes, I'll be there in my chauffeur's hat and name sign." Quinn chuckled, "It'll be good to have you back. The kids listen to you way better than me."

Delaney laughed imagining their store clerks causing chaos for her friend, "That's because you're the fun parent and I discipline them. I'm excited to get back and get everything finalized for Graham Jacob's event."

Quinn blew out a raspberry making her giggle, "You worry too much. Everything is going to be fine and you'll have your moment to fangirl all over him."

"It's like you don't even know me. I'm going to get off here and try to relax for the rest of the evening. I'll see you tomorrow. Love ya sis."

"Love ya too."

The call ended and Delaney let out a long sigh. Sometimes she wished she could be like Graham Jacob and disappear from society. Living in solitude, writing books and making a career of it. As much as she loved her family, friends and bookshop, she would give it all up for a cabin in the woods with no one around her. Delaney opened her text thread with the Fangirl authors.

I think my social battery is tapped out for the night,
however I would be up for breakfast before we all
leave. Let me know if that works for everyone.

Emerson: Great idea! Rest up my friend and
we'll see you in the morning. Meet up at 8AM
in the hotel restaurant.

Raelyn: Sounds like a plan! See y'all then :)
Enjoy your evening Delaney!

Laurel: Zeppelin says breakfast is on him and
I quote, "When will I ever be able to buy four
sexy ladies breakfast again?" *rolling eyes*

Laurel: He also suggested this playlist for
relaxing. He plays it whenever touring gets to
be too much. He hopes it helps :)
http://ytvid.com/melancholicinstrumental

Thank you... everyone, I really appreciate it and I'm
glad you all are here for me. See you tomorrow
morning.

Delaney clicked on the playlist seeing various ambient videos with classical or instrumental music that was somber, slow and immediately put her at ease. She would have to thank Zeppelin personally for sharing this playlist with her. She had it playing on repeat as she showered and got into her pajamas. The last thing she remembered was lying down beneath the fluffy comforter and closing her eyes for a moment.

Before she knew it her alarm was going off the next morning. After getting ready, packing all her things into her carry on and meeting the group for breakfast. True to his word, Zeppelin insisted on paying for everyone's breakfast. Delaney still couldn't believe she was sitting at a table with not only her favorite actor, but one of her favorite singers as well.

"How did that playlist work for you?" Zeppelin asked, pulling

Laurel up from her seat next to Delaney.

Delaney laughed as Laurel rolled her eyes never breaking her conversation with Raelyn and Austin.

"It worked like a charm, thanks. Hard to believe you have any sort of social anxiety though. You always seem to love the crowd when you're performing."

Zeppelin shrugged, "I fake it 'til I make it. Honestly, ninety percent of the time I'm fine especially when Laurel is on tour with me. However, I've definitely had moments of sheer panic where it feels like my heart will explode if I go out on stage."

"I feel like that in groups of people." Delaney admitted.

"Hopefully, you'll hang out with us more and we can become a little safe space for you. I know we seem intimidating, but we're all really a bunch of nerds who love one another."

"Speak for yourself Foster!" Leigh called out, making everyone laugh.

Delaney, Emerson and Pacey headed off to the airport after saying goodbye to everyone. She watched Emerson and Pacey say goodbye at his gate taking him back to Vancouver, Washington. Delaney felt like she was intruding on their moment, but she couldn't look away. Pacey wiped away a stray tear falling down Emerson's face while her hands clutched the sides of his shirt. He placed his hands on either side of her face, kissing her one final time before whispering something against her lips. For a moment, Delaney felt a moment of longing to have what Emerson and Pacey had.

While Emerson would fly back to Chicago with Delaney. The flight from New Orleans to Chicago was filled with them exchanging book recommendations and talking about some upcoming promotions for her book.

"Do you mind sending me some photos and videos of you with your book in the bookshop. I think those would be great to start really building out your social media pages." Emerson was writing down some ideas in a notebook.

Delaney let out a small sigh, "I will have Quinn send you some things. I'm sure she would be willing to torture me with a camera for an hour or so."

Emerson chuckled, "I know you hate social media, but we all can't be Graham Jacob."

"I wish. Not only for the privacy but being on the New York Times list would be amazing." Delaney took out her phone taking a photo of Emerson's list for Quinn.

When they landed, Delaney and Emerson made their way towards the main entrance where they found Quinn dressed in a black suit, white button down shirt, tie and chauffeur's hat. She was holding a sign with their last names on it. Emerson started laughing as Delaney wished for the earth to swallow her whole.

"Miss Holbrook, Miss Bishop, your chariot awaits." Quinn bowed, holding out her arm towards the door.

"Oh, I like her… she's my kind of people." Emerson chuckled as they followed Quinn out to her car.

"If you like her that much then she's yours. Free of charge."

Delaney winced as Quinn smacked her arm, "You couldn't give me up. You love me too much and would miss me."

"Mmhmm…" Delaney smiled as she put her things in the trunk, "But really, Emerson, if you want… OW!"

Quinn took off her flip-flop and smacked her, "Stop trying to give me away! You're stuck with me."

She rolled her eyes as Emerson continued laughing getting into the backseat.

"Hey Emerson, do you think the Fangirl authors would ever be interested in doing an event at Scattered Pages?"

Delaney narrowed her eyes on her best friend, "I think they have a full convention schedule, and they have books to work on or content to create for multiple platforms."

"Of course we would! Are you kidding me? Raelyn would do it just to visit your shop again. She really does have a thing for small town bookshops. I think it's a great idea."

"I told you so." Quinn not so quietly whispered.

Emerson placed her hand on Delaney's shoulder, "Did you think we wouldn't do it?"

Delaney shrugged, "I'm always surprised when authors say yes to an event at our shop. If I keep expectations low then I don't get my hopes up."

Emerson squeezed her shoulder, "We'll have to work on that, but yes I think once we all have our next projects done or thought of then we should gather for an event here. You should definitely tell Leigh about it and I'm sure she would work with Quinn on setting it all up."

Delaney felt her shoulders squeezing in towards her ears, "We'll see. I want to get through Graham Jacob's event first. It will be the biggest event we've ever had and if we can get through it smoothly then I'll be more open to having fangirls flood our shop."

Quinn pulled up in front of the Scattered Pages and Delaney relaxed feeling at home finally. Their bookshop was a corner, two story building. Large windows with displays of books on either side of the main lobby doors. The lower level was the retail store with books, selected movies and merchandise for sale. The upper level was office space and event area. They could fit up to two hundred and fifty people in the space but had never had an event to fill it completely.

Currently, the store front was decorated for fall even though mother nature was insisting that summer have an extended stay in the Chicago area. Thankfully, they were close enough to Lake Michigan that the lake breeze cooled their small little town just outside of Evanston. Even though Delaney would love to live alone in a cabin in the woods, all her pride and joy was sitting in front of her now.

"Em!"

The three of them looked over to see a man running across the street towards them. As he got closer, Delaney recognized Everett Holbrook from photos Emerson had shown her. The siblings hugged as Quinn nudged her in the side.

"Who's the hottie?"

Delaney rolled her eyes, "That's Emerson's brother, Everett. He's finishing up his second degree at Northwestern. Yes, he's single and yes he's off limits."

Quinn huffed, "You never let me have any fun."

"Almost like I know you or something. Also, I thought you were talking with some guy online?"

"I like keeping my options open, but yes we've been trying to set up a time to meet up. He travels a lot for business." Quinn put on her best smile as Emerson and Everett walked towards them, "Are you sure he's off limits?"

Delaney noticed that Everett was obviously checking her friend out. She would never stand in the way of her friend dating a great guy, but she didn't want anything to affect her relationship with Emerson.

"For right now, yes."

Quinn sighed, "Fine, but if he asks me out then it's all fair game."

"Deal." Delaney waved to Everett as Emerson pulled her into a hug.

"We're taking off. Dad is cooking and I need to go make sure the house doesn't burn down. Hopefully we can hang out the next time I'm in Chicago."

Delaney nodded, "Absolutely, I would love that."

"Let me know how your event goes, especially if you get to have your own fangirl love story." Emerson smiled.

"I doubt that will happen, but I'll let you know. Have a safe drive to Elmhurst." She waved goodbye then followed Quinn inside the shop.

They were normally closed on Mondays in order to restock and freshen up the displays. Today, Quinn and Delaney were working on finalizing all the details for the author event. Quinn was working on her questions for the event while Delaney double and triple checked her order for his books. They were to be delivered three days before and in case of an emergency she had an in with a local book distributor that could get her books fast.

She was changing out the front table display with all of his backlist titles when Quinn decided they needed to call it a day.

"Come on, we're going to go home, order our favorite Chinese takeout and drink wine. Then you can tell me all about the convention and what Emerson meant by fangirl love story."

Delaney groaned, "Fine, but we're going to need bourbon for that."

Quinn chuckled as they locked up and walked out of the shop, "Don't need to twist my arm."

2
Two

ASHER

Asher Graham looked out the window of the airplane. The clouds were floating by as they traveled from St. Louis to Chicago. He wasn't going to be in the air long enough to sleep but that didn't keep him from shutting his eyes. The last three and half weeks had been a whirlwind of people, places and his body was feeling it.

"How are you holding up?" Dom Kincade asked beside him.

He gave his agent a pointed look then closed his eyes once more hearing him chuckle.

"Noted. This is the last stop and we're going to be staying an extra day, so you'll get some beauty sleep. Our hotel is in downtown Chicago, but the drive to Evanston isn't bad."

Asher was missing the beach and ocean from his Wilmington home. In the week leading up to this tour he had been able to make it feel a little more like home. Besides his office, his favorite spot was on his deck looking out to the private beach leading into the ocean. After multiple hotels and towns, he was ready to go back home.

"Out of curiosity, is our hotel on Lake Michigan?" he asked, hoping for some resemblance of what he had waiting for him back home.

"Yeah we are and we have all day to relax there. Your event is scheduled for tomorrow evening with a signing line after the panel. I'll warn you that Quinn Larson is excitable and chipper."

Now he opened his eyes, narrowing them on Dom who refused to look up from his laptop, "Chipper?"

He shrugged, "You're the writer, take that for what you want. I just wanted to warn you before you meet her. I've heard her partner, Delaney, is quite the opposite. Maybe that's an author thing. Her book is being released today as well."

He looked back out his window letting the silence fall between them. The moment Dom had said her name, his heart had leaped. It was weird to feel such a reaction for someone he had never met. For some reason her name burrowed itself within his chest and he couldn't think of why. He shook his head as if he could shake her name from it. Grabbing his headphones he decided to listen to an audiobook and watch the world past beneath him.

Once they had landed in Chicago, they made their way towards the pickup entrance where a tall woman with long wavy chestnut hair was standing with a sheet of paper with his pen name on it. She was lean, athletic wearing a pair of dark jeans, bright pink blouse and black leather jacket. Conventionally, she was an attractive woman and for some reason he felt like he had seen her before.

"Hi, Mr. Kincade and Mr. Jacob?" She asked, holding out her hand.

Dom took it first, "Please it's Dom and Graham"

Asher took her hand next, trying to study her features up close, "It's nice to meet you Miss Larson."

For the life of him he couldn't place where he knew her, but his stomach was twisting in a way that told him he did. Maybe from his college days when he was a sophomore he had more than a few one night stands at parties.

"Please call me Quinn. I'll be taking you guys to your hotel and going over the itinerary for the event tomorrow. We've completely sold out and have a long waiting list, so we're excited for you to be here."

He followed her out to a SUV that was obviously a rental. He decided to sit in the back so Dom could take care of all the details with Quinn. He had always wanted to visit Chicago. A summer of hearing Laney, his one and only summer romance talk about the magic of the city he had made it a goal to visit. As they drove out from the airport and into downtown, he could see why she felt it was magical. The city skyline was impressive and beautiful. Massive skyscrapers that were modern steel wonders with a classic feel to them.

"Graham are there any preferences you have as far as singing markers, snacks, drinks. Anything that will make you comfortable during the panel and signing." Quinn asked him, looking back through the rearview mirror.

"Your basic black Sharpie will be fine. I'll have my water bottle with me so that should be all I need. If there are any local snacks I should try then please feel free to have those. I like trying local food."

She laughed, "I don't know if we can outdo St. Louis's toasted ravs, but Chicago deep dish is a must. I can give you a suggestion for a place downtown to check out. In Evanston we have a little mom and pop shop that has the best Chicago style popcorn. I will definitely pick up some."

Asher couldn't help the small smile spreading across his lips. Quinn's positivity and joy was infectious, and it was nice to be around someone who was genuinely happy. He was once again reminded of Laney. He thought about her all the time even after he had met his ex-wife. Suddenly his chest tightened as the word flashed in his mind... *ex-wife*. Add that to the pile of failures he had.

"This SUV is for you guys to use while in town. I have my car waiting at your hotel, but I didn't want you to waste any money on Uber or anything. Tomorrow, we would like to have you at the bookshop by three o'clock to get you all set up. You'll get to meet Delaney, my partner in crime and soon to be famous author."

He looked up at Quinn, "This is her debut, right?"

Quinn nodded excitedly, "Sure is! Her book is amazing. Being her best friend since grade school, I've read everything she's ever written. I really think she has found her niche with romantic thrillers. She has blended the two beautifully and keeps you on the edge throughout the book. I was sure I knew the twist and then *BAM!* She hit me with something completely out of left field."

Asher smiled as Quinn pulled into their hotel, "Sounds like a book I would love to read."

"That would be music to Delaney's ears. I'm not supposed to say anything because she wants to keep everything professional, but…" Quinn parked in front of the entrance then turned back towards him handing him a copy of her book, "She's a huge fan of yours. She has your entire backlist of books and has read them multiple times."

He found himself matching Quinn's wide smile and an all too familiar ache spread across his chest. He leaned forward whispering to her, "I'll make sure to keep that between us. Thank you for your hospitality so far. I truly appreciate the warm welcome to your beautiful city and can't wait to see your bookshop."

Asher didn't think it was possible for her face to light up brighter, but it did. Dom was giving the valet the keys to the car while Asher grabbed their bags. Quinn waited for them on the sidewalk to make sure Dom had all the information for the reservation.

"Would you like for one of us to walk you to your car?" Asher asked.

She shook her head, "Nah, I'm good. The parking garage is attached to the building so it's not far. I'll see you both at three o'clock and if either of you need anything please don't hesitate to call me at any time." She waved goodbye to them as they walked inside to the front desk.

Asher noticed Dom's eyes were glue to Quinn's ass, "Really?"

"What? I bet she's perky in so many areas…"

He hit Dom in the shoulder, "Maybe if you treated women with respect then you wouldn't only have your hand to please yourself."

Dom scoffed, "Whatever. I'm a gentleman when I need to be."

"Come on, let's get checked in. I need a shower after this conversation."

Once Asher settled into his room, he took a nice, long, hot shower. The water pressure was surprisingly good in this hotel, and he let the water beat down on his tense muscles. It was too early for dinner yet and too late for a nap. Deciding he needed to do something to keep him from falling asleep he grabbed his laptop and decided headed out to his balcony.

The cool lake breeze made it the perfect temperature for a hoodie and jeans. He sat at the small table and pulled up his book document. Dom had been concerned with his book synopsis and outline, which he should be since it was definitely not something Asher would ever write. Westerns weren't too far off from mystery thrillers but cowboys in space were. Honestly, he just wanted to see if they would let him go with it or if they would shoot him down. Of course, it was the latter and now he had to come up with a real project.

He had lived in the *Lost and Abandoned* world for so long that now he couldn't imagine leaving it for another one. Living side by side with his main character, Detective Martin Williams, for the better part of fifteen years. He often thought that a good transition would be a spin off book with one of the support characters in the series. However, the way trends were going in thrillers, he needed something new and different to keep up with the other authors. More and more the thriller and horror genres were blending together and the thought of writing a horror novel was intriguing.

He started typing out a few notes about characters and setting. He thought it might be a great chance to add a paranormal aspect into it as a red herring. The next thing he knew, Dom was knocking on his door to grab him for dinner. They decided to walk to the pizzeria that Quinn had suggested and grabbed a table. After they each had a slice of deep dish which Asher thought was alright preferring New York style.

"So, have you given your next project any serious thoughts while we've been out on tour?" Dom asked while Asher rolled his eyes.

"Wow, I'm surprised you waited until we finished a whole slice before starting your interrogation."

Dom flipped him off as he laughed, "I'm hungry so my stomach decided for me. Now answer my question."

"I was actually working on it when you knocked on my door. I know trends are pulling towards more horror thrillers these days. I was thinking of writing a thriller with horror and paranormal aspects in it."

Dom seemed interested until he mentioned paranormal, "Space cowboys have been done before, thank you Star Wars. Explain exactly how the paranormal would be used in your story."

"Two words… Red. Herring." Asher smiled as the realization was visible on Dom's face, "Everyone loves a ghost story. I think I can use that to create some truly terrifying scenes and still stay in my wheelhouse of procedural thrillers."

"So, Ghost Hunters meet Law and Order. I'm not gonna lie, I like it. I think I can definitely sell that to the publishers. When do you think you'll have a synopsis and outline done?"

Asher took another bite of his pizza before answering, "I think once I'm back home I should be able to have them both knocked out within a few days and then start drafting within a week after that."

"Sounds like we finally have a good game plan. Which is good because I was getting scared that the publisher would give in to your space cowboys idea." He shivered as Asher wadded up a napkin and threw it at him.

"I don't care what you say, space cowboys are cool."

Once Asher was back in his room, he decided to go ahead and start working on his synopsis. After an hour, he had to take a break, or he was going to smash his head through the hotel wall. He hated writing a synopsis and since he had been writing a series for the last ten books he hadn't needed one.

Asher went to pull out Delaney's book and saw the large envelope he had stuffed in his bag before he left Wilmington. He didn't need to open it already knowing what was in it. He pulled it out anyway and stared at it for a long while. Within it was a large packet detailing one of his biggest failures and the aftermath of it. Pulling the envelope open, Asher pulled out the papers and read the header of the document.

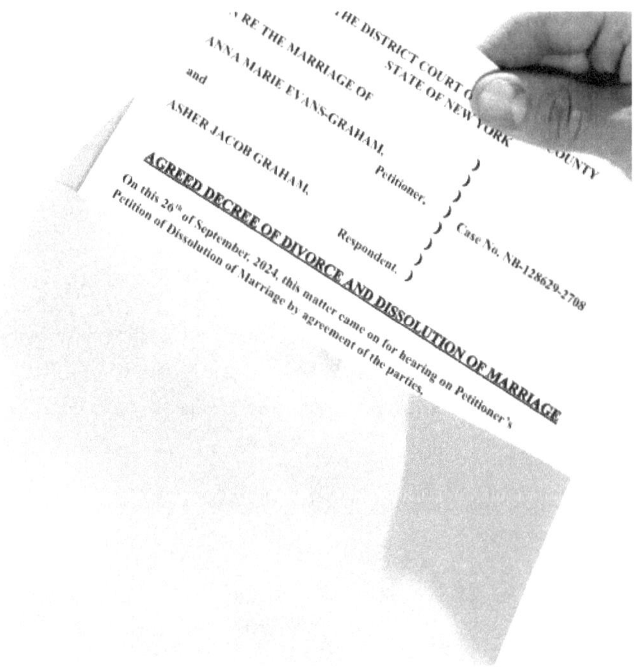

Stuffing the papers back in, he shoved the envelope back in his bag and pulled out Delaney's book. Reading the back of the book, he was intrigued by the hook and flipped to the author page. Delaney Bishop's smiling face looked up at him and his heart immediately began picking up pace. Flipping through the book and skimming a few pages he set it down and opened his laptop once again. Deciding to look at the Scattered Pages website seeing a link to a recent fan convention panel she had moderated.

He watched as three women walked out on stage then Delaney

followed behind them. Her dark red hair was pulled into a ponytail over her shoulder and she wore muted colors. She reminded him of a librarian wearing dark brown pants and an olive blouse. She stood out from the other ladies on stage. One dressed in teal sundress while another was in jeans with a punk rock band tee, and finally there was the baseball fan wearing a ballcap, jeans and team shirt. Delaney had tried to blend with the background when she actually made herself stand out more.

He watched the entire panel amazed at the crowd that had gathered for the three authors on stage. Apparently they all had released a book inspired by their real life romances with famous men from TV, music and sports. They were all represented by the same agent along with Delaney. They had started talking about her living out her own fangirl romance when meeting him.

"She would be better off staying single." He chuckled.

Asher could tell talking about herself or her book made her uncomfortable and that was something he could relate to. The one author, Emerson Holbrook, who had fallen in love with her baseball hero spoke.

"So, from everything I've heard there's still a chance to live out your own fangirl love story."

"We'll see, but for now I would love for everyone to give a round of applause for Raelyn Burton-Jameson, Laurel Adler and Emerson Holbrook!"

"Nicely done Miss Bishop. You're a pro at redirecting the conversation." He said, turning off the video and deciding he was done working for the night.

The whole time he watched the panel, he got the same feeling as when he met Quinn. He knew Delaney from somewhere and his theory of knowing them from his college days was looking like a real possibility. He would have to ask them if they ever went to Princeton when he arrived tomorrow. Asher grabbed Delaney's book, *To Have and To Hold* and soon got lost inside the world of Hope and Alex.

3
Three

ASHER

The next day, Asher slept in until midmorning. He couldn't remember the last time he had not only slept in but had stayed up all night to read a book in one setting. Delaney was truly talented at weaving words together to immerse her readers into the story. Her book was atmospheric and creeped him out at key moments. Rather she intentionally meant to add subtle elements of horror or not they were beautifully written in there. He immediately went on his Goodreads account and wrote up a review for it.

Promptly at two o'clock, Dom came to his room to get him. Asher was showered and dressed in a pair of comfortable jeans, with a black button down with a plain white tee underneath and his dress boots. He tamed his unruly wavy hair with some styling product leaving the finishing touch to truly turn him into Graham A. Jacob. Slipping the dark rimmed glasses over his eyes he looked up into the mirror. No longer was Asher standing there but his alter persona Graham. Grabbing his things Asher headed out the door to an impatiently waiting Dom.

The drive to Evanston was thirty minutes and Asher insisted on driving. One thing he loved more than writing or reading was driving. The temperature was cool enough the have the windows down. Turning the music off, he listened to his surroundings. Cars honking their horns in an effort to move traffic faster. He could hear boats off in the distance on the river that flow through town. For thirty minutes he was a normal guy driving through the Windy City. That was all he needed to relax him before having to turn on his author persona.

Turning onto the street where the bookshop was Asher couldn't believe his eyes. A line of people was wrapped around one side of the building and down the street. Hundreds of people were there, and his mind would not simply believe they were all there for him.

"Holy shit…" He mumbled as he pulled into the back parking lot where Quinn had directed them.

Dom patted his shoulder, "My friend, if you don't feel loved after this then I'm worried that you may truly be soulless."

He let out a halfhearted chuckle, "For once, I have no words or argument."

Now Dom let out a loud bark of a laugh, "Well mark this day on the fucking calendar! Asher Graham… wordless!"

"Shut up asshole."

Quinn came bouncing out a back door to greet them, "Hello and welcome to the Scattered Pages! Can you believe the line? I'm thinking a lot of folks are going to hang around the shop downstairs just to catch a glimpse or hear you. It's pretty amazing, right?"

Asher nodded, "It's something alright." Immediately several synonyms for overwhelmed popped into his mind

Bewildered. Confounded. Dumbfounded. Surprised. Astonished.

"Well follow me and I'll introduce you to everyone." Quinn held open the door for them to enter what was some kind of delivery and mailing room. Boxes, packing papers, bubble wrap and label station filled the small room.

"This is Jay's area. He's our online clerk who processes all of our mailing orders. We've got a pretty steady online presence and run specials for Blind Date with a Book or special editions."

They continued walking through the back room where three workers wearing Scattered Pages shirts were prepping goodie bags.

"Graham Jacob and Dom Kincade, these are our amazing shop clerks, Gen, KC and Shep. Delaney and I affectionately call them our kids." Quinn introduced them and Asher could see why they called them kids.

"It's nice to meet you all. Thank you for all the hard work you're doing for this event." He said as they each nodded at him.

Quinn led them through one last door then they were inside the main shop area. Asher immediately loved the little bookshop. It reminded him of the central library located on Princeton's campus. It was classic academia with a modern touch of technology. The Scattered Pages was exactly that as well. The built-in bookshelves were filled with books from all genres including a large classics section. There were small display tables including one featuring his books and then there were tables in the back of the shop with power supplies on the tabletops.

"That's our writer's section. Anyone is welcome to come in and sit at our tables to study or write the next great novel. It was important to Delaney that there was a spot for writers." Quinn explained, "Speaking of the devil…"

Asher looked up and felt all the air escape from his lungs. Delaney Bishop was more beautiful than any photo or video he had seen of her. Her long, dark copper hair was braided down her back and round frames outlined her beautiful blue eyes. She had on a black skirt with black tights, a pale blue sweater and black knee high boots. She was holding a couple of his books tightly in her arms as she walked up to them.

"Delaney Bishop, this is Graham Jacob and his agent, Dom Kincade. Gentlemen, this is the next bestselling author, Delaney

Bishop.”

Delaney rolled her eyes before locking them onto his. They widened as she froze for a moment. He held out his hand to her trying to come off as friendly as possible.

“It’s a pleasure to meet you. Your bookshop is amazing. I love the vibe you have going in here.” He smiled as she took his hand.

An electric current surging up his arm making him shiver. Seeing her standing before him now, he knew without a doubt that he knew the woman in front of him.

“Have we ever met before? You seem so familiar.” He asked.

She dropped his hand and her eyes turned into a cold stones, “No Mr. Jacob, I don’t believe we have.”

He was sure if her eyes could have shot out frost he would be a solid block of ice as she turned her attention to Quinn.

Dom leaned in whispering, “What the hell was that about?”

Asher shrugged, “I truly have no idea.”

Once everyone was seated, Quinn had him and Delaney standing off to the side out of sight. Asher could feel the air around them charged and tried to ignore it. He also kept his eyes on the stage resisting the urge to look over to Delaney. However, his eyes betrayed he wishes and glanced over at her. Her eyes were focused on the stage while her hands fiddled with the note cards. Quinn took center stage welcoming their audience and setting the ground rules for the night.

“Ladies and gentlemen, thank you all for being at the Scattered Pages bookshop. We're excited to be hosting the last stop on Graham Jacob’s first ever book tour.” The crowd applauded as Quinn continued her speech, “Not only do we have the honor of hearing from a New York Times bestselling author, but he will be in conversation with our very own, Delaney Bishop! She is the founder of Scattered Pages and her debut novel, *To Have and To Hold*, released today as well.”

The audience cheered once again, louder this time and he noticed her cheeks deepen in color.

"Please welcome to the stage Delaney Bishop and Graham Jacob!"

They walked out onto the small stage in front of a crowd of two hundred and fifty people with even more piled into the shop downstairs. Sitting in chairs next to each other, he watched as Delaney took a breath and squared her shoulders. Meanwhile he stared out into the crowd and immediately felt sweat gathering in his armpits now making him question if he remembered deodorant or not.

"Hello everyone! As Quinn said, we are incredibly honored to be hosting this event tonight with New York Times bestselling author, Graham Jacob. Graham, how are you feeling tonight?"

"I'm feeling a little overwhelmed with gratitude for everyone being here tonight." He answered, trying to keep his emotions from falling down his face.

Delaney went through her opening questions about his latest book and how he felt about the series ending. At times, Asher would lose himself talking about the inspiration for his Lost and Abandoned series. How Detective Martin Williams was inspired by a real life New York City detective that he shadowed during his research stage. How he never imagined the series having ten books in it but never felt like Detective Williams' story was over until now.

"I just want to say that your book, *To Have and To Hold*, is amazing. I stayed up way too late to finish it. I couldn't put it down. You're incredibly talented." Asher said, never taking his eyes off her.

Delaney fiddled with the note card in her hands, an obvious tell for her nervousness, "Thank you. I'm proud of Hope and Alex's story. I loved finding their voices and telling their tale. Graham, what's next for you?"

"Well, I've actually been thinking a lot about that. I'm not quite sure what my next project will be."

She smirked as if there was an inside joke that he wasn't in on, "Do you think you'll jump into another series?"

He shook his head, "No, I definitely think I'll work on a standalone title. Unless I find the right story to tell that needs a series. I've also been thinking that maybe I would like to co-write with another author. I would have to find the right partner though."

His eyes met hers and watched them widen in surprise, "Well I'm sure anyone would love to work with you."

"What about you? Any ideas for your next project?"

She smiled, "I'm thinking of writing another romantic thriller but this time set in summer on a private beach. Maybe two people meet randomly on a beach, fall in love and then one of them goes missing. Something similar to Gone Girl."

Delaney looked over at him with a spark in her eyes. She was trying to tell him something and he couldn't figure it out. He watched as disappointment filled them as she looked back down at her note card. He knew he had just failed some kind of test and that bothered him.

"That would be amazing. I would definitely read it and hey if you ever need to do research on private beaches let me know. My family owns a house with a private beach. Be more than happy to help in any way I can."

The smile that appeared on her lips never came close to reaching her eyes, "I think this would be a great time to start the audience Q&A."

The next hour went by as equally quick and agonizingly slow. Audience members asked them questions about their books, their writing processes and inspirations. When the panel ended, they both made their way to the signing tables. For the next two hours they talked with fans and signed books. The one thing Asher found he loved about the book tour was talking with the fans. He loved hearing their theories and love for his characters. Finally, when the last patron left for the night and the doors were locked he watched as Delaney let out a long, relaxing sigh.

"Delaney, I wanted to thank you again for hosting me here. Your bookshop is wonderful as well as everyone who works with you.

Definitely my favorite stop on this tour." Asher said, holding out his hand to her.

She shook his hand, with a firm finality in it, "The pleasure was all ours. I hope you have a safe trip back into the city and back home tomorrow."

He watched as she turned away and walked over to the counter speaking with one of the clerks. Quinn was skipping over to them with the biggest grin he had ever seen. Seeing the two best friends celebrating brought back a strange memory from the summer before he left for Princeton. A memory of a girl he fell head over heels for talking excitedly on the phone with her friend. He couldn't shake the similarities between then and now.

"Our work here is done. Let's get out of here and head back to the hotel."

He shook the memory from his head before nodding, "Right behind you." Asher took one last look at Delaney Bishop smiling before making himself turn following Dom out of the bookshop.

Later that night, he found himself sitting outside on his balcony staring out over Lake Michigan. There was something deep in his gut, made him unsettled. He knew at the center of it was Delaney Bishop. The mere thought of her name made his stomach clench and his heart flutter. How could one woman he had never met before today bewitch him so quickly. Opening up his laptop, he watched her panel he had found from the day before.

"Delaney, where do you write most of the time? An office or favorite coffee shop?" Raelyn Burton-Jameson asked her.

Delaney chuckled, "Well I do have an office space at my bookshop that I sometimes use to write. A lot of times I write in my bedroom at a little desk I have set up in there, but when I'm truly in the mood to do some all-night writing, because I'm a night owl."

Laurel Adler raised her hand, "Me too! Zepp and I stay up late writing all the time.”

Delaney smiled, “I’ll go to my favorite hole-in-the-wall twenty four hour diner and sit in my favorite booth. I’ll order a big basket of fries and a strawberry milkshake without the cherry. I’ll sit there until the sun rises, getting lost in my work.”

Raelyn and Emerson Holbrook were laughing as Laurel sat with her jaw nearly to the floor, “ME TOO! I have a favorite little diner back in Springfield that I would meet Leigh at all the time. It was that very diner that I decided to go out on tour with Heartstrings, forever changing my life for the better.”

All four girls were laughing on the stage when Asher paused the video. His fingers itching to type into a search bar for local twenty four hour diners near the Scattered Pages. When his willpower failed, he found that there was only one diner near there that was open twenty four hours. Then a thought occurred to him and he shook his head.

“Asher, get a hold of yourself. You’re dangerously close to stalker-like behavior.”

He closed out of all his browsers and shut down his laptop. Emptying his glass, he walked back inside and decided all he needed to do was get a good night’s sleep and then he would wake up ready to head back to Wilmington.

That’s when he remembered Delaney’s project pitch from their panel and once again the nagging feeling was pulling at his heart once more.

“I’m thinking of writing another suspense romance but this time set in summer on a private beach. Maybe two people meet randomly on a beach, fall in love and then one of them goes missing. Something similar to Gone Girl.”

Two people meeting randomly on a beach and falling in love. That was exactly what happened between him and Laney all those years ago. There was no way of Delaney knowing that about him unless… then a wild thought popped into his head that nearly made his knees give out from him.

“No way… no fucking way that they could be the same girl…” he murmured then pulled out his phone looking up a picture of Delaney.

Her hair was long and red like his Laney but darker. They both had blue eyes, but so did a lot of people. Yeah their names were similar as well, but he was sure there were a lot of women named Delaney or Laney. He closed his eyes trying to push his memory as far back as he could to remember his Laney. He remembered her being full of joy and light. Always smiling at everyone that would pass by her. Jumping in to help anyone who was in need if it was giving money or the jacket off her back. She was playful and smarter than her own good. She would constantly knock him off kilter with her knowledge of literature.

He opened his eyes looking down at the photo of Delaney. The woman he met today was stand-offish, cold and hardened. There was no way she could be his Laney. Even after all these years, he couldn't imagine his Laney changing that much. Staring at her photo, there was something pulling him towards her and he knew until he figured that out there would be no rest for him.

"This is a colossally stupid idea, but what the hell." Asher grabbed his wallet, phone and the keys to the SUV.

DEAR DIARY,

May 2007

I hate that my dad shipped me out to my grandparents. I mean sure a summer at the beach is ideal but not without my BFF. Instead I'm stuck with Dillon who will annoy me to no end… like a brothers do. Quinn and I had big plans to hang out at the mall and watch the football team practice. Speaking of… Ty Wallace had asked me out right before summer break. I was shocked he did since I had no idea he liked me. I mean… only in books does the quarterback like the nerdy bookworm. Quinn says I'm selling myself short, but I'm just being real. Of course I had to tell him no since I wouldn't be home all summer, but told him maybe we could go out when school started back up.

I really wish I could have just stayed home while my parents went on their little anniversary trip to Europe. I mean, I'm 16 and shouldn't need a freaking babysitter. Though, it will be nice to paint with my grandma again. It's been a long time since I've painted for fun. I just need a sign from the universe that this summer will not be a complete bore. Crap, my grandma is calling for me… I'll write more later.

When you ask the universe for something she answers in a big way. Holy cow… our grandparents took us for a special dinner at some beach restaurant. It's not too far from their house so I asked if I could walk on the beach back to their house. Dillon of course wanted to come with me, but my grandma could tell I needed some me time. As I was walking, I saw the hottest guy sitting on the beach reading. Of course, me being me, I was too shy to talk to him, but he called out to me. Of course he didn't know me so I told him I was visiting my grandparents for the summer and he pointed up to his house that is right on the beach. We ended up sitting and talking for a couple of hours until Dillon came to find me since grandma was worried.

He invited me over to his house to hang out and I could hear Quinn's voice screaming at me, "SAY YES! HANG OUT WITH THE HOT GUY! YOU ONLY LIVE ONCE!" So of course I said I would love too. Oh! I didn't even tell you about him…

His name is Asher, he's 18 years old and just graduated high school. He loves books and writing. He is planning on going to Duke University for creative writing and wants to become an author like his father who is M.W. Graham. He loves the ocean and libraries that have an old feel to them. He has wavy golden blond hair, hazel eyes and is super tall… like SUPER tall. He's hot and definitely out of my league, but for the summer maybe I'll take Quinn's advice to live wild and free.

Smile :) Until next time,

Laney

DELANEY

How had she not put it together before now? Delaney stood completely stunned to her core at the man standing in front of her. Not by the fact that he was her favorite author and she had read every book that he'd ever written. Not by how handsome he was, however, that did fuel the raging fire flowing in her veins that he was devastatingly handsome. No, she was completely taken aback by the fact that they had meet one summer in Wilmington, North Carolina when she was visiting her grandparents. She was sixteen and he was eighteen, they had fallen in love and then he left only leaving behind a letter with empty promises.

"Have we ever met before? You seem so familiar." He asked her.

Her heart immediately dropped to the pit of her stomach and shattered, "No Mr. Jacob, I don't believe we have." She didn't mean for her words to come out so cold, but for the second time in her life this man broke her heart by not even recognizing her.

Delaney averted her eyes to Quinn pleading with her to take the lead and she nodded, "Graham, would you like to follow me then I can get you all set up in my office upstairs."

His warm hazel eyes didn't leave hers as he walked past, "Absolutely, that sounds great."

The moment he was walking up the stairs, Delaney finally took a breath. Asher Graham, of all the men that could have walked through the door it had to be him. There were only two men on this planet she never wanted to see again, and he happened to be one of them. The other, her ex-husband, but she never had to worry about seeing him again. Delaney closed her eyes, counted to ten then started working on the next task on her to-do list. Focusing on the work was what she could do to help distracted her from going upstairs and giving Asher a piece of her mind.

Fifteen minutes later, she was in the back stockroom when Quinn came back there and asked the clerks to start setting up all the chairs.

"Okay, what the hell was that? You did not fangirl like I thought you were going to. Actually, you looked like you wanted to rip his face off. What gives?"

Delaney shook her head, "Nothing. I think I was overwhelmed by meeting him."

By the look on Quinn's face, she had sounded as convincing as the time she lied to her parents about sneaking out for a party her senior year. Quinn placed her hands on her hips and Delaney knew there was no way of getting out of this.

"You wanna try that again." Quinn said.

"I promise to tell you everything tonight when we're home. The short of it is, I may know Graham Jacob from a long time ago and it's obvious that he doesn't remember me at all. I would like to keep it that way to ensure that our event goes smoothly. So, I'm going to ask you to drop this for now. Please."

Quinn studied her face for a moment, "Okay, but I definitely want to know the full story with all the gory details when we get home. No locking yourself in your room or hiding. Deal?" She stuck out her hand.

Delaney took it and pulled her into a hug, "Deal."

The panel and signing had gone off without a hitch. Delaney was proud that she could keep her professional mask firmly on hiding the array of emotions happening inside of her. Asher and his agent had left about an hour earlier and their clerks were still working hard to clean and balance everything.

"Guys, let's call it a night and locked the money in the safe. We can balance everything and take inventory tomorrow before we open. Thank you for all your hard work today. We couldn't have done it without you guys and I'm proud of everyone. Go home, rest up and I'll see you tomorrow."

Everyone waved goodnight to Delaney and Quinn as they left out of the employee entrance. Quinn wrapped her arm around Delaney's shoulders.

"Come on bestie, let's go home, drink wine and you can tell me all about how you know Graham Jacob."

Delaney groaned, "Alright, but I think we're going to need something stronger and some greasy food."

"Say no more. I'll grab the food and you grab the alcohol. See you at home."

After their favorite meals from Lake Bay Diner and half a bottle of whiskey, Delaney felt ready to finally talk about her summer with Asher Graham. They both settled in on the couch covered by their favorite fuzzy blanket and Red Moon playing in the background.

"Okay, now tell me how in the world you know Graham Jacob and I don't because I'm having a hard time believing that you met him without telling me."

Delaney drained the last of her whiskey holding the glass out to Quinn to refill it, "Asher Graham."

Quinn cocked her eyebrow, "Why does that name sound familiar?"

"The summer before junior year when I went to Wilmington to

spend the summer with my grandparents…"

Her best friend's eyes widened, "Oh my god, the hot boy you fell in love with that ghosted you. That's…"

"Ding, ding, ding! Graham A. Jacob is his nom de plume which is his full name rearranged. Asher Jacob Graham."

Quinn looked at her curiously while taking a drink, "You remember his full name from fourteen years ago?"

Delaney looked down shrugging, "I can't remember what I ate yesterday but I can remember the full name of the boy who broke my heart."

"That's kind of fucked up, but that's part of the reason why I love you." Quinn set her glass down, "Why didn't you tell him who you are. Seems like the perfect opportunity to not only throw what he missed out on in his face but to get some overdue closure."

Delaney shrugged, her shoulders suddenly feeling heavier, "I don't know…"

Quinn grabbed her hand, "I don't believe you. Why didn't you tell him who you are?"

"I didn't say anything because it hurt realizing that he didn't recognizing me. It was a reminder of how little I meant to him and how much he meant to me. The fact that he's not only successful but also I was charmed by his writing without even knowing it was him."

"Hey," Quinn squeezed her hand, "You're incredibly successful and it's his loss at the chance of being with the most wonderful woman in the world."

Delaney smiled, feeling the weight on her shoulders lift ever so slightly, "Thanks. Honestly, I don't really blame Asher for not contacting me after our summer. He was going off to Ivy League school, and I was in high school. The only thing I wish had been different was me being more confident in myself and not falling for my douchebag ex."

Her ex-husband, Ty Wallace, flashed before her eyes. A sudden sadness filled her chest. Even the thought of her ex after five years still made her feel like a huge failure. After nine years together, he filed for divorce and moved all of her things into a storage unit while she was on vacation with Quinn. She still had the email he sent to her about all her stuff saved and every now and then she would reread it to remind herself of why she would never be in relationship again.

It wasn't too much later Delaney sat at her desk in her bedroom, staring at her cursor blinking on her screen. Bringing up memories of Asher and Ty had her mind spinning and unable to concentrate on writing. She tried reading over the outline she partial had written and sighed in frustration.

"I need a change of scenery."

She packed up her notebook, laptop and pen pouch. Writing a note to Quinn in case she woke up in the middle of the night, Delaney headed out the door and walking down the street towards her favorite late night spot. It wasn't long before the bright neon sign of Lake Bay Diner came into view and the smell of greasy food filled her nose as she stepped through the door.

"My favorite author!"

Delaney looked over to see the overnight waitress, Louisa, coming from behind the counter. She held a copy of her book in one hand and a marker in another. Delaney smiled as she set her things down in her favorite booth.

"Louisa, you know I would have given you a copy. You didn't need to buy one."

Louisa scoffed, "You won't make no money if you give it away. This way I contributed to your rising fame. Now, while you sign it I'll go get your order in."

It was still surreal to Delaney that not only did people have her book and were reading it, but they were asking for her autograph. She wrote out the catchphrase then a sweet note for Louisa finishing with her autograph. Setting the book and marker on the edge of the table,

Delaney started to set up her spot to let the inspiration start flowing.

Louisa brought out her normal order of large basket of fries and a strawberry milkshake. Thanking her, Delaney put her headphones on, dipping a fry into the milkshake and went back to her notebook. The one thing she loved about the diner was that Delaney lost all concept of time while sitting in there. The later it was the less people would come in. By the time it was one in the morning, Delaney was the only one in the diner and she relaxed a little more in her booth.

She was in the middle of researching most commonly visited beaches by couples when a shadow came over her table.

"Louisa, could I please have a glass of water?" She asked without looking up until the shadow moved closer to her.

Delaney was shocked to see Asher sitting across from her. Only a few people actually knew which specific diner she went to late at night and she always made sure to never mention the name of it when speaking about it causally. She wasn't afraid to be out at all hours of the night, alone, at a hole-in-the-wall diner. However, she didn't need to broadcast it either.

"W-What are you doing here?"

5

ASHER

What was he doing here? It was a question that had been bouncing around in the back of his mind the whole trip up here. What was he trying to accomplish by coming up here to her writing sanctuary? Other than looking like a crazy stalker.

"I… uh, couldn't sleep and I remembered from a panel you recently did that you said you liked writing at a diner late at night. I thought I would give it a shot."

Asher could tell immediately that she could see through his bullshit answer, "You do know you probably drove past hundreds of diners on your way up here. Seems a little odd for you to choose this specific diner."

"May I?" He pointed to the basket of fries taking one after she nodded, "Honestly, I can't shake the feeling that I know you from somewhere. I know that's weird and me coming here is creepy…"

"To say the least…" She chuckled.

"Whenever I can't figure something out then it festers and bothers me until I do. For some reason, I need to figure this," he waved his finger between the two of them, "out."

Something that he said had made her smile the same one she had given to the waitress. Now, all he wanted to do was make her smile like that over and over again.

"Like I told you before, we've never meet before today." The light from her smile left her eyes and that cold stare returned.

"Maybe we met a long time ago. I went to Princeton for college. Did you go there or visit friends there?" He was taken back when her icy stare suddenly turned into a fiery rage.

"No. I've never been to Princeton. I went to Northwestern here in Evanston. I didn't have any friends who went to Princeton either."

Something about her reaction told him that she wasn't telling the whole truth, but he didn't want to push her. He was good at reading people. He had to be for writing thrillers and was an avid people watcher. Right now, he knew if he pushed this too hard then she would shut down completely. He didn't want that.

"Oh, I don't suppose you've ever been to upper New York State or the Hamptons either?" he asked, knowing it would be his final question.

She shook her head then grabbed her headphones, "Nope, now if you don't mind I'm trying to work through some ideas I have so I can pick my next project."

"I thought you were going to write Gone Girl summer romance?" He asked, trying to swing the conversation back into his favor.

Delaney sighed, "That was a joke… kind of. I honestly don't know what I'm going to work on. I have a few ideas that are not fleshed out and honestly aren't capturing my attention fully. So, I'm trying to free write my ideas down to see what might stick."

He gestured towards her notebook, "May I see? Promise I won't steal any of them for myself."

She was hesitant but slid her notebook towards him, "Shouldn't you be sleeping for your flight home tomorrow? I'm sure your family won't want to see you exhausted when you arrive home."

Asher kept his eyes focused on the page before answering, "No family waiting for me at home. Just an empty house and beach side view."

He glanced up to see pity in her eyes, "Oh, I'm… well I assumed you would have a wife or girlfriend, maybe even kids waiting for you. Very little is known about your private life."

"I'm well aware," Now he felt exposed and wanted to change the subject as soon as possible, "None of these seem like tropes or story arcs that match your style. A lot of these are contemporary romances where your strengths are in the suspense genre."

"Really? You got that from reading my book once?" She scoffed.

He finally looked up at her smirking, "Yes. My father was a bestselling author, and I've been in this industry since I could write my name. I'm also just good at reading people and finding their niches. The romance arc of your book was well written, intriguing and heart wrenching."

She smiled that smile again, "Thank you."

The tension in his chest melted, "However, what made your book stand out was the suspense you weaved between the romance. I felt like I was living in Alex's shoes or beside Hope when your antagonist was hunting her. I was immersed in that world and felt true danger senses when your characters were in peril. How you blended the two can't be taught but only come naturally from true talent."

He felt a sense of satisfaction when her cheeks turned a lovely shade of pink and she averted her eyes down to the table. Delaney Bishop was not used to being praised and that was a tragedy.

"That's very nice of you to say. It means a lot for an author of your caliber to give that kind of feedback." She took her notebook back from him and set her pen on top of it.

He could tell she was struggling to say something to him by her hands fidgeting with her papers. He noticed it during their panel with her note cards. For some reason he was fine tuned to noticing every little tell or quirk she had. It was maddening and comforting at the same time.

"Do you…" She started to say.

"Delaney, whatever you want to ask me go ahead. I'm not going to bite." He joked making her laugh.

"Do you think you could brainstorm with me to help with my next project?"

Her beautiful eyes finally locked with his and he reached over giving her hand a squeeze.

"I would love too."

Asher always thought that writing was an isolating, solo adventure. Since the first book he wrote in college, he spent hours in a dark corner of Princeton's library writing page after page alone. His father would never have worked with another author, and he definitely would never have brainstormed with them either. His father wouldn't even share his manuscripts with him fearing that even his own son would steal his ideas.

Sitting here working with Delaney was the most fun he had brainstorming a new project. It also made him want to work with her all the time. He found himself trying to work up the courage to see if she would even entertain the idea of working with him.

Louisa, the late night waitress, brought over a pot of coffee and a fresh basket of fries for them. Asher held his cup for her to refill with the fuel for all night owls.

"Delaney, would you like anything?"

She shook her head, "No thank you, Louisa. I drank my caffeine before coming here. I'll stick with my water."

"You don't drink coffee?" Asher asked her completely shocked by the revelation.

"Nope and yes I'm well aware that it makes me less of a writer for not. I've come to terms with not being as great as the amazing Graham Jacob."

He chuckled, "You know, Quinn told me that you were a big fan of mine. I'm starting to think she was pulling my leg."

He watched Delaney's tense shoulders relaxed for a moment, "I am a fan of yours. I have been since your debut novel released. I've admired your work and need for privacy. I'm sorry if I've given you any other impression."

He could tell she was being genuine which gave him hope that maybe she would be willing to work with him.

"Apology accepted. I'm glad someone understands my need for privacy." He looked back down at her notebook writing a few more story points.

"May I ask you a personal question?"

Asher looked up, "Sure, but I may not answer it."

She smiled while rolling her eyes, "Fair enough. Why have you never made public appearances before? I mean, nowadays authors are basically social media influencers to sell books. Obviously, times were different when you sold your first book."

He flinched, grabbing his chest, "Damn, you make it seem like it was eons ago. I'm not that old yet."

"I know you're not. You're only a couple of years older than me-" She suddenly stopped, biting her bottom lip nervously.

"So, you are a fan!" He laughed, "You do keep tabs on me with what little information is available online. Good to know Quinn is not a liar."

"No, she's not. She'll tell the whole world your entire life story and all your secrets. Tread lightly…" She warned, "Now are you willing to answer my question?"

He pretended to think about it for a few seconds before answering her, "As I mentioned before my father was a bestselling author. He was always going out to promote his book on tours and readings. He would do interviews and talk all about his life, his family."

For moment Asher was taken back to living in The Hamptons and a fan being in his bedroom when he came home for Christmas. She had scared the crap out of him and his dad came into his room shocked to see her. He knew her by name and was so familiar with her that Asher accused him of cheating on his mom.

Delaney squeezing his hand brought him back to the present, "Graham, are you okay? You don't have to answer if you don't want to."

"Asher, my name is Asher. Graham A. Jacob is my pen name," He shook his head, "And it's okay I want to answer. My father being so public about everything brought a lot of enthusiastic fans into our lives. Towards the end of his career, he had one particular fan who felt entitled to knowing everything about my father and turned violent towards my mom. It was the last straw for my mom and ultimately what ended everything."

"You don't mean…" she paused for a moment, and he watch as realization of his words set in.

Asher nodded, "His guilt was too much for him and one night driving home with my mom he veered off the road. He crashed into a ditch, and they were both instantly killed. It wasn't until I moved into our home in Wilmington that I read a letter from him explaining everything."

Delaney's hand squeezed his tighter and he realized that she had never let go. For the first time since finding out the truth about his parents' death he felt comforted.

"I'm so sorry for your loss. I won't lie; it scares me to live so publicly. I want my books to sell but I really hate being the center of any kind of attention." She chuckled.

"Thank you." He squeezed her hand back, "Now let's get back to brainstorming."

Asher starting writing in her notebook again. He could feel her eyes on him as he wrote. Taking a chance, he glanced up using the blanket of his curly hair as cover. Her bright blue eyes were trailing down from the top of his head to where his hand was resting on her notebook. Surprising her eyes glazed over as if lost in thought.

"Delaney?" His voice brought her back to this moment, "What do you think of this?"

She looked down at her notebook seeing what he had been working through.

- Protagonist 1 (P1)- Female, mid 30's, beautiful, starting new life in small beach town
- Protagonist 2 (P2)- Male, late 30's, handsome, owns local shop in small beach town, hires P1 to do bookkeeping
- Support Character- male, late 30's, P2 BFF, voice of reason
- Antagonist- Male, mid 30's, douchebag, P1's ex, hunting her
- Attempted kidnapping, threatening voicemails, [insert suspense stuff]
- P2 protecting P1
- P1 staying w/ P2, [insert romance stuff]

Delaney chuckled, "Suspense stuff? Romance stuff?"

"What? I figured you would get the gist of it." He shrugged, leaning back against the booth, "So what do you think?"

The concept was pretty basic, but he knew she could build off it. However, he watched her nose scrunch up over something that she didn't like.

"What if the antagonist was a serial killer. Instead of a man, she's a woman who hunts women she is jealous of. Smarter, more beautiful, more talented women." Delaney started writing her thoughts down.

"See, a little teamwork never hurt. However, I still like the whole they meet on a beach randomly." He laughed.

His laugh died off seeing Delaney stared at the piece of paper, gripping her pen tightly. Her icy stare was back, and she closed her notebook suddenly. He had said something wrong and didn't even know what it was that set her off. It was almost like she was holding a grudge against him, but why?

"Well, I think that's enough for tonight. I should probably get home."

"Wait," He placed his hand on top of hers, "Please give me two more minutes and then I can drive you home."

Delaney looked down at the table before sighing, "I don't need a ride home. I live close by and walk at this hour all the time."

"Okay, heard loud and clear. I would like for you to consider something before you leave. Then I promise to leave you alone."

She nodded, "Go on, I'm listening."

Asher took a deep breath, "You're truly talented. It's been a long time since a book captured my attention like yours did. I really think that your talents and mine would blend beautifully together in a dual POV book. I would love to co-write a book with you. You would be the main author, and our agents can work out all the details. I've enjoyed sitting here with you tonight and would love to continue this.

Professionally, of course."

She was looking down at her lap with a sadness in her eyes before looking up at him, "I really appreciate that offer. I do, but I want to make a name for myself on my own first. I hope you can understand that."

"I do. Maybe one day, we can work together."

Delaney stood up slipping her backpack on, "Maybe. Have a safe trip home. Goodnight Asher."

"Goodnight Delaney."

He watched as she pulled her hood up and started walking down the street vanishing into the darkness of night. He put his own notebook into his bag and sat there for a moment feeling more lost than ever before.

6

DELANEY

"Asher, my name is Asher…"

Delaney kept replaying her night with Asher over and over in her head. He had told her his name still unaware that she knew who he was. No matter how hard she tried she couldn't let go of the resentment she was holding onto for him. How could he not remember who she was? Now she felt even more foolish about not confronting him in the first place.

"Delaney?" She looked up to see Quinn standing in the doorway of her office.

"Sorry, what's up?"

Quinn's warm eyes were filled with concern, "You tell me? You've been hiding up here all morning. Are you okay?"

Delaney looked down at her phone to see it was already noon and had indeed been moping in her office for hours.

"I didn't realize I had been sitting up here for so long. Who needs a break downstairs? Does Jay need help pulling orders or packing them? Maybe I should do a quick run through the shelves and do a book order."

"Whoa, whoa, slow your roll. First off, everyone has had their break. Jay is all caught up and prefers to work alone. Our shelves are fine especially since today has been slower than molasses in December." Quinn pulled a chair next to her desk, "Tell me what's going on with you."

She knew she wouldn't be able to fool Quinn, "Asher came to the diner last night."

Quinn perfectly sculpted eyebrow arched, "How did he know you were there? Did you finally tell him you know who he is?"

"Apparently he watched my panel with the Fangirl authors, and I mention going to a diner late at night. I'm sure it wasn't too hard to search for the nearest diner to the bookshop."

"That's kind of creepy." Quinn cringed.

Delaney chuckled, "He said the same thing. I really thought he was going to remember me, but he definitely didn't. He told me his real name and still no recognition."

Quinn slump back into her chair, "So what did he want?"

"You're truly talented. It's been a long time since a book captured my attention like yours did. I really think that your talents and mine would blend beautifully together in a dual POV book. I would love to co-write a book with you. You would be the main author, and our agents can work out all the details. I've enjoyed sitting here with you tonight and would love to continue this. Professionally, of course."

Delaney still couldn't quite process that her favorite author and ex-summer romance wanted to work with her. Of all people he could work with, he wanted to hear her ideas, read her writing and create a whole world together. It was flattering, exciting and completely infuriating since he couldn't remember who she was.

"He wants to work with me."

"Work with you? Like mentor you with your next book?" Quinn asked.

Delaney sighed, "Not quite. He wants to co-author a book together. We would work closely together. Building new characters and a world together."

A small smirk curled on her friend's lips, "Rather he remembers you or not seems like to me that he's still attracted to you."

"I don't think that's the case." The spark that ignited in her heart drove her brain into protective mode, "If he was attracted to me then I think it would spike the memories from our summer together. Like it did with me when I saw him again. That didn't happen."

Quinn stood walking toward the door, "Maybe, but I think you should give it some serious thought. Working with an author of his caliber would be great for your career. Take the rest of the day off. Go home or to the diner and really consider what he's offering. Push out your feelings and think about this from a business perspective."

She shook head, "I can't take the day off. What if you guys get busy?"

"We'll handle it. Now, as your business partner and friend, I'm commanding you to go home." Quinn blew her a kiss and walked out of her office.

Delaney sighed knowing Quinn was right. She needed to process everything that had happened. She began packing up her things thinking that a nice walk would help clear her mind. Looking out her window, she smiled seeing families walking along the sidewalk. It was a picture perfect autumn day with clear blue skies, leaves drifting over the ground and a cool breeze.

Grabbing her bag, she made her way down to the main floor when the chime on the door rang as a family walked in. Delaney stopped suddenly as all the air left her lungs. Apparently the universe wanted her to deal with all her past traumas as her ex-husband and new family started browsing their children's section. Everything around her was fading in the background except for her rapidly beating heart. Between seeing Asher, who didn't remember her, and now seeing Ty, who had clearly moved on as quickly as possible was too much for Delaney.

She tore her eyes away from the happy family as she looked for the quickest path out of the shop. Right as she was about to walk down the rest of the stairs, Ty's eyes locked onto hers. She almost laughed at the shock that fell over his handsome face. He said something to the woman holding a baby and pointing out a book to young boy holding onto her skirt. Delaney knew there was no way she could sneak away and swallowed the emotions lodged in her throat for the incoming confrontation.

"Delaney? Wow, I didn't know you worked here."

She tried to push a smile on her face, "I'm actually one of the owners. Quinn and I opened it about five years ago."

The satisfaction flooding her body from Ty's surprised expression boosted her confidence. They had put everything into opening their bookshop right after she and Ty had divorced. It was the baby she could have instead of wallowing in her grief of the baby she would never have.

"Oh wow, that's amazing. My…" Ty paused glancing over to the woman and kids again, "wife loves coming here. Strange we've never seen you before."

Delaney's hand began to shake hearing the condescending tone, "We'll I spend a lot of time in my office doing the business side. I'm also a full time author. My first book just released, and I have been traveling for book events."

Ty's eyes rolled and she knew the nice act was over. His true colors always showed themselves whenever she pushed back against him.

"So, you actually finished writing a book. That shocks me since you could never finish anything you started when we were together."

"Honey, who is this?" Ty's wife walked up to them with their children.

Delaney immediately stuck out her hand to her, "Hi I'm Delaney Bishop. I'm-"

"Oh, my goodness you're the author of '*To Have and To Hold*'. My book club is reading it right now. So far, your book is absolutely amazing. Do you two know each other?"

For a brief moment, Delaney wanted to air out all of Ty's dirty laundry that he obviously had buried from his family, but then an overwhelming wave of compassion came over her. She looked over to Ty whose eyes were wide with fear. She sighed putting on her best smile before picking up one of her books on a nearby table.

"No, your husband was coming over to see if I would sign a copy of my book for you." She walked over to the main counter where Quinn was standing wide eyed, "Who can I make out to?"

"Oh honey, you're so sweet for asking her. You can make it out to Danielle. I appreciate you taking the time to do this."

Delaney couldn't help to smile as she signed her book then handed it over to Danielle never taking her eyes off of Ty, "Yes it was very nice of him. I hope you enjoy your time in our bookshop."

Ty smiled at his wife, "Anything for you. Why don't you pick out a couple more books for the kids."

Danielle thanked her again before walking away. Ty's eyes snapped to hers as his mouth opened about to speak. Delaney held up her hand having no interest in hearing whatever he wanted to say.

"I could have been a complete bitch and told her who I was. I decided to be the bigger person and allow her to live in her delusion that you're some kind of loving, wholesome husband. I only hope that you treat her better than you ever treat me." She stepped up beside him and whispered, "Don't think I didn't notice that your son is too old for you and her to have been together. He's what, six or seven? That would mean he was born while we were still married."

Ty narrowed his eyes, "He's seven."

"Husband of the year." She looked over at Quinn grinning from ear to ear, "Quinn, their copy of my book is on the house."

"You got it. Come on Ty, let me show you where we keep the true crime section to give you a preview of what happens if I see you again." Quinn led Ty away from Delaney and she was able to take a long breath letting out the tension in her body.

She walked out of the bookshop and took one last look at Ty and his family checking out with Quinn. The perfect family that she had always dreamed about having with him when they were married and never did. Flashes of the day she had told him she could never have kids and how disappointed he was in her. Blaming her for never taking care of herself and never being able to do anything right. Turning away from them, she started walking towards her apartment now wanting to crawl into her bed and cry herself to sleep.

Delaney immediately went into her room and flopped onto her bed. Staring up at the ceiling she tried to think about anything other than seeing Ty. Asher's handsome face appeared in her mind and his charming smile as he wrote ideas in her notebook. Looking over to her desk an old familiar shoebox sat there. She grabbed it and bit her bottom lip before opening it.

The first thing she saw was a photo strip of her and Asher from their summer together. On the back in her handwriting was the date and their names. The first photo was of them awkward smiling as she sat on his lap. The second photo they were laughing from bumping their heads together. The third photo Delaney was looking at the camera grinning while Asher was looking up at her smiling. She could see the love in his eyes as he looked at her, and she felt her heart flutter. The final photo was of them kissing. Not just any kiss but their first kiss. She touched her lips as if his lips were still pressed against her. A wave of loneliness washed over her, and she put the photo aside continuing to look through the box.

A photo of her and Ty from their senior prom was in there. They were both standing stiffly next to one another and barely smiling. During the ride over to prom, they had argued about what they were going to do afterwards. He wanted to go to a hotel party with a bunch of his football friends. She wanted to go home and told him he could go to the party. He had not been happy with her answer and pressured her into going. The whole night had been a disaster.

Delaney pulled out a folded sheet of paper seeing Asher's handwriting on it. It had been one of the many letters he had written to her that summer. She ran her fingers over the words as droplets stained the paper. She wiped tears from her face as she read his letter.

…You are my girl, Laney. Forever and always. No matter the distance between us or how much time goes by. You will always be the only one for me. You have my heart in your hands…

The loneliness sat heavily on her chest, and she laid in her bed letting the tears run freely. Taking in a shaky breath as more tears rushed down her face. The emptiness in her chest was nearly unbearable for her to handle. It was a painful reminder of why she never lets anyone in her life get too close. Never again did she want to feel the pain of being abandoned or discarded again. She would never allow anyone to make her feel unwanted and forgotten again.

She sat up hastily putting everything back into box and sliding it under her bed. Pulling the covers over her head, she closed her eyes and tried to forget about the men who broke her.

AUG. '07

DEAR LANEY,

THIS IS THE HARDEST LETTER I'VE EVER HAD TO WRITE. RIGHT NOW, YOU'RE LAYING BESIDE ME IN THE VERY SPOT WE FIRST MET. LAST NIGHT WAS THE MOST AMAZING NIGHT I'VE EVER HAD. BEING WITH YOU, FALLING ASLEEP NEXT YOU, I CAN'T IMAGINE LIFE ANY OTHER WAY. I WANT NOTHING MORE THAN TO STAY WITH YOU FOREVER. TO GO TO SCHOOL IN CHICAGO TO BE CLOSE TO YOU, GO TO YOUR PROM AND WATCH YOU WALK ACROSS THE STAGE WHEN YOUR GRADUATE. BOTH OF US GOING TO THE SAME COLLEGE, LIVING IN AN APARTMENT TOGETHER AND BUILDING OUR LIFE TOGETHER. I WANT YOU TO HAVE THE VERY BEST LIFE BECAUSE YOU MORE THAN DESERVE IT.

THAT IS WHY THIS LETTER IS LITERALLY RIPPING MY HEART TO SHREDS. IN ORDER FOR YOU TO HAVE THE BEST LIFE, IT MEANS THAT I HAVE TO BECOME THE BEST MAN FOR YOU. WHICH MEANS I NEED TO FOLLOW MY FATHER'S PLANS FOR ME. I WANT TO HAVE THE CAREER HE HAD AND TO BECOME A BESTSELLING AUTHOR LIKE HIM. THEN I CAN GIVE YOU ANYTHING AND EVERYTHING YOU WANT. BY THE TIME YOU WAKE UP AND FIND THIS LETTER, MY FAMILY AND I WILL ALREADY BE GONE. I'M GOING TO ATTEND PRINCETON LIKE MY FATHER WANTS ME TO DO. I WILL LIVE WITH THEM IN THE HAMPTONS UNTIL I CAN AFFORD MY OWN PLACE OFF CAMPUS.

To

Laney,

'ove you.

—Asher

I'm doing this because I love you... I'm deeply, madly in love with you. I want to give you everything in the world and this is the first step to me accomplishing that. I promise I will write you letters every day, since I know you find them more romantic than texts or emails. I will send you a new bookmark with every letter as well. Then when I can, I will come visit you in Chicago and we can plan for you to come visit me at Princeton. Though, I have a feeling I will get into a lot of fights trying to keep all the college guys away from my girl.

You are my girl, Laney. Forever and always. No matter the distance between us or how much time goes by. You will always be the only one for me. You have my heart in your hands. That is another reason why I'm writing this letter instead of telling you in person. I don't have the will power or strength to say goodbye to you. I wouldn't do what I know I need to and would just follow you to the ends of the earth. I know this will hurt you and I hope you can find it in your heart to forgive me. Please know that I love you more than anything in the universe. Until my next letter.

Always & Forever Yours,
Asher

Seven

ASHER

The buzz of an airport usually was comforting to Asher as he sat waiting for his plane. He would let it drown out any thoughts running in his mind and concentrate on whatever project he was working on at that time. However today, he was staring absentmindedly out the windows and watching the planes fly up into the air. Something inside of him felt unsettled and urging him to stay in Chicago. He knew it had to do with Delaney and how familiar he was to her. He had never felt so comfortable with anyone before especially when talking about writing.

He looked down at his notebook on the seat next to him. He wanted to pick it up to look at her handwriting in an effort to feel close to her somehow. Asher shook his head at himself.

"Pull yourself together, Graham."

Grabbing his notebook, he flipped it open to the next blanket page when something fell to the ground. Looking down, his heart nearly stopped seeing the drawing on it. His hand shook picking up the piece of card stock and staring at it.

Asher leaned back in his chair as the memory of the day he drew the beach scene on the front of the bookmark filled his mind.

***

Asher looked down at Laney lying on a blanket reading one of his dad's books. It was the perfect day to go swimming in the ocean or lay around on the beach. All Laney wanted to do was hang out at his house on the back deck and read. When she looked up at him with those deep blue eyes he couldn't say no to her. Now, he sat on the deck with his project notebook trying not to stare at the girl who had recently laid claim on his heart.

"I can feel you staring at me. Work on your outline." She said not looking away from her book.

He chuckled, "Who needs an outline. I have it all right up here." He pointed to his temple.

The beautiful laughter flowing from her lips gave him goosebumps as Laney glanced in his direction, "You can barely remember what you did yesterday. How are you going to remember the entire plot of your short story?"

He laid down beside her, running his hand down her back, "I remember clearly what I did yesterday. I believe it went a little something like this."

Asher leaned over gently pressing his lips to hers. Laney rolled onto her back, wrapping her arms around his neck and pulling him closer to her. Suddenly he was enveloped by coconut and the ocean as he deepened their kiss. She sighed as he pulled away for a moment to catch his breath and immediately kissed her again. This time she giggled against his lips threading her fingers into his hair.

"Yep, exactly what happened yesterday." He chuckled looking down at her.

Laney's cheeks were bright red as she rolled her eyes, "I don't know... I remember it a little differently."

She pushed him on to his back and swung her leg over his waist. The sun reflected off the strands of her copper hair making orange streaks. Pulling her hair over to one shoulder, she leaned down kissing him. He ran his hands over her smooth legs coming to rest on her hips. She was right that this was exactly how they been when his dad had walked in on them in his bedroom. Laney had jumped off of him and tumbled off his bed landing on her ass.

"Are your parents home?" She asked suddenly pulling away from him.

He shook his head, "Nope. They're at some fundraiser dinner in Raleigh. They won't be back until tomorrow."

"So, we're alone? All night?"

His eyes immediately went up to her hope filled ones, "Laney..."

***

It was the first time in their month long romance that they had a disagreement. She wanted to go to the next step and so did he, but he wanted to do it right. He didn't want it to be teenagers having sex because of their out of control hormones. He wanted it to be because he loved her and to show her he loved her. It had taken him all night to convince her that nothing was wrong with her, and he very much wanted to sleep with her. After that night he spent the next three weeks planning out the perfect night for her first time. It was also the last time he saw her before moving to The Hamptons and attending Princeton.

Looking down at the bookmark the realization hit him as the only person who could have placed it in his notebook. How hadn't he seen it before or maybe he was trying to rationalize that there was no possible way for him to be lucky enough to find her again. Thinking about it now, he felt foolish not to realize it earlier.

Laney, his Laney, was Delaney Bishop and she was within his reach once more. Immediately he pulled out his phone and called Dom.

"Are you so bored at the airport that you have to bother me?"

"Funny, but no. I need more time in Chicago. I really want to see if working with Delaney Bishop is a possibility. I would like to stay for two more weeks. I promise I'll be working on my manuscript while I'm out here. I think there is something here."

The silence on the other end made Asher nervous. Either Dom was going to be a nice guy and go along with this or an asshole. Asher's bet was on the latter.

"Fine. Two weeks and that's it. I want you back in Wilmington and pounding out chapters instead of pounding into this chick."

There he was, the asshole, Asher took a deep breath before speaking.

"It's not like that but I wouldn't expect you to understand. I'll let you know where I settle in at." Asher ended the call before Dom could say anything else.

He searched for hotels in Evanston and picked one closest to the diner. He ordered an Uber to take him there and finally felt the uneasiness in his body settling. Once he was in his hotel, he text Dom where he was and sat outside on his balcony. His first instinct was to go to the bookshop and confront Delaney there, but he knew that was the wrong move. There was only one other place he knew she would be and it would be several hours before she would be there.

Asher held the bookmark in his hand thinking about how much his life would have changed if his father had simply allowed his letters to be sent. He wished he had been smart enough to mail letters to her from school, but he never thought his father would interfere with his life that way. The anger he had felt when reading his father's letter when he found it with all his letter filled his chest.

Asher's phone buzzed in his pocket. He was shocked to see the name on his screen and for a moment he considered letting it go to voicemail. At the last possible second, he picked up the call.

"Hello Anna."

"Hey Asher, I wanted to make sure it received your copy of the divorce papers."

He looked back at his bag, "Yes, but that's not why you're really calling. What do you want?"

There was a long pause, "Don't be like that Asher. You don't have to be cold."

He sighed, "I'm sorry. Thank you for checking to see if I got them."

"You're welcome. You know I still care about you, but our marriage was going nowhere. We had been drifting apart for a while." She sighed, "I saw a video of you doing a panel for your book. I never thought you would actually give in to Dom."

He chuckled, "It wasn't him. My publisher pushed for me to go out on tour and there wasn't an option to tell them no. It was... an experience to say the least."

There was a long silence making Asher check his phone to see if the call had dropped, "Anna?"

"Was that her? The interviewer in Chicago."

Now it was his turn to be quiet. Neither of them would ever admit it, but one of the many reasons their marriage failed was because he still harbored feelings for Laney. She had followed him throughout college and when he had met Anna during his senior year at Princeton. She had been in the back of his mind when they had their first date, first kiss, first everything. He had even thought about her when he proposed to Anna and when he watched her walk down the aisle.

"I think so. Though it wasn't until today that I realized it might be her."

"Asher, may I be honest with you?"

Her question surprised him, "Of course."

He heard her take a deep breath, "I know I lived in her shadow. From the moment you told me about her over a bottle of whiskey, I knew I would never compare to her."

"Anna…"

"Let me finish. I always figured that at some point you would forget about her and focus on us. When I realized that would never happen I began distancing myself from you to see if you would notice."

Asher pressed his fingers to his forehead pinching them together, "But I didn't."

"No, you didn't notice me slowly moving my things out of our home. You didn't notice me spending more time in L.A. or going weeks without talking to one another. At first I thought it was me. That I was overreacting or not being an attentive wife. I blamed myself for the longest time."

The guilt pressed against his shoulders, "Anna, I'm so sorry. You have to know now that it was never your fault. I was a terrible husband and partner."

"I wish I could blame you Asher. God knows I tried to be angry with you, but honestly I feel bad for you. Never being able to move on properly and allow other people to love you. You hide away in your office and behind your books. So, if I may I want you to do one thing for me."

"Jump off the nearest bridge?" He asked, trying to make it sound like a joke.

"No, I want you to find her and tell her the truth about what happened with your letters. Beg her for forgiveness and then for the love of God be happy."

Asher smiled, "I can't promise that I'll do that, but I'll promise to try."

She laughed softly, "Good. Take care of yourself Asher and don't be a stranger if you're ever in L.A."

"You too, Anna. If you ever need anything let me know and I'll be there."

"Thank you. Oh, and Asher?"

"Yeah?"

"I loved your book. It was a beautiful ending for Detective Martin Williams."

He grinned, "That means a lot to me, thank you. Talk to you soon."

The call ended and Asher stared out to the small town of Evanston. A cool breeze blew by bringing a feeling of change coming his way. He didn't know what was going to happen, but he was certain that this was the beginning of a new era in his life. For once, he was excited to see where the future would take him.

After a long afternoon nap and an early dinner, Asher tried to work on his manuscript to kill time before heading to Lake Bay Diner. The more he wrote in his new manuscript the more he hated it. His mind had already determined that he wanted to work on the project he outlined with Delaney. He created a new folder on his shared drive and created a new word document. The notes he could remember from the previous night he typed out. He added a few new notes of ideas he had and even wrote out a few scenes that he couldn't get out of his mind.

Before he knew it, Asher looked to see it was nearing 10:30 pm. He figured it might still be a little early for Delaney to be at the diner, but he was starting to get antsy. Packing up his things, he headed out of the hotel and started walking towards the diner. He could see why Delaney loved to walk to and from the diner. The leaves crunched under his boots, the breeze blowing through his hair and the stars bright in the sky. It was the perfect autumn night.

When he approached the diner, he stopped seeing Delaney already sitting in her booth. Her computer was open and her head was resting in her hand. She glanced down at her notes and made a disgruntled face causing Asher to laugh. Seeing her now, knowing who she was, he couldn't believe he didn't know it was her. Her mannerism were the same, her hair was a little darker and her eyes were a deeper blue than he remembered. She held her pen against her lips before writing a note in her notebook. He pulled out the bookmark from his bag and headed inside.

Delaney never looked up from her notebook as he approached her table. He was envious of her focus but knew he was about to destroy that. He placed the bookmark on the table and slid it towards her capturing her attention. She looked up at him almost with an expectancy and bit her lower lip like she always had done with she was nervous.

"Hi Laney."

DELANEY

Delaney had been in the diner for hours. Louisa was surprised when she had shown up before midnight. She had already eaten a basket of fries and had three refills of soda. After sleeping all afternoon and having nothing to distracted her at home, she grabbed all of things to head off to the one place that always brought her comfort. For the last few hours, she had focused in on finishing her outline and writing out a few scenes as they came to her. She was going into hour four when she hit a block. Using a tried and true exercise, she began to free write in her notebook.

That's when a familiar hand drawn bookmark slid across her table and a pair of familiar forest green eyes stared down at her. She had been hoping he would find his bookmark when he was on the plane heading back home. Apparently the universe had other plans in mind.

"Hi Laney."

She flinched, "No one calls me that anymore."

Asher slid into the seat across from her, "That's what I always called you. Well, that or baby."

"Don't even think about it." She shook her head, "So, now you know who I am. What are you doing here?" She asked her tone flat and cold.

"When did you realize it was me? Did you know the whole time? Playing the role of a fan but knowing it was me the whole time."

Delaney tried to ignore the anger slipping in between his words. She leaned back against her seat doing her best to not to look into those beautiful eyes she knew would break her walls.

"I had no idea who you were until I saw you the day of the event. I honestly believed that I was going to be meeting my favorite author Graham A. Jacob. It wasn't until I saw you that it all hit me. Asher Jacob Graham, rearrange it and you get your pen name."

"Why didn't you tell me when you met me?" He crossed his arms over his chest, "I even asked if we knew each other and you say we didn't."

"Well, what did you expect Asher? When I realized that you didn't even remember who I was I kind of took offense to it. Obviously, that summer meant more to me than to you. I figured you would be gone within twenty-four hours, and I would never have to see you again. So why bring up the past."

Delaney picked up the bookmark. It was her favorite one of all the ones he had made for her that summer. He drew a beach at sunset from the night they met.

"I can't believe you kept my bookmark." He mentioned, looking down at it fondly.

She sighed, "Well, what can I say? I guess I'm sentimental."

There was no reason to tell him that she had kept all his bookmarks and letters he wrote to her that summer. Even though any time she looked or thought about them she would fall deeper into the dark well inside of her. The same well that she was currently circling the edge of the longer he sat across from her.

"Well, thank you for returning this. I guess you can go back home now."

Asher shook his head with a familiar stubborn look in his eyes, "Actually, I'm staying here in Evanston for the next two weeks."

"What? Why?"

"Well, yesterday I met this incredible author who impressed me with her talent. It's my mission to convince her to work with me on a book." He smiled, infuriating her.

"Really? You still think we would work great together?" She asked with sarcasm dripping off each word from her lips.

His smile turned into a full grin, "Now knowing who you truly are I believe it more than ever. I think you know it too. We always complimented one another."

"That was nearly two decades ago. I've changed and I'm assuming you have as well." She looked down at her notebook, "Plus I'm already starting my new project and my agent loves it."

She watched as he peeked over to her notebook, "Seems like you're a little stuck. Freewriting, right? You always would do that when you were frustrated or stuck on something."

"Sure, now you remember…" she mumbled.

"Lane-"

"Don't call me that." She snapped, "No one has called me that since you. I'm not Laney anymore and haven't been since the morning I read your final letter."

"Everything okay?" Louisa walked up to the table looking directly at Delaney.

She smiled watching Asher lean away from the waitress. At least he knew better than say anything.

"We're fine, Louisa. I promise."

She walked away as Delaney looked back at Asher who was watching Louisa go back behind the counter. "I do believe that woman would cut my balls off if I upset you."

Delaney laughed, "Yes she would so don't make her do that and go back home."

He turned back towards, hurt filling his face, "I can't."

"Why not?"

She clenched her fists in her lap frustrated that he kept pressing her. Why was he so insistent? Why did he care? Why, why, why? Finally, Delaney couldn't take not asking the question on her mind since the end of that summer in 2007.

"Why didn't you write to me? You promised you were going to write to me. You promised to visit me. Instead, you forgot all about me and smashed my little, fragile heart into a million pieces."

She took in a sharp breath surprised to see the pain in Asher's eyes and face. It was like she had physically struck him. His eyes darted to the table in front of them. When he spoke, his voice was remorseful and quiet.

"I'm sorry that none of my letters reached you. I'm sorry for breaking all of my promises. I'm sorry for hurting you."

"What do you mean your letters never reached me?"

Being a writer, word phrasing was a specialty of hers and she knew of his. He didn't say he never wrote to her, but that his letters never reached her. That would mean he had written to her. That meant the last decade of heartache and turmoil could have been prevented. Suddenly Delaney's head was spinning with all the possibilities of what ifs.

"When my parents died, I inherited their house in Wilmington. When I was going through their things, I found all the letters I had written to you bundled together with a letter from my father. I wrote to you all the time and would ask my mom to mail them off for me. It ended up that my father was taking the letters and keeping them."

Delaney didn't want to believe Asher, "Why would he do that?"

"That last night we were together. My father had come back home early to get me and take me to our new house in The Hamptons. He…" Asher's cheeks turned a slight pink, "He saw us in my room."

Now her cheeks were burning, "Oh god…"

"Yeah, when I went down to the kitchen to get you a cup of water, he was waiting for me. He told me if I really wanted to do what was right then I would let you go to become the man you deserved. To go to Princeton and create a life worthy of you. I believed him. What I didn't know was he was lying to me. He thought you were beneath us, beneath me and the talents I was developing. He knew if he told me that I would rebel, so he told me what I wanted to hear."

Her heart dropped, "Asher, I'm so sorry."

His eyes softened, "You have nothing to be sorry about. There was nothing either of us could have done since we had no idea what was truly going on. You thought I forgot all about you, which is the furthest thing from the truth. I thought about you all the time. Even after I met Anna and married her. I thought about you and ultimately it ended my marriage. Again, not that you had anything to do with that. It was all on me."

"You shouldn't have had to go through that though. How long were you married?"

Asher sat back with a small smile on his lips, "Seven years and together for ten years. She's an architect and now lives in Los Angeles starting her own firm."

Asher pulled out his phone and showed her a picture of Anna and him from their honeymoon. She was a beautiful, petite woman with warm brown hair and matching brown eyes. Her smile was filled with pure happiness while his was guarded.

"She's beautiful."

"Yeah, she is and I'm sure she is even more beautiful now that I'm not dragging her down."

Delaney couldn't help to reach over and squeeze his hand, "I'm sure you didn't drag her down. Honestly, you probably were never your true self around her thanks to what your dad did. It wasn't your fault."

He squeezed her hand back and she quickly withdrew it back into her lap. The familiarity and comfort it brought to her was too much. She couldn't allow herself to fall for him again. She had to guard her heart.

"That may be true, but it doesn't mean it wasn't my fault." He shook his head, "I'm sure you had men lining up for the privilege to be with you."

A chill went down her spine, "No. Not even close."

His eyebrow arched, "Wasn't there a guy who had asked out you right before that summer? I'm sure once you realized what a loser I was that you would have ended up with someone better."

Her veins burned with anger. Not towards Ty or Asher, but towards the man that caused all this. Her life suddenly out of her grasp all because one man felt she was unworthy for his son. As quickly as the anger burned through then came the icy realization that Asher's father was right. She was unworthy of him. Ty had proven that she was a terrible partner and it was actually Asher who had dodged the bullet.

"You're not a loser. Your dad was right. I was beneath you and you deserved better. Hopefully now you can realize that and move on with your life to find happiness."

Delaney closed her notebook and laptop. The inspiration that usually flowed through her sitting in the diner now vanished. For the second time that day all she wanted to do was go home, get under her covers and cry herself to sleep.

"How can you say that? You are definitely not beneath me and I, no we, deserved the chance to see what would have become of our love." The passion in his eyes scared her. "What happened to make you think that you are beneath anyone?"

Delaney looked down at her hands on the table, "You really want to know?" Her hands began to tremble.

"Of course I do."

"I waited for your letters. I waited while Quinn told me to move on and the most popular boy in my school chased after me. I waited because the only boy I ever wanted to be with was you. Ty was used to getting what he wanted and kept persisting on asking me out. Finally, I said yes when he asked me to homecoming that year."

She remembered it like it was yesterday. Ty walking into the library she worked at after school. He was wearing a tux and had a bouquet of flowers. He held a sign asking her to homecoming with a check box with yes or no. Not wanting to embarrass herself or him she gave in and checked yes.

"We went to homecoming and for the first time I was able to push you to the back of my mind. Ty and I dated from that moment on. When we were in college, he asked me to move in with him and when we graduated from college he proposed. He wanted the whole white picket fence and kids as soon as possible."

The never wavering heaviness on her shoulders pressed further down onto her as she continued, "I was married at twenty-two and by the end of our first year I found out I could never have my own children. My body would never produce healthy eggs to have a pregnancy. Ty couldn't except that his perfect little life was being tarnished by my failures of doing what a woman is naturally supposed to do."

"Delaney…" Her name was a whisper on his lips, and it broke her.

Tears welled in her eyes, "He became distant and eventually he filed for divorce after three years of being married. He now has the life he always wanted with the woman he had an affair with throughout our entire marriage. They have two beautiful kids including one that was born before we were divorced."

She watched Asher's fist clench into a ball, "Bastard…"

"No, he wasn't. He wanted what any other man wants which was a wife that wasn't a complete failure and broken beyond repair. I was damaged already when he asked me to homecoming and I continued to deteriorate throughout our relationship. My failed marriage was my fault. My body's failure to do one simple task that all woman do is my fault. All of it because one summer I threw caution to the wind and fell in love with a boy who was way out of my league. So my broken heart afterwards was my fault and how my life turned out is my fault."

She took a deep breath feeling the weight on her shoulders lift ever so slightly from finally speaking her truth. She almost giggled from the release but instead allowed the tears to fall down her cheeks.

"Delaney, you can't possibly believe that. You have to know deep down that none of this was your fault. Right?"

It was more of a plead than a question and all she could do was shake her head.

"I'm sorry." Asher reached across the table and wiped away her tears cupping her face, "I'm so sorry for everything."

She couldn't help but lean into his touch but then back away, "It's fine."

"No it's not…"

Delaney shook her head and began packing up her things, "No, really it's fine. I learned a valuable lesson from all of it that has led me to being the person I am today."

"What is that?" He asked as she stood up from the booth, "Delaney wait, please."

She turned around steeling herself, "I learned that I can never trust anyone with my heart. That it's better for me to be alone in this world than allow anyone close to me that could break my heart for good. Goodnight Asher."

She quickly made her way out of the diner and jogged down the street until the diner was out of view. That's when everything hit her at once and she had to stop to gasp for air as a sob ripped from her chest. Seeing him again, him knowing who she is was all too much for Delaney. When she walked into her apartment and saw Quinn sitting in the living room she broke down to the only person in the world she trusted wholeheartedly.

ASHER

Asher flipped onto his right side pulling the scratchy comforter over his shoulders. He was staring at the red lit wall reflecting the digital clock color on the end table. He tried closing his eyes again and Delaney's beautifully sad blue eyes appeared. The tears falling down her cheeks that sliced right through his heart. All the pain creasing through her forehead and around her eyes. The shell of a woman who was vibrant and the center of attention wherever she went now blended into the shadows.

He flipped onto his back and stared up at the ceiling. Now that he knew she was his Laney there was no way he could not have her in his life. The universe was giving him a second chance, and he had to do everything in his power to take it. Sitting up he turned on the light beside him and grabbed his notebook. He began writing her a letter like he did when they were teenagers and soon he found his body relaxing enough for him to fall asleep.

***

"Asher… Ash-sher…"

A sweet, warm voice pulled him from his sleep. Peeking open his eyes he found a curtain of red surrounding him as soft lips kissed down his neck. He groaned running his hands down her sides to rest on her hips.

"Are you awake?" She whispered into his ear, "Today is a big day."

He smirked, "It is? Isn't it Tuesday? Nothing exciting ever happens on Tuesdays. Ow!"

Delaney smacked his arm as she sat up, "You know good and well what today is. Don't play dumb with me Asher Graham."

He brought his hand behind her neck and pulled her back down to kiss her. Instinctively, he rolled his hips against her making her moan. She pushed her hands against his chest breaking their kiss.

"Don't you dare try to distract me. We have to get up and get ready for our event at the bookshop."

"Oh, I'm up…" He grabbed a hold of her rolling Delaney onto her back and making her squeal.

"Asher!" She laughed as he trailed kisses down her body, "Seriously Asher, we don't have time."

He made it down between her legs, kissing her inner thighs, "Babe, there is no event without us, so we have all the time in the world. Plus, I think this will relieve a lot of pressure that we both have built up from the release of our book."

Asher pressed his lips against her panties before pulling them down her legs, "I promise to be quick."

The soft moans slipping through her lips urged him to continue until she tugged on his hair to get his attention.

"Y-You're right… this will help us." She pulled him back up to her pressing her lips against his, "but don't be too quick."

He grinned before reaching down between them and pushing inside of her…

***

Asher's eyes snapped open seeing he was back in his hotel room. Alone. He groaned, pushing his blanket off and heading to the bathroom. It was nearly five in the morning and decided he might as well get up and get ready for the day. Once he was dressed, Asher headed out to a local coffee shop that was close to his hotel. He was surprised that at seven o'clock in the morning the place wasn't that busy, but he was grateful as he took that first sip and sat down at a table.

Pulling out his laptop and headphones, he text Dom to set up a meeting to discuss next steps. Dom was more than eager to hop on a call with him.

"Please tell me you've changed your mind and are headed back to Wilmington."

"Not quite." Asher rolled his eyes hearing Dom groan, "I want you to draw up a contract for Delaney Bishop to co-author a book with me. I want her to be the lead author on the book and all royalties going to her."

There was silence until Dom's booming voice rang in his ear, "You want me to do what! Absolutely fucking not. People are expecting a big title from you after ending your main series. They're not going to buy a book from some unknown author that has your name in the small print."

Asher sat there for a moment letting Dom stew for bit, "Then I will return my advance for the next book, end my contract with the publisher and you then work solely with Delaney's agent on a book for us to co-author. Maybe under a different pen name or maybe even my real name. I will get my lawyer started on all the paperwork."

"Wait."

He sat there waiting for Dom's counteroffer which he knew was coming. Over the last fifteen years of working with Dom, they had developed the type of relationship that was friendly but brutal. They never bullshit one another and always find a way to compromise with what each of them wants. He knew he was asking for a lot especially when Dom was right. His publishers were expecting a big book from him after ending his series. He also knew his publishers would agree to whatever he wants since he brings them a lot of money in with his sales. Dom, on the other hand, was the one he had to play hardball with.

"I'll work on a contract, but the royalties will be split accordingly. I believe seventy percent to you and thirty to her is fair. She is a debut author, and you are a New York Times Bestseller. She needs to pay her dues like you did."

"Eighty percent to her and twenty to me. I'm not going any higher. She may need to pay her dues, but she also needs to make a living. I've made enough off my books to live comfortably. Plus think about it from a PR perspective. I'll be mentoring a new author and bringing them up from the ground floor. Maybe this will finally convince me to get an online presence to promote our project."

Asher knew he had hooked Dom when he didn't immediately shoot down is idea. For the last five or so years everyone on his team had been trying to get him to be on social media. He hated the idea of being so vulnerable and available to everyone in the world. He also hated that his team was right and he would sell double or triple the books if he had more of a presence online. His small book tour had proven fruitful as his book soared to the top of the New York Times list.

"Fine, I'll write it up and send it for you to review. Should I send a copy to Leigh Meyer as well?"

He grinned mentally patting himself on the back, "Not until I've read it. I'll let you know when to send it."

Dom began laughing, "You haven't convinced her to work with you yet? Oh my god, you've got it bad for this chick."

"Shut up while you're ahead, Dom. I'll talk to you later."

Asher ended the call finishing his coffee which tasted even better with the small victory over his agent. Now he needed to convince Delaney that his intentions of working with her were truly professional and not because he couldn't imagine his life without her again. He looked at the Scattered Pages website to see that they opened at nine o'clock. That meant he had at least an hour before he could go there and try to talk with Delaney again. He knew it would be pressing his luck with her, but he had to keep trying. He decided to take the time he had and write a list of pros as to why they should work together.

He finally made his way to the Scattered Pages and saw they already had quite a few customers inside. Knowing at least one good thing came out of all the heartache she experienced was her bookshop brought a warm sense of pride in his chest. He walked inside to see one of the clerks, Gen, standing at the register.

"Hi, may I help… oh Mr. Jacob." Her eyes widened as he stepped up to the counter, "H-How can I help you?"

"Nice to see you again Gen. I was hoping to speak to Delaney if she's available."

Gen went to speak but a voice from behind her chimed in, "She's not available."

Asher watched Quinn walk up and knew she was the first step to getting back on Delaney's good side. He motioned for them to step off to the side and smiled at Gen.

"Thank you Gen." She nodded at him with a worried expression then went up to the front of the shop.

Quinn led him to beneath the stairs where the entrance for the back room was. She turned around quickly and stuck her finger into his chest.

"You have a lot of nerve coming here and wanting to speak to Delaney. Haven't you caused her enough pain and suffering?"

"Yes, I have. I want to start mending everything I broke with her." Asher took a half step back to keep out of striking distance of Quinn, "I promise my visit today is purely professional, but I won't lie to you or her. I want Delaney to be part of my life in any way I can. Be professional or friends. I care for her."

Quinn's eyes softened slightly, "Is the story about what your dad did true?"

He nodded as she continued, "You had no idea he felt that way about her?"

"If I had known then that he felt that way then I would have given up everything to be with Delaney. I didn't care about going to an Ivy League school or the money my parents had. The moment I met Delaney all I knew is that I wanted to be by her side forever."

She crossed her arms over her chest, "And now? What are your intentions now?"

He paused for a moment. He knew the right answer was to tell her that he wanted to be friends with her and help support her in any way he could. That he wanted to work with her and write books with her. Neither reason was a lie, but at this moment he knew being completely honest with Delaney's best friend was the best first step to being back in her life.

"I want to show her that she is worthy of being loved. I want her to know that never once did I ever think she was beneath me but the other way around. I was never good enough to be with her. I want to be by her side in any capacity she'll have me."

When he saw Quinn's shoulders relax Asher knew he had yet another small victory. She motioned for him to follow her upstairs and led him into her office. He couldn't help to chuckle seeing the complete difference between her office and Delaney's. Quinn's was bright, slightly messy and well lived in where Delaney's office was orderly and almost sterile.

"Delaney's not here today. She didn't get a lot of sleep last night. Between seeing you again and then running into her ex yesterday here. Her emotions have been put through the ringer."

"She didn't tell me she ran into her ex yesterday. No wonder she was on edge." Asher sat down across from Quinn, "I came here to try and convince Delaney to write with me. I truly believe that we could have an amazing writing partnership and create some truly remarkable stories. I know she's going to think that this is a charity case or trying to make up for what happened in the past. Honestly, I only want the chance to get to know her again and work together for now. If she so chooses to being friends with me then I would consider myself very lucky."

She smiled, looking to a framed picture on her desk, "You would be lucky. I don't know if you'll be able to convince her to work with you. Seeing you again really threw her for a loop, and she's been spiraling ever since."

It hurt to hear he was causing her pain, "It was never my intention to hurt her. Not then and definitely not now. I can't help to think that the universe is giving us a second chance and it's the only thing I have been thinking about since seeing her again."

"You really loved her, didn't you?"

"Yes." The answer came immediately out of his mouth without hesitation, "To be honest, a part of me still loves her. I know that may sound ridiculous or creepy, but it's the truth."

Quinn leaned back in her chair with a sigh, "You know, I really wanted to hate you. I want to tell you to fuck off and stay away from my best friend."

He chuckled, "You would have every right to do that."

"I swear to god if you hurt her again I will make sure even God himself can't find your body." Quinn started writing on a sheet of scrap paper, "Here's our address, she should be home still unless she decided to go to the diner. Good luck."

Asher took the piece of paper like it was a golden ticket, "Thank you, I appreciate you not telling me to fuck off."

"It's still earlier. Now go before I change my mind."

As he walked out onto the sidewalk in front of the Scattered Pages, Asher had a new pep in his step. Winning over the best friend was crucial. Now he had a little more confidence and hope as he walked to Delaney's apartment. When he stepped in front of her building his phone ding with an email notification. Dom had sent the rough draft of the contract over and he took it as a sign from the universe that he was headed in the right direction. He quickly skimmed over it before heading up to Delaney's apartment. Standing outside her door for a moment, he rapped his knuckles against it and held his breath.

The door didn't open but her voice traveled through it, "What are you doing here?"

"Delaney, please give me five minutes and then I promise I'll leave."

He waited counting the seconds in his head. Thirty. Forty-five. Sixty. He almost went to knock again when he heard the bolt unlock and the door cracked open.

"Five minutes and I have a timer set." She pointed to the microwave where a timer was indeed counting down.

"Thank you."

She shut the door and folded her arms across her chest sitting at the small table in the kitchen. "No need to thank me. Say what you have to say so we can both move on."

"No matter what happened in the past I still believe you're one of the most talented authors I've read in a long time. I love your style and out of the box thinking. I want you to seriously consider writing a book with me."

She sighed, "You can't be serious."

He pulled up the contract on his phone and slid it towards her, "I am. I had my agent draw up this rough draft contract. You'll be the main author on the project. You will have creative decision making in all aspects of the book. Eighty percent of the royalties will go to you while the other twenty will come to me. Whatever press or advertising you want for the book I'll happily participate in. You'll have almost all control over everything."

Her eyes were skimming through the pages, "Why?" She looked up at him handing his phone back.

"Why what?" He asked, not knowing what she was referring to in the contract.

"Why do you specifically want to work with me? There are plenty of talented debut authors that would die for the chance to work with you. Why are you pushing so hard to work with me?"

This was his moment. He knew what he said next would make or break the opportunity to have Delaney back in his life.

"I want you to be in my life again. Right now, professionally makes the most sense. I know you have changed a lot since we were teenagers as have I. Working together will give us the opportunity to get to know each other again and for me to prove myself to be your friend. No matter how long it takes, I want to prove to you that I can and want to be by your side encouraging you in any way I can."

Delaney loosened her arms allowing them to rest on the table, "It says in this contract that I would have to work in Wilmington. Did you put that in there or your agent?"

Asher looked at the contract again specifically for that part, "Damn it. I'm sorry that was Dom. I have a really good set up at my house in Wilmington and he has a little more control over getting me to write there. I would completely understand if that would be a deal breaker and I will have him change it for the official contract."

A small smile appeared on her lips, "It's not necessarily a deal breaker."

His eyes met hers with a spark of hope igniting in his chest, "Well, as you may remember, there is more than enough room in the house if you wanted to stay there. You could definitely have your own room and work space. Being in the same town would help with collaborating."

"Plenty of authors co-write on opposite sides of the world. Technology is great for that." She looked over to the timer which was showing he still had two minutes left. "Have your agent send Leigh a copy of that contract and I'll see what she says. I make no promises that I'll agree to this."

"I appreciate you even considering it. I'll make sure she has a copy of it by the end of the day. I'm still going to stay in Chicago for the next couple of weeks if you could have a decision by then it would be great."

She nodded, "You're not going to show up at the bookshop everyday asking if I've made a decision, are you?"

"No, but I make no promises that we might run into one another at the diner. I really love the vibe there and even looked up the closest diner in Wilmington." His timer went off as he stood from the table, "Thank you for the five minutes."

She walked him to the door, "If Leigh thinks it's a good idea for me to work with you then I'll definitely consider it. Right now, I'm not sure if spending so much time with you is good for me. Either way, I promise to give your offer serious consideration."

"That's all I ask. I hope you have a great rest of your day."

He walked out of her apartment hearing door close and lock behind him. Taking a shaky breath, he text Dom to finalize the contract and send it to Leigh Meyer. Then immediately followed with another text calling him an asshole for saying they had to work in Wilmington. Asher decided to calm the anxious nerves in his body by going on an extended walk before heading back to his hotel. He knew the next couple of weeks were going to be the longest ones in his life. All he could do was hope that the universe cleared a path for him to reconnect with Delaney.

Dear Diary,

Remember how I was complaining about being at my grandparents for the summer? Yeah... I take it all back. The last couple of weeks have been the best in my life. Asher and I hang out every day and he even includes my brother, which I kind of find endearing even though Dillon can be annoying at times. I think him hanging out with Asher will be good for him. Asher is so mature and really chill about everything. Also, he is always coming up with something new for us to do. During the day the three of us will go swimming or out on his parents boat. Then at night, he and I will go to the movies then walk around town.

Today, while we were walking back home, he asked me if I had a boyfriend back home. I didn't really think anything about it when he asked. I told him about Ty and how he likes me, but I don't really like him back. Like it feels like I should like him since he's popular and what not. I told him I didn't have a boyfriend. He mentioned that he didn't have a girlfriend either. Now thinking about it, I wonder if that was his way of asking for me to be his girlfriend, but that seems unlikely. I mean... come on. Guys like him don't like girls like me. Especially since he's going to college and I'm still in high school.

Don't get me wrong, if he asked me to be his I would say yes in a heartbeat. Every time I'm around him my heart races and my stomach gets all fluttery. He makes me feel special like no one else has. I'm really scared that I really, really like him and maybe getting my hopes up that he would feel the same.

Tonight he gave me one of his dad's books to read. Within the pages was a bookmark he made with the ticket from our first movie and our favorite line from the movie. Isn't that sweet? Man... I really like this guy. Fingers crossed that he might like me too.

Smile!! Until next time,

Laney

DELANEY

The airport was surprisingly empty as Delaney made her way to the baggage claim. She couldn't believe she was in North Carolina. After a week of Leigh and Quinn encouraging her to work with Asher. Delaney was now back in the city that started everything to write a book with her teenage summer boyfriend. She stood by the conveyor belt waiting for her suitcase feeling the invisible rope around her chest tighten. She pulled out her phone, calling the one person she blamed most for her being there.

"This is crazy. I can't do this."

Quinn chuckled, "Hello, I'm glad you made it safely to Wilmington."

Delaney saw her suitcase and quickly grabbed it, "Not funny Quinn Larson! I'm serious, I can't do this. I can't work with him. I can't be here with him. I. Just. Can't."

"Take a breath, Delaney." She mirrored Quinn's breathing, "You can do this. You are going to write an amazing book. You are going to work through a lot of trauma that has been burdening you for decades. And you're going to satisfy all that pent up energy and frustrations with your hot summer boyfriend."

Delaney stopped in the middle of the terminal not only from her best friend cackling on the phone, but from a man in a black suit holding a sign with her name on it.

"I hate you so much right now. I have to go."

"I love you too! Have fun and do everything that I would do." Quinn's laughter was still echoing in her head after the call ended.

She approached the man, "Hi, I'm Delaney Bishop."

He looked up from his phone smiling, "Hello, Miss Bishop. I'm Liam and I'll be driving you today."

Liam took her suitcase from her and led her out the main entrance to a waiting SUV parked on the curb. Delaney expected Asher to be in the car but was pleasantly surprised to find that he wasn't. Getting into the backseat, she watched as Liam drove them down the highway heading towards the beach.

"Have you ever been to Wilmington before?"

Delaney watched the world pass by as she answered, "Yes, a long time ago."

She allowed her mind to wander back to the last time she had taken the familiar drive to the Wilmington Beach community. The closer they were getting to the community entrance the more memories were flashing through her mind. She saw the diner they would spend countless night hanging out at and where her love for strawberry milkshakes began. She couldn't believe her eyes when she saw the small taco hut still standing on the beach as a memorial where the new taco hut was now a large restaurant that sat next to it.

Before she knew it, they were pulling up to the large metal gate that held the beach side community within it. She remember them seeming a lot bigger at sixteen. Now they looked like was over glorified garage doors. However, knowing they were closing behind her as Liam drove through tightened the rope around her chest once more almost making her gasp for air.

She was near to a full blown panic attack when her grandparents humble little beach house came into view. The rope around her loosened and slipped from around her chest. After the summer with Asher, Delaney never came back to visit her grandparents and once they had passed she had regretted allowing her anger towards him keep her away from their beautiful oasis.

Liam pulled into the driveway of Asher's home, and she immediately got out walking into the cul-de-sac towards her grandparents' house. Swimming with Dillon in their pool or watching him and Asher play beach football with some other guys. Late nights of sitting on the beach talking and making out. Looking back now, she had nothing, but good memories of Wilmington and her cheeks burned with foolishness for staying away for so long.

"The Murphy's now own it." His deep, husky voice sent chills down her spine, "They have twins, boy and a girl, who around eight or nine."

She laughed softly, "What are the odds…"

Asher walked up beside her, "It is quite the coincidence. They're a lovely family and in the summer the kids were always coming over to swim in my pool."

She turned towards him, "Just like Dillon and I used to do that summer."

"Yeah." He looked off as if searching for someone then shook his head, "Well, let me show you to your room and let you get settled in. I don't cook much, so I was planning on ordering Chinese for dinner. Is that alright?"

Delaney nodded, "Sure that sounds fine. Maybe I could go grocery shopping and cook a meal or two. At least letting me feel like I'm contributing something around here."

A big sticking point for them both was Delaney staying there for free. She knew Asher was well off and could take care of it all, but she wanted to pull her own weight as well. Asher had put his foot down since she was willing to indulge his agent's insistence on her working in Wilmington with him.

"If I let you buy groceries and cook will that make you feel better?" he asked with a hint of a smirk curling on the corner of his lips.

Delaney nodded, "Yes it would and I would probably do it regardless. I can't live on Chinese takeout anymore. I have to have some balance of junk and healthy."

Asher held out his hand to her, "Deal."

"Deal."

She took his hand; the hairs on her arm standing as sparks surged up it. Hearing him chuckle and shake his hand after she let it go was a sure sign he had felt it to. Asher went to the car and grabbed her suitcase taking it inside the house. Delaney looked back at the house one last time before following him inside.

"I didn't know which room you would prefer so I figured you might want more privacy than not."

She followed him down the stairs to the lower level of the massive house. She could remember having movie nights in the theater room with her brother and Asher. Thinking of Dillon now, she made a mental note to call him later to update him on everything going on. She was positive he would have encouraged her not to go back to Wilmington. After that summer, Dillon had vowed if he ever saw Asher again he would punch him in his pretty little face. An image of that made her giggle catching Asher's attention as they walked down the hallway.

"Something funny?"

She shook her head, "Just lots of memories coming up being back here. Movie nights with Dillon and what not."

He flinched hearing her brother's name, "I remember how cool he thought I was. I'm sure now he would have a different opinion after everything that happened."

Delaney chuckled, "Yes he does. The bond between fraternal twins is strong and my pain back then was his as well."

"So, he hates me. I figured as much." Asher's laugh was filled with sadness which made Delaney feel the slightest bit bad for him.

"I don't know about hate, but he's not your biggest fan." She followed Asher into the second room to the right, "Wow…"

Looking around, she couldn't believe he had fully furnished an entire bedroom within a week. There was a queen size bed in the center with pale green bedding and pillows. On either side were end tables one with a reading lamp and the other with a charging station for her phone and earbuds. A large dresser with a mirror was on the left side of the bed while a closet with a shelving unit was on the opposite wall. A few framed pictures filled up the blanket space of the white walls. Delaney stepped up to one of the photos instantly recognizing it.

"Is this the Taco Hut?"

Asher smiled, "Yes it is. My mom used to love taking photos when we lived here. Anytime we were at the beach she always had her camera out. When I moved in I found all her framed pictures in the storage area. I decided they needed to be displayed throughout the house. If you don't like them feel free to take them down and replace them with whatever you like."

Delaney turned to see Asher nervously looking down to his feet, "She was very talented. Why didn't I know she was a photographer?"

Asher's gaze dropped to his feet. "She was very talented," Delaney said. "Why didn't I know she was a photographer?"

"Well, I think they're beautiful and would like to keep them right where they are."

Asher tapped Delaney on the shoulder. "Dom wants to meet for dinner at seven. Do you want to come, or would you rather order room service and relax? It's all covered, so you don't need to worry about anything."

They walked across the hall into another bedroom that indeed looked like an office. There were two large windows looking out towards the beach and ocean. In front of them was a large L-shaped desk that was bare except for two large monitors. On the wall across from the desk was floor to ceiling bookshelves. They were mostly filled with Asher's dad's books then his books followed after that. There was also an oversized chair in one corner with a blanket and pillow.

"Do you have a rewards membership to Ikea or something?" She asked, looking at all the book spines.

Asher laughed, "I'm actually their customer of the year in Charlotte. I didn't want to keep any of my parents' things. I donated them to locate charities or homeless shelters. I wanted everything to be new."

"That's understandable. Is this your office normally? You didn't have to rearrange everything for me. I'm fine with sitting on a bed or couch and writing on my laptop."

"Honestly, there was nothing in this room until you decided to come to Wilmington. My office is upstairs in the master bedroom." She turned towards him as he continued, "I couldn't imagine sleeping in my parents' old bedroom, so I turned it into an office. I did some updates to my old room and sleep in there."

A memory of the last time she had been in Asher's room popped into her mind, and she felt her cheeks heating up, "Oh… o-okay. Good to know."

"You're always welcome to work in my office if you want. There's a large bay window that has a fantastic view of the ocean. I didn't know if you would want to work in my office or not, so I played it safe. We can always move this desk upstairs because there is plenty of room up there."

Delaney could tell he was nervous about making sure she felt welcome and comfortable. Part of her really loved that he was working so hard for that but the other part of her felt like an inconvenience.

"This is fine for now. I appreciate everything you've done to make me more at ease being here." She truly meant that and was rewarded with one of Asher's brilliant smiles.

"I'm glad, well I'll let you get settled in and order the takeout. Beef and broccoli with an egg roll still your order?"

She chuckled, "I can't believe you still remember that. Yes, that's still my favorite. Though I have grown a fondness for ramen as well."

His eyes widened in mocking shock, "You? Ramen? How you've changed Miss Bishop. Lucky for you, I happen to know of the best ramen place in Wilmington. One night we'll have to check it out."

"Sounds good to me. Okay now get out so I can put my own touch on these two rooms. Right now, I feel like a damsel trap in a dungeon." She gently pushed him out into the hallway that was filled with his rich laughter.

"Alright, alright, I'm leaving." When he reached the stairs he turned back towards her, "Seriously, if you need anything let me know. Amazon is my best friend, and I have Ikea on speed dial."

Delaney watched him walk upstairs then went into her room and flopped down on the bed. Her social battery was running on empty, and she needed some time to process everything going on. The whole time she was flying towards Wilmington, driving through the town and being inside Asher's house now. A sense of calm had been spreading over her. A sense of belonging and home now settling into her chest as she laid on the bed knowing that Asher was so close to her. It felt like the bed was cradling her and she felt her eyes getting heavy. Curling onto her side, Delaney closed her eyes relaxing against the soft mattress slipping into the darkness.

When she opened her eyes again, it was dark within her room. She was covered with a blanket that she recognized from the office. Wrapping it around her shoulders she made her way up the stairs and towards the kitchen. She surprised herself by remembering exactly where it was as if she had never left. On the refrigerator there was a note for her.

Delaney,

I didn't want to wake you up. Your food is in the fridge and help yourself to anything else you want. I'm going to be working in my office if you need anything.

-Asher

Pulling out her food out, Delaney warmed it in the microwave then stepped outside onto the deck. The breeze from the ocean made her shiver but it was worth watching the sun set over it. She watched as a family was walking on the beach together. Kids were giggling and the parents were talking to one another. Suddenly, her chest ached watching the family continuing their walk and knowing she would never have that. Movement from the corner of her eye caught her attention.

Asher was pacing in front of his office window. She could see he was wearing a pair of headphones over his ears. She couldn't help but admire his form now looking out towards the ocean. His lean body was covered by a hoodie and sweatpants. His hair was curling around his headphones, and his glasses were nearly falling off the tip of his nose. His strong jaw was covered by a few days growth that made her shiver in a way she had long forgotten about. He stepped away from the window and headed further into the room until out of view. The sudden urge to go to him pushed her up from her spot on the deck and abandoning her food on the counter.

Walking down the hallway towards the master bedroom, the door was cracked open allowing low light to seep out from it. She gently pushed the door open and saw Asher sitting at an antique wooden desk with his back to her. His head was bopping to whatever was playing in his headphones. He was looking down at his notebook and bouncing his pen on top of it. His shoulders were tense as well as his back. The urge to touch him was nearly overwhelming and she found her foot taking a step towards him. Taking a deep breath, she knocked on the door frame before walking in. He didn't flinch and she almost giggled at the opportunity to scare him. She slowly walked up behind him and tapped his shoulder. The room filled with a shriek as Asher quickly turned around.

"Fuck me running, Delaney! You scared the shit out of me." Asher was breathing heavily as he placed his hand over his heart, "You shouldn't scare people like that especially at my age. I could have had a heart attack or cardiac arrest."

Delaney was now fully laughing at him, "Oh my god Asher stop being so dramatic. You seem to be healthy and in good shape. I'm sure your heart is fine. It's good to know that your still easy to scare."

He scoffed, "You're an evil, evil woman."

Delaney began to look around the room now noticing that the only things in this room were the desk and bookcases that were mostly empty. One thing she did notice right away was her book facing out on one of the shelves beside Asher's newest book. A surge of pride swelled in her chest, and she couldn't help the smile spreading across her face.

"You weren't kidding that there's a lot of space up here and the view is much better." Delaney walked over to the window the night sky starting to twinkle with stars.

She watched Asher's reflection as he took off his headphones and stepped behind her. His dark eyes were traveling the length of her body and the tether she once thought was severed now tightened pulling her towards him.

"Yeah, I really don't know how I want this room to look. I keep it simple."

She turned towards him hoping the tether would loosen, "Do you think…" she paused taking a step closer to him.

"What?" Asher took a step towards her, and it took everything in her to not close the distance between them.

"Do you think that maybe my new desk would fit next to this window?"

The smile that spread across his face made bubbles of joy and happiness pop in her chest. The warmth flowing down her veins was comforting and terrifying. She wanted to run away and leap into his arms. The only time she ever felt safe and at home was in his arms. She glanced up into his eyes and could see the happiness shining in them.

"There's only one way to find out, if you're feeling up to it."

She nodded and followed him back into the kitchen towards the entrance to the garage. Grabbing a set of tools, they both went back down to her office to take apart the desk and bring everything up into Asher's office. It was a little after midnight when they finally arranged the office to both their likings. Her desk facing the windows while his was against the wall next to hers. They brought all the books back up to his office and Delaney spent a couple of hours arranging them. Finally, she connected her laptop to the monitors and brought up her project folder.

Looking over to Asher she smiled, "Are you ready to get to work?"

ASHER

Three Weeks Later

Asher was standing in the kitchen as Delaney was writing in the living room. Over the last few weeks, they had developed an outline which was now on a large whiteboard in their office. Delaney was finishing up the second chapter for him to write the third chapter in his point-of-view. Asher had a new favorite past time of watching Delaney work. He found himself mesmerized at how she allowed her writing to consume all five of her senses. Hearing her character's voice, seeing their face in her mind's eye, tasting their favorite foods, smelling their musk and touching the things they touched.

He was always left in awe seeing her immersed within her character. Much like now standing in the middle of his kitchen and watching her from afar completely awestruck. It was only when the doorbell rang that they were both pulled from their trances.

"Shit! I forgot Leigh and Thomas were coming!" Delaney gathered her things up and looked back at him, "Asher entertain them while I put on real clothes."

Internally he groaned loving seeing her in her short-shorts and hoodie, "You got it."

She rushed down to her room while he headed to the door. Leigh Meyer was standing with her arms crossed over her chest while her boyfriend, Thomas Reed, was hanging his head low as Asher heard him whispering to her.

"Give him a chance before you rip his balls off, sweetheart."

"Hi, welcome to Wilmington. Please come inside and allow me to keep my balls for at least the next few hours." Asher stepped aside as they walked in.

Leigh turned towards him, "You're safe for now. Just know I could ripped them off at any time I feel you're hurting or taking advantage of my friend."

"You would have every right to do that and more." Asher felt her gaze bore into his before she finally relaxed and allowed him to take a breath.

"Busting his balls again, Leigh?" Delaney walked into the room with a pair of jeans on with the same hoodie, "I told you last week he's been nothing but a gentleman."

Leigh's eyes narrowed on him for a moment before she turned towards Delaney smiling, "I know but I love reminding him that I have the power to end him."

The girls hugged as Asher held out his hand to Thomas, "Asher Graham, it's nice to meet you."

"Thomas Reed, please don't piss off my girlfriend."

Asher chuckled, "I will try but I have a feeling that no matter what I do I'll piss her off."

They all made their way into the living room while Asher went into kitchen to grab everyone something to drink. When he came back in the only spot available was on the love seat next to Delaney and for a moment he wondered if he should just stand.

"May I?" He asked motioning to the spot next to her.

She nodded, "Yeah, of course. It's your couch silly."

He leaned back resting his arm on the back of the couch. Asher figured if he kept quiet then there was less of chance of Leigh causing him physical harm. Plus, he loved listening to Delaney talk. Even when they were teenagers, he loved it when she would go on a rant about something her brother did or read part of a book to him. He always found her voice soothing in a way he hadn't remembered until spending hours listening to her talk about their characters.

"I know you guys said you were coming out here for a vacation, but usually people come out here during the summer months. You weren't checking up on me, were you?" Delaney gave Leigh a pointed look.

"You didn't tell her?" Thomas asked.

Delaney glanced over at him before asking, "Tell me what?"

Leigh smiled before holding her hand out to Delaney. On the left ring finger was a beautiful diamond ring and Delaney's gasp filled the room.

"Oh my god… you're engaged…"

Asher looked at Delaney who was smiling from ear to ear, but her eyes were shining with tears. Not tears of happiness that she was trying to portray but tears of sadness. She stood up to hug her friend and Asher reached across to shake Thomas's hand.

"Congratulations to you both."

"Thank you. We've been engaged for a couple of weeks now. Delaney was talking about Wilmington to Leigh when she was making the decision to come out here and we wanted to see about having our wedding out here." Thomas pulled Leigh into his side as she sat back down.

Delaney almost seemed to curl into herself as she sat down beside him again. Absentmindedly, Asher reached out to rub her back. Feeling her flinch, he went to pull his hand away until he felt her lean back against him. He continued to rub small circles in the middle of her back until he saw her shoulders relax.

"Wilmington is beautiful in the summer. I don't know what you had in mind, but you are more than welcome to use the private beach I have with the house for the ceremony. My parents would allow people to use the beach all the time for summer weddings."

A small smile was on Delaney's lips as she glanced over at him. A vivid memory of them crashing the reception of a wedding that took place that summer while his parents were out of town. Snatching a bottle of champagne and drinking it on the deck while making out.

"Thank you for the offer. I'll definitely keep that in mind. I have a few meetings scheduled at venues here that I was hoping to steal Delaney for." Leigh smiled, "I know it's not your thing…"

"I'd be honored to come with you. If for anything, I can take excellent notes for you."

He felt Delaney's back tense again and he started running his fingers along her spine gently. She wiggled ever so slightly before relaxing against his touch again. He knew he should stop but couldn't bring himself to. He wanted to take every opportunity he could to feel close to her.

Thomas looked over to him, "This leaves us to entertain ourselves. If you need to get writing done I totally understand. I can always busy myself with band stuff."

"We could go into town and have some lunch. Maybe grab some food to cook up for these lovely ladies." Asher suggested looking to Leigh for approval.

"I think that sounds like a lovely idea. A girls and boys day. For now, we wanted to check in with you before heading to our hotel." They all stood heading towards the door.

Delaney pulled her friend into a hug, "You know there's plenty of room here. You guys could have stayed here."

Leigh chuckled, "That's sweet of you, but I don't think either of you could handle us on vacation." She wiggled her eyebrows making Delaney blush deeply.

Asher laughed seeing Thomas rolling his eyes, "How is that I fell in love with the most blunt and honest woman in the world?"

"Because I'm basically the female version of Zepp and you're practically in lo-"

Thomas covered her mouth, "Alright enough of you. We'll see you tomorrow. Have a good night."

Asher and Delaney stood on the porch watching them drive down the road until they were out of sight. Delaney turned heading inside towards the couch. He watched her flop face first onto it.

"You okay?" She mumbled something that sounded like yeah, but he didn't believe her, "It's okay if you're not."

She lifted her head as he sat on the love seat across from her, "I'm very happy for them. I just don't do the whole giddy over engagements or pregnancies thing."

"I think she would totally understand if you weren't all giddy."

She sat up crossing her legs beneath her, "I know she would. I would feel like a bad friend if I wasn't giddy for her. It's a me thing."

Asher stood up holding his hand out to her, "Would you like to distract yourself with finishing your chapter and helping me write the beginning of mine? Murder and mayhem only for now."

She placed her hand within his and a warm buzzing current flowed up his arm. He watched as goosebumps covered her arm and smirked down at her as he pulled her up.

"Murder and mayhem sounds pretty good." They started walking towards the office when she turned around, "Thank you for calming me down earlier. I didn't realize I was that tense."

"No need to thank me. Any time you feel tense or uncomfortable

I'm here for you."

She smiled with a hint of pink on her cheeks and Asher's heart soared.

The next day, Asher dropped the girls off at their first venue while he and Thomas went to grab lunch nearby. At first they were both distracted by their phones. Dom was sending him threatening texts about the first few chapters being due. Asher told him to shove his threats straight up his asshole and he would get the chapters as soon as they were done. Thomas must have been dealing with someone equally as annoying from the frustrated groan that came from him.

"Asshole problems?"

Thomas nodded, "Kind of. My best friend, Zepp, is being a pain in my ass about his next album."

Asher took a drink of his beer, "Album?"

"Yeah, I'm the manager for Heartstrings. My best friend is the lead singer…"

"Zeppelin Foster is your best friend?" Asher asked suddenly a little starstruck, "As in the same Zeppelin Foster that was featured in Rolling Stone this past month?"

Thomas nodded, "The very same. Us plus Zeppelin's girlfriend, Laurel, have all been friends since grade school. Our little summer love triangle inspired her fangirl book."

Asher remembered a pretty blonde woman on the panel with Delaney, "Ah yes, the fangirl authors. I watched their panel with Delaney."

"You know they're all hoping that Delaney will have her own fangirl love story with you. Emerson keeps texting their group that second chance romances are gaining popularity." He chuckled.

"I don't think that will happen, but you never know what they universe will throw at you. I never expected to see Delaney again and here we are working on a book together. I guess anything could happen."

Thomas leaned back in his chair, "How are things going with the two of you working together? Is it weird?"

Asher shook his head, "I wish it was weird, but it's not. It almost feels like no time has passed at all. We fell right into a routine and enjoy working together. At least, I do."

He took a long drink trying to keep his thumping heart under control. He knew Thomas was going to ask him the question he had been asking himself the last week or so.

"Do you think there's a chance for you two to get back together?"

There it was. That question on repeat in his head and driving him crazy. Everything with Delaney was so easy like breathing except when it came to feelings. He didn't want to push her away, but he also wanted to show her that he definitely had feelings for her. From the moment he woke up one morning and saw her cooking breakfast in the kitchen. He knew he wanted to be with her forever. His feelings came back nearly knocking him down.

"Honestly, I have no fucking clue and it's driving me crazy." He let out a shaky laugh, "My feelings came back for her almost immediately, but I don't think I'll ever be able to earn back her heart. I hurt her too deeply."

Thomas looked out to the ocean, "I kind of thought the same thing with Laurel except about our friendship. I was an ass trying to win her like some fucking prize. Honestly, all I really wanted was what her and Zepp have. That feeling of home when you're near that person. Someone who doesn't make things more difficult but like you could breathe easily. I didn't realize I didn't feel that way for Laurel until I started to get to know Leigh. Only then did my friendship with Laurel start going back to the way it had always been. Maybe there's still hope for you and Delaney."

Asher thought about what Thomas said for a moment, "Maybe, but it'll have to be on her terms. I won't push her out of my life again just because I have feelings."

"You also can't expect her to do all the work either. That's a two way street my friend." Thomas's phone chimed, "Speaking of the devils, they're ready for their next venue."

Thomas pulled out his wallet and Asher stopped him, "After all the advice you just gave me the least I can do is pay for lunch."

After dropping off Delaney and Leigh to their next venue, they headed to the local grocery store to pick up some food for dinner. Thankfully it sounded like Delaney had already written out a list for them while the first venue coordinator had bored them with the history of the location. As they walked inside, Thomas stopped him pointing to a flyer on the bulletin board.

"What do you think? I know Leigh would be down for it, but would Delaney?" Thomas asked.

"Honestly I have no idea. I'll text Delaney to see if she would be up for it."

Asher was surprised when Delaney said yes to going to the Fall Festival. He had figured that her social battery would be empty and in need of recharging. However, it had seemed like a little girl time with Leigh was all she needed. By the time, they picked them up both girls were already discussing all the stuff they wanted to do there. They still had a few hours before the festival and decided an early afternoon nap was in order before going.

Arriving home, Delaney headed down to her room and Asher headed to their office. He knew taking a nap would be a terrible idea for him, but working on his chapter to appease Dom would be in his best interest. He was surprised when a few moments later, Delaney was sitting at her desk with her laptop.

"No nap?"

She shook her head, "No. I'm pretty sure if I took a nap I would want to stay in bed for the rest of the day. Better if I work on our project especially after the text Leigh got from Dom."

He snapped his head up, "What text?" He swore if Dom was a dick to Leigh he would chew him a new asshole.

"Don't worry, Leigh put him in his place. He was demanding that I send my chapters to him now so he could approve them. Leigh told him to taking a flying leap and he would get our chapters when we're ready to send them." They both started laughing, "She may have also called him an entitled prick as well, but we both assumed you've told him this as well."

"Indeed, I have many of times. I'm glad Leigh stood up for you. His been threatening me all day and I told him to stick it where the sun don't shine." He turned in his chair towards her, "Are you sure you want to go tonight? They would understand if you needed to recoup from a day of wedding talk."

The smile that spread across her face melted his heart. He wanted to be the cause of the smile all the time and now made it his mission to do so.

"I forgot how well you could read me." She laughed, "I appreciate you asking me. Leigh asked me the same since she knows social gatherings stress me out. Honestly, I had a lot of fun with her today and it would be nice to hang out with her and Thomas."

"Okay, but if want to head back here at any point let me or Leigh know. We'll make it happen."

Asher was surprised when she reached over and squeezed his hand, "Thank you."

Around five o'clock, Asher and Delaney headed out to pick up their friends. The Fall Festival was being held throughout the center of town leading all the way out onto one of the docks. There were rides, games and food vendors everywhere. A stage was set up where local bands were playing throughout the night. It felt like everyone in Wilmington was there.

He and Thomas grabbed some food from one of the food trucks while the girls had secured a table for them. A special moment happened as they were finishing their meal when a couple of young women came up to Delaney asking her to sign their books. Leigh took a picture of them and asked permission to post on Delaney's social media.

"I'll never get use to that." Delaney muttered as the fans walked away.

Asher leaned in so only she could hear him, "I think you might have to because you're incredibly talented and are only going to become more popular with every book you release."

Her cheeks deepened in color, "Thanks Ash."

Hearing her say his little nickname only for her sent his heart into overdrive. He wanted to reach out and take her hand or put his arm around her. He wanted her to be his and to be able to show the world that he was hers.

As they walked around the festival, Asher couldn't keep his eyes off of her. Every time she would let out a bellowing laugh from participating in a silly game. When her and Leigh decided to take part in a line dance to win a funnel cake to share. Seeing her happy had him falling even harder for her and he didn't know how to turn it off.

"Asher Graham, I challenge you in a water shooting game." Thomas declared loudly, "Prize to go to our ladies."

He saw Delaney's eyes go wide as Leigh pulled her into her side.

"Challenge accepted."

For the next hour he and Thomas played multiple games winning little trinkets and stuffed animals for the girls. In the end, Asher had won more gifts for Delaney but only because Thomas let him win a few games. As they were walking to the car, Leigh pulled Asher back away from Delaney. Thomas had kind of given him a heads up that this would be coming and he tried to prepare himself.

"Do you have feelings for Delaney?" She hooked her arm with his.

"Yes, I do." He knew honesty was best when it came to the people closest to Delaney.

Leigh glanced over at him, "Do you promise not to hurt her?"

"I promise to never intentionally hurt her, but I can't promise that I'll never hurt her. I'm human and male. I will make mistakes."

"Boy ain't that the truth." She laughed then stopped walking, "You bring out something in Delaney that I've never seen since getting to know her. Something that is good for her and I want to see more of. If you hurt her then you'll have to deal with me, my authors and I'm sure her best friend, Quinn. So, do us all a favor and don't hurt her. We're all rooting for you two to get back together."

Now Asher chuckled, "Yeah, I heard second chance romance are all the rage."

"Exactly! Now you get it." She let go of his arm and hurried up to Thomas.

Delaney looked back at him with a questioning look when he stepped up beside her and answered her silent question.

"Leigh threatening my balls again. Nothing to worry about."

She rolled her eyes, "I swear to god all my friends are losing their minds."

Much like rubbing her back, Asher instinctively reached for her hand, "They all care about you and don't want to see you hurt. I don't blame them one bit for threatening me and I will take whatever they give me because I don't want to see you hurt either."

Delaney bit her lower lip then nodded as they continued walking to the car. Asher's heart beating rapidly as she continued to hold his hand as they walked.

The next morning when he walked into their office, he smiled noticing all the little prizes he won for her lined along the window's ledge by her desk. For the first time since reuniting with Delaney, he felt like he might actually have a chance of winning her heart again. That small ember of hope was all he needed to keep going down that path.

DELANEY

Delaney was anxiously pacing behind Asher's chair as he finished the last few pages of his chapter. Their self-imposed deadline was tomorrow, and he was cutting it close. Her poor fingernails were paying the price of his perfectionism.

"The more you pace the slower I will go." Asher chuckled.

Delaney smacked his shoulder playfully, "If you don't hurry up then I'm going to finish it for you. We have editors for a reason."

"The more I edit while drafting then the less they have to do and the less we have to do later on." He looked up at her with smug smile, "Oh and by the way, I've been done for ten minutes now. I just wanted to make you suffer a little."

The instant relief and annoyance fought for space in her body, "Asher Graham, you're a horrible partner!"

She walked over to her computer to see their shared document ready to be submitted to their agents. The first nine chapters in Project Murder and Mayhem was completed. The relief finally pushed out any annoyance with Asher when she hit submit to Leigh. Almost immediately she received a dancing GIF from her agent. Now, Delaney could focus on act two of their project and the big midpoint moment.

She glanced up when she heard Asher on his phone. His forehead was furrow and his shoulders tense from whoever he was talking to. She had one guess and knew it was right when Asher voice raised slightly.

"You haven't even read it yet. How could you possibly have an opinion on it?"

She rolled her chair closer to him. He looked up rolling his eyes and mimicking talking with his hand. She giggled then wrote in his notebook.

Asher chuckled then stopped suddenly, "Seriously? You know you're the one who pushed for me to be in Wilmington to write and now you're scheduling meetings in New York for me."

Delaney suddenly had a sinking feeling in her stomach. She didn't like the idea of being his house alone. Over the last month she had grown accustomed to being around him. Not that she would ever admit it to anyone else, but for the first time in a long time she felt more at home with him than with anyone else. It equally relieved and terrified her.

"If you're insisting on me being there in person then I would like to bring Delaney with me." Asher looked towards her, "It'll be great experience for her to observe meetings with the editors and publishers. We can also meet with the cover designers to put our input for the cover."

The smile spreading across her face was matched by Asher's. She had never been to New York but had always wanted to go. Her publishing house was based in Chicago, so she's wasn't new to meeting with the publishers and editors. However, Asher was a big four author at one of the largest publishing houses in the country. To be able to network with them would be immeasurable for her career. All because Asher believed in their project and her talent. Suddenly her heartbeat was pounding in her ears.

"Dom, this is non-negotiable. Either the meetings are virtual so I can stay in Wilmington to write, or Delaney comes with me to observe the other side of large publishing houses. You decide."

The smile on Asher's face made her believe that she would finally be crossing off an item on her travel bucket list.

Deciding to take the night off to rest and regroup from finishing nine chapters, they ordered takeout from the Taco Hut and watched rerun episodes of Red Moon on TV. Delaney spent most of the time laughing at Asher who couldn't believe she had access to not only a rockstar god, but an TV actor and baseball player. Being friends with the Fangirl authors definitely had some great perks.

Lying in bed, Delaney was unable to sleep. Looking at her phone she wondered if Quinn might still be up at midnight.

"Delaney, there better be a damn good reason for why you're calling me right now."

She laughed, "You don't sound like you were sleeping so are you at someone else's house for the evening?"

There was a loud groan, "If you must know, yes I am with someone, but we're in my bed instead of his."

"Alright Quinn, no more details needed. Call me tomorrow

whenever you're done with the boy of the night." Delaney couldn't help the disappointment in her words.

"Delaney wait. Give me a minute to go out into the living room."

She could hear Quinn whispering to someone before hearing her closing the door, "What happened?"

"You first, who's the guy?" Delaney asked trying to figure out exactly what she wanted to tell her.

Quinn's silence worried Delaney. It was either some douchebag she had dated before and hooking up with out of comfort or...

"Quinn... are you hooking up with Emerson's brother? Please tell me you're not hooking up with Emerson's brother."

"You said if he asked me out then he was fair game."

Delaney could hear the pure joy in her friend's voice, "Yes, yes I did. Does he treat you right?"

"Yeah, he does and really makes me happy. Not to mention he's definitely the best in bed..."

"Whoa! Nope, I don't need to know that." Delaney sighed, "As long as you're happy and he treats you right then I'm super happy for you."

"Your turn." Quinn's voice was in full serious mode, "What happened? Do I need to come out there and punch Asher in his pretty face?"

Delaney sat up in her bed, "No. Honestly, Asher has been great. We've finished nine chapters and work really well together."

Quinn silently waited for her to continue but she didn't know what was wrong or why she couldn't sleep. All she knew was that she really wanted to be in the office with Asher even if they weren't writing or working. The realization that she wanted to be next to Asher was startling and suddenly felt like she couldn't breathe.

"Delaney, I don't know what's happening, but I can assume you're freaking out about something. Take a deep breath and count to ten."

She tired, but a short gasp came out instead, "Shit…"

"Come on, take a slow breath in count to five then let out and count to five." Quinn's soothing voice helped her to take a breath in, "Great Delaney. Take another breath."

She could feel the tension around her chest loosened, "T-Thanks Quinn."

"You're welcome. When you feel ready tell me what sent you into a panic."

Delaney appreciated the patience and love her best friend had for her, "I don't want to keep you from Everett."

Quinn chuckled, "He's fast asleep since he has to be at the hospital early in the morning. I'm all yours for as long as you need me."

"Have I told you lately how much I love ya and how amazing you are?"

She started laughing, "You never need to tell me that because I know it already and feel the same about you. Now spill."

"Do you believe in second chances?" Delaney asked.

There was definitely a small audible gasp from her best friend, "You're falling for him again."

"I… I don't know. I think I might and it terrifies me." Delaney swung her legs over the edge of her bed.

"Is that what triggered your panic?"

She knew she didn't need to answer because Quinn knew the answer. For some reason, Delaney really needed to get it off her chest and say it out loud to know if what she was feeling was true.

"We decided to take the night off and relax since we've worked hard on the first act. We ate dinner and watched Red Moon. We talked about the Fangirl authors and their celebrity men. I went to bed and haven't been able to sleep tonight. I couldn't figure out why my body is restless. That's why I called you and then I had a thought."

"What thought? I'm dying here, tell me the thought!" Quinn excitedly said making her chuckle.

Delaney took a deep breath again to calm her nerves, "I really wish I was in our office with him just to be next to him or close to him. He makes me feel comfortable and relaxed all the time. It's easy to be around him."

The squeal that erupted from her friend was deafening, "It's about damn time! I've been telling you that you need to get out there and find your person. Looks like the universe did it for you."

"Calm down. I'm not even sure what I'm feeling or what I should do. Bringing feelings into a working relationship could really mess things up. Not to mention he invited me to New York to-"

"He what?!" Quinn squeaked, "He invited you to New York? You're number one bucket list travel spot."

"It's a business trip. He's going to meet with his agent, editors and publishers about our book. He thought I might like to go to observe how things work in a big four publishing house. Well, more like his agent schedule meetings making him leave Wilmington. His agent doesn't like my writing or that Asher is working with me. Anyway, Asher told him that if I couldn't come with him then he wasn't going to leave me behind in Wilmington."

Her friend let out a low whistle, "Oh my dear, dear friend… he's got it bad for you."

Delaney scoffed, "I don't think so. I don't know and that what's tripping me up about everything. I have no idea how to read men or act around them. I don't know how to be with someone because my track record isn't exactly stellar."

"Delaney Bishop, you listen to me," She paused as Delaney flopped back onto her bed, "You are a wonderful woman who deserves men to worship the ground she steps on. It was the men in your relationships that messed up, not you.”

She laid there for a second letting her friend’s words sink in, “Quinn, am I dumb for wanting a second chance with Asher? Honestly?”

“Not at all and I’ve been rooting for it since the moment you realized who he was. It’s always be apparent to me that your heart has always belonged to him. I think you should absolutely give him a second chance. Go to New York and enjoy a free trip to a city you’ve always wanted to see. And for the love of god…”

Delaney started giggling knowing what her crazy, wild spirited best friend was about to say.

“Let go of your inhibitions and let him fuck you senseless.”

“And with that I’m going to get off the phone now. I love you.” Delaney laughed.

Quinn’s quick words were coming through as Delaney ended the call, “You know I’m right! Let go and fuck freely! LOVE YOU!”

She shook her head still laughing as she put her phone back on the end table. Deciding there was no way she could go to sleep, Delaney decided to go up to office and start outlining some plot points for Asher to review later. Reaching the top of the stairs she saw the light in the office was already on.

Peeking around the corner, she smiled seeing Asher sitting in his chair with his notebook resting on his lap. What she hadn’t expected was to see him in only a pair of plaid pajama pants. He pushed his glasses back up the bridge of his nose then ran his hand through his unruly wavy hair. His bicep flexed and Delaney realized she needed to take a breath. His dark green eyes looked up widening when they landed on her. His lips parted as if he were going to say something, but nothing came out. His eyes drifted down her body and suddenly she was all too aware that she was standing there in only an oversized t-shirts and her underwear.

“S-Sorry… I was, um, I was going to write some notes for act two.”

She tugged on the hem of her shirt nervously.

Asher stood walking over to her desk and she couldn't take her eyes off him. The way he always carried himself with purpose and what she could only describe as grace. He grabbed her blanket shaking it loose before walking over to her and wrapping it around her shoulders. Looking up, his lips were close enough for her to push up on her toe and kiss them. The urge to do just that and wrap her arms around him nearly knocked her off balance.

"Better?" His raspy voice sent shivers down her body.

She nodded, "Yeah, thanks."

He took a step back but kept one hand on her elbow, "I guess great minds think alike because I came in here to do the same thing."

"I know it's late, but do you think…"

His full attention was on her, "Think what?"

Let go of your inhibitions…

Quinn's words echoed in her mind, "Do you think maybe we could work in the living room with the fireplace going?"

His lips curled into a beautiful smile, "You were always the smart one between the two of us. Of course, that's a great idea."

Asher grabbed his notebook along with hers then held out his hand to her, "Shall we?"

Delaney nodded placing her hand into his and following him out into the living room. It was a small step, but to her it felt like a giant leap of faith she had taken, and she wanted to do it again.

JUL. '07

DEAR LANEY,

I HATE HOW FAST THE SUMMER IS GOING. I NEVER WANT THIS SUMMER TO END. THINKING ABOUT LEAVING YOU MAKES MY HEART FEEL LIKE IT'S RIPPING. I KNOW THIS IS GOING TO SOUND CREEPY OR EVEN STALKERISH, BUT I SWEAR I WAS THINKING ABOUT THIS BEFORE THIS SUMMER. I WAS THINKING OF MAYBE TAKING THE SEMESTER OFF AND APPLYING TO NORTHWESTERN. I LOOKED INTO NORTHWESTERN BEFORE, BUT MY PARENTS DIDN'T LIKE THE IDEA OF ME MOVING SO FAR AWAY. I CAN'T... I CAN'T IMAGINE SPENDING A SINGLE MOMENT WITHOUT YOU. I KNOW I SOUND CLICHE AND LIKE EVERY MALE MAIN CHARACTER IN ROMANCE NOVELS BUT...

I'M FALLING IN LOVE WITH YOU.

YES, I SAID IT. I LOVE YOU. I'M FALLING IN LOVE WITH YOU. I WANT TO BE WITH YOU. AT LEAST IF I WENT TO NORTHWESTERN WE COULD SEE EACH OTHER AT NIGHT, ON WEEKENDS. WE COULD GO ON DATES AND YOU COULD BE THE TALK OF YOUR SCHOOL BY DATING AN OLDER GUY LOL. I DON'T THINK WHEN THE TIME COMES THAT I'LL BE STRONG ENOUGH TO SAY GOODBYE TO YOU. I DON'T WANT TOO.

OKAY, I'M RAMBLING. I HOPE YOU LOVE YOUR BOOKMARK. UNTIL MY NEXT LETTER.

ALWAYS & FOREVER YOURS,
ASHER

ASHER

The last few days had been some of the best Asher could remember. He and Delaney seemed to cross some kind of barrier where she was becoming more and more comfortable around him. Even as excited as he was to be getting closer to her it was also slowly killing him. Before she always made sure to have on sweatpants or leggings whenever they were writing in the office. Now, it was nothing for her to be in her chair only in a t-shirt and pair of shorts that left little to his imagination. He wanted nothing more than to pull her into his arms and run his hands all down her body.

"Asher?"

He shook his head trying to get the image of her naked body out of it. "Yeah, sorry I wasn't listening."

She chuckled, "Obviously. I was asking if I could have the window seat."

"Uh, I don't know if you know this or not but only VIPs get the window seat. Maybe next time." He smirked trying to get her riled up because he loved seeing her pop off.

"Well, I don't know if you know this or not but I'm kind of a big deal. If you think about it I'm more of a VIP than you because people know who I am. They don't know you from a random dude on the street. The window seat goes to me."

He glanced back at her sitting proudly in the backseat. He held his fist on top of his other hand narrowing his eyes on her.

"Paper, rock, scissors for the window seat. Two out three."

She mirrored his position with a fierce determination in her eyes, "You're on."

The first round went to Asher when his rock beat her scissors, "Always with the scissors."

"Oh, I have new tricks, don't think you know me." She laughed.

The second round went to her when she threw rock onto his scissors. They both leaned in further neither of them wanting to lose to the other.

"Now kids, don't make me pull this car over." Liam chuckled.

Asher assumed she was going to throw scissors again, so he went back to rock. Her tiny hand covered his fist as she shouted in victory.

"HA! I won fair and square! Window seat is all mine."

The beautiful grin spreading across her face was well worth losing the game and the window seat. "I admit defeat and bow to your greatness."

What she hadn't known was he was going to give her the window seat no matter what. He would give her anything she asked for because since she had been in Wilmington he was falling for her more and more.

Once they were on the plane, they both settled into their seats with their headphones on. Asher had his laptop out trying to work on his chapter for the start of act two. His mind was wandering about the romance elemental of the book since he had never written romance. Delaney was looking out her window with her notebook and pen on the tray. He picked up the pen and wrote a question for her. He watched as she giggled writing her answer with a smirk on her lips.

She laughed shaking her head and went back to looking out her window. He grabbed her pen again and wrote a real answer to her question. Her smile softened as read his answer, writing a response next to his. He loved seeing their handwriting next to one another.

IS OUR BOOK GOING TO HAVE SMEXY TIMES?

Do you want it to have smexy times?

I'M A GUY… WE ALWAYS WANT SMEXY TIMES 

I THINK IF IT MAKES SENSE FOR THE PLOT AND STORY THEN YES. I'VE NEVER WRITTEN ROMANCE OR SEX SCENES SO…

I agree. We'll see if it naturally comes up in the story. I haven't written explicit scenes but I've written enough to get the point. We can always have a close door scene.

He drew a smiley face letting her go back to looking out the window. She looked at peace watching the clouds drift below them. She was leaning her head against the frame watching the world go by without a care. He wished he could be that for her. A constant point of peace in her life where she felt safe enough to relax fully. He wanted nothing more than to be her safe haven.

The flight was just long enough for him to drift to sleep until he felt someone shaking his shoulder. Suddenly the commotion of the plane hit his ear when Delaney slid one of his earpieces off.

"Wake up sleepy, we're landing."

He took his headphones off and put them in his bag. Delaney was looking out the window as they descended through the clouds. He leaned over looking out the window as well. She lifted her arm wrapping it around his shoulders and suddenly his was wrapped in a glorious mix of mint gum and flowers.

"Wow… look at the city." Delaney pressed her finger against the window, "It's beautiful."

Asher's eyes went from looking at the city to the woman beside him, "Yeah, it is really beautiful."

When they were walking off the plane, he became hyper aware of the sheer number of people and chaos within LaGuardia Airport. Asher reached out for Delaney who tightly gripped his arm pulling it against her body. They both had packed light since they were only staying a couple of nights. Each of them had one carry on and their backpacks. He slipped his arm around her shoulder, pulling her into his side and headed towards the pickup area. People were bumping into them at all angles and at one point Delaney wrapped her arm around his waist as to not get knocked out of his grasp.

Finally, they found the driver Dom has arranged to take them to the hotel. Once they were both in the car, he pulled out his phone sending a text to Dom that they had landed. Asher had picked a hotel with a great view of the New York City skyline making sure Delaney's room was the one with the view.

He looked over at her and chuckled seeing her wide eyes looking out the window. The sun was starting to set and the city lights were starting to light up the city. Her cheeks were pink from the wide smile on her face. His phone buzzed bringing him out of his trance watching Delaney.

Dom Kincade: Lets meet up for dinner. Our normal place at 7pm.

See you then

Asher tapped Delaney on the shoulder, "Dom wants to meet for dinner at seven. Would you like to go, or would you prefer to order room service and relax? Everything is paid for, so you don't need to worry about anything.”

She sat back in her seat thinking for a moment, “I think I’d like to join you if that’s okay.”

“Of course, I would love for you to join us. It will keep Dom on his best behavior.”

She scoffed, “I doubt that but glad I can give you that illusion.”

They checked into their hotel with their rooms a few doors down from one another. He had hoped they would be next to one another but at least they were on the same floor. He walked inside her room to set her carry on suitcase down. The floor to ceiling windows gave an impressive view of the skyline. The lights twinkled off all the reflective surfaces in the room and created a wild vibe. Asher began to question if maybe it would be a little over stimulating for her then he looked over to Delaney. Her bright blue eyes were shining, and her face was nearly pressed against the glass to see the street below.

“This is amazing! I always dreamed of staying in New York City.” She turned towards him, “Thank you for inviting me to come with you.”

His heartbeat rapidly echoed in his ears, “Y-You’re welcome. I’m glad I could make one of your dreams come true.”

He left her to settle in and relax before dinner. Walking into his own room, Asher leaned against his door trying to get his heart to stop pounding in his chest. How the hell was he going to keep himself in line around Delaney when he was teetering the edge of falling for her completely. Things were going so well between them, and he didn’t want to ruin it by acting rashly with his feelings for her. However, the more he was around her the more he wanted to throw caution to the wind. Closing his eyes for a moment, Asher decided a hot shower was in order before getting ready for dinner.

At quarter to seven he walked down to her room knocking on the door. When she opened it his jaw nearly dropped seeing a totally different woman standing there. Her long wavy curls were cascading down her back. She had put on a little bit of make-up to highlight her natural rosy cheeks and full lips. What had stopped him dead in his tracks was the little black dress with a plunging neckline that hugged her curves. Covering her shoulders was a lacy shawl that gave the illusion of being covered up when really, she was bare for the world to see.

"Is something wrong? This was the only nice thing I had with me and that's only because Quinn insisted I take it with me." She pulled the corner of her bottom lip beneath her teeth, and he wanted to cancel dinner.

"Nothing's wrong. You're stunning. Absolutely gorgeous." He smiled watching her cheeks turn pink, "However I'm thinking I should have worn a different shirt in case I have to fight guys off of you."

Delaney rolled her eyes, "I'm sure you won't have to do that."

He held out his arm to her, "Let's hope so because I really don't want Dom to bail me out of jail."

They got into the elevator and suddenly the air around them was super charged. Delaney anxiously moved from foot to foot while Asher had to inconspicuously adjust his pants. When they stepped out into the lobby both of them laughed breathlessly.

"By the way, you look very handsome tonight." Delaney slipped her arm through his again.

He smiled feeling his own cheeks burning now. He felt like he was on a first date in high school again. The nerves bouncing around in his stomach and every little touch heightened. Maybe it was because he hadn't been with anyone since Anna and it felt good to have a beautiful woman beside him.

The walk to the restaurant was only five minutes from their hotel. It was a little family owned Italian place that was Asher's favorite. Anytime he was in New York he would go there at least once for dinner. The owners, Enzo and Camilla Gallo, knew him and Dom by name. When they walked in, Camilla was waiting for him.

"Asher, my love! How good to see you." She kissed both of his cheeks, "Who is your beautiful lady? Trying to make me jealous."

He let out a nervous laugh, "This is my friend and co-author for our next book, Delaney Bishop. Delaney this is Camilla Gallo. Her and her husband own Casa di Cuore, passed down through generations of Gallo's."

"It's lovely to meet you." She yelped as Camilla pulled her into a hug.

"It's about time this handsome man settled down."

Asher shook his head, "Oh we're not… we're only friends…"

Camilla hit his shoulder taking Delaney arm within hers, "Do not listen to him. He says only friends which means he's madly in love with you. Trust me on this."

Now he was wishing the ground would swallow him whole before his lovely friend ruined any chance he may have with Delaney. She led them to a back table where Dom was already drinking a glass of wine. When he looked up, his eyes immediately went to Delaney followed by a frown on his lips. Asher gave him a pointed look before holding Delaney's chair out for her.

"Ever the gentleman." Camilla whispered before heading off towards the kitchen.

Dom looked back down at his menu, "I wasn't expecting a party of three."

"Oh, am I interrupting a meeting?" The panic in her voice made Asher's foot slide right into Dom's shin.

"Not at all. We normally have dinner together when meeting in New York. This is nothing but dinner between friends." He glared at Dom, "Right?"

Dom put on his best smile, "Of course. Maybe we can discuss standards and expectations of high quality novels."

Asher wanted to reach over and punch his friend in the face, "How about we discuss what looks good on the menu and order a bottle of wine."

Camilla was already two steps ahead of them bringing out bottle, "This is a special Vietti Barolo Cerequio that Enzo only serves for special occasions or special people. I feel like this is a moment for celebration seeing our old friends and making new ones."

"Thank you, would you mind showing me to the ladies room." Delaney stood, following Camilla towards the back of the restaurant.

Asher looked at Dom, "What the fuck is your problem?"

"She's my problem because she's distracting you. You should be working on the next bestselling thriller/horror novel but instead you're playing house with an amateur fanfiction writer."

"You've been against her from the moment I suggested working with her. You're not giving her a fair chance. She's talented and smart with her writing." Asher could feel the rage building deep his gut.

Dom leaned forward, "She's not. I've read her chapters and they're mediocre at best. She has nothing on your talent. A talent that you're wasting while trying to get in her pants."

"Well then I guess you need to make a decision because I'm working with Delaney and publishing this book with or without you." Asher crossed his arms over his chest.

"We'll see about that." Dom scoffed standing, "I'll see you tomorrow morning. I suggest leaving the missus at the hotel."

Asher watched him walk out of the restaurant when Delaney's voice brought his attention back to the table.

"I'm sorry. Maybe I should have stayed at the hotel." The defeat in her words killed him.

He shook his head, "No. Dom just has his head up his ass. This has absolutely nothing to do with you, I promise."

She nodded, staring down at the table, "I think I would like to go back to the hotel."

Asher said his goodbyes to Camilla and Enzo before joining

Delaney outside. The wind was picking up, and he could see her starting to shiver. He pulled off his blazer wrapping it around her shoulders. On their way back, they walked in silence as Asher thought of a thousand ways to make Dom's life a living hell.

"Do you mind if we go inside?" Delaney asked pointing to a bookstore.

"Not at all. Let's go." He took her arm within his.

He watched as her shoulders lifted and her happy demeanor returned. He loved watching her in her element surrounded by books. She ran her fingers over the spines and would tell him little tidbits about titles or authors. She was not only a talented writer, but she knew the business from all sides. Never before had he been more impressed by her as when she would explain how booksellers pick and choose what books to buy or feature. He was in awe of her knowledge. They were heading towards the thrillers and mystery section when a couple of people came up to them.

"You're Delaney Bishop, right?" A young woman asked.

"Y-Yes, I am."

She pushed the young man beside her, "I told you! I'm here picking up a copy of your book. I've read all the other Fangirl authors and only had yours left to read. Would you mind signing my book?"

That breathtaking smile appeared on Delaney's face again and Asher took a step back to admire her. She spoke with the young couple for several minutes before more people started to come up to her wanting their books sign. Finally, the manager of the store came up and ushered the crowd back giving Delaney the opportunity to head back to him.

"Wow."

"How's it feel to be famous?" He asked, leading her outside again.

That smile never faded only shining brighter beneath the city lights. "Overwhelming but exciting. One of them said it's their favorite book of the year. Another said that they could really relate to Hope and Alex.”

Delaney continued to talk excitedly about the fans until they reached the hotel lobby. She only grew quiet as they stepped into the elevator and she stood next to him resting her head on his shoulder. His body was nearly vibrating with pent up energy. The buzz didn't release when the doors opened and they stepped out onto their floor. When they reached Delaney's room, she turned around hugging him.

“Thank you for everything. It may have started off rough, but it ended up being one of the best nights ever.”

When she looked up at him with those beautiful ocean eyes, Asher couldn't hold himself back anymore. He placed his hands on either side of her face, leaning down and gently pressing his lips against hers. The world, for one singular moment, stopped and everything felt like it was meant to be.

14

Fourteen

DELANEY

Had he read her mind? How did he know she was thinking about kissing him? After overhearing him standing up for her to Dom and then listening to her gush about the fans she met. Protecting her in the airport and making her feel comfortable at every possible moment. All she wanted to do was be close to him. He was the gentleman she remembered from when they were teenagers and that made her fall head over heels for him again. The whole elevator ride up to their floor all she kept thinking was how she wanted to kiss him. Now they were standing in the hallway doing just that.

Delaney went to put her hands up into hair when he suddenly pulled away from her. Her lips tingled and her skin was on fire. Asher's head hung low as he took two steps back.

"I'm sorry… shit I'm so sorry Delaney. I genuinely got caught up in the moment."

A cold wave washed bover her, "I-It's fine. I get it. Um, goodnight Asher." She quickly opened her door going inside, hearing him call out to her.

Delaney leaned against the door as tears sprung to her eyes. Had he not meant to kiss her? Was it instant regret he felt? Her mind scolded her for allowing herself to get close to someone again. Her body was urging her to go to his room and finish what they had started. She ignored both and went to change into her pajamas. She pulled the covers over her head and prayed to the universe to pull her into a deep sleep so she could forget about everything.

After laying there counting to one hundred, she pushed the covers off her. Getting up she began to pace in front of the bed. Delaney stopped pulling the curtains open to look out at the city below. It truly was the city that never slept. Bright lights shining at all hours and people covering the sidewalks. People moving on in their lives while she was freaking out over a man she didn't completely understand.

The last few weeks had been some of the best in her life. She finally felt like she found a safe space that wasn't working herself to death. She could relax and be herself when she was around Asher. That was why she had originally fell in love with him at sixteen. Even though he was eighteen and headed off to college. He never once looked down on her for her age or social status. He didn't care that she had been whimsical and idealistic. He always supported her. Encouraged her. Treated her as an equal. Even now, he was the successful author and her the amateur. Yet, in his eyes they were the same.

She looked towards the door as if someone was calling out her name. Her feet were taking a step closer to it. To him. Her mind screaming at her not to go. To protect herself. To protect her heart at all cost. To be alone was to be safe. Yet, Delaney found herself at the door turning the knob. Walking down the hall she stood outside his door for a full minute. Raising her hand several times to knock but chickening out. Finally, she pushed herself to rap her knuckles on the door holding her breath.

She was just going to talk to him. Get all the awkwardness and feelings out of the way. If she said it out loud to him then they could go back to how they were earlier in the night. She didn't even need to come inside; she could say everything in the hallway and then retreat to the safety of her room. The door unlocked and her eyes widened as Asher came into view.

"Delaney? Are you okay?"

His hair was slicked back and his glasses nowhere to be seen. Water droplets were rolling down his broad chest to his stomach and disappearing into the towel wrapped around his waist. She couldn't take her eyes off the beautiful human in front of her and suddenly her brain went quiet. Quinn's voice ringing clearly in her mind.

Let go of your inhibitions…

"Delaney…"

Her eyes snapped up to his dark, mischievous green eyes and suddenly words were not enough for what she wanted to convey. She stepped up to him wrapping her arms around his neck and pulling his lips down to hers. Her fingers threading through his wet hair as he lifted her legs around his waist. She pressed herself against him bringing her lips beneath his ear. A low growl rumbled in his chest fueling her confidence to gently nip at his neck.

"Fuck Delaney…" He moaned pressing her back against the door, "Hold on a second."

She shook her head, "No. No more seconds. No more waiting. I want this. I want you."

The smile that appeared on his face was magical, "I agree whole heartedly, but I want to do this right."

"What's more right than you and I together? I'm tired of fighting it and I'm tired of being alone." The tears started to fall and she hated it, "Man, the only crying I wanted to be doing was crying out your name."

Asher's deep, rich laugh filled her with a warmth that could only come from loving someone. He placed her feet on the floor taking her head within his hands.

"Oh, there's plenty of time for that." He wiped the tears from her cheeks, "You're sure you want this? Because I'm in this for the long haul. You're the only woman I want to be with for the rest of my life. If you're not sure you want that then I don't want a taste of the forbidden fruit only to have it taken away."

His intense stare stirred something deep within her that she thought had been lost forever. She had only ever felt it the night her and Asher had made love for the first time. It was like a bind tying them together. She brought her fingers down the side of his face to his chest coming to rest over his heart.

"I've always been yours. Then, now and forever." She whispered, never breaking eye contact.

He leaned his forehead against hers, "Forever."

She nodded, "Forever."

She barely had the word off her lips when his lips pressed against hers. His hands reached down slipping beneath her t-shirt and pulling it over her head. A moment of insecurity hitting Delaney hard as her breasts were bare for the world to see. She went to cross her arms when Asher's hands grabbed each of her wrists.

"Oh no, there's no hiding your beautiful body. I want to see all of you."

She didn't know how it was possible, but his low voice made her knees wobbly. He let go of her wrists placing his hands on the waistband of her shorts. Kneeling before her, he pulled her shorts and panties off with one motion. The cool air hit her burning skin making her shiver. Delaney glanced down to see Asher's tongue dart out slowly over his bottom lip. He lifted one of her legs to rest on his thigh as he leaned over kissing her inner thigh.

"Ash…" She whispered.

"Mmhmm." He hummed moving further up her leg.

The realization of what he was about to do snapped her brain back into reality and she pressed her hands against his shoulder.

"You don't have to do that. I mean, it's not well kept or anything." She felt her cheeks burning with shame.

"If you think that a little grass on the field…" Asher stood up chuckling his hand rubbing small circles against her, "is going to keep me from eating you out like you're my last meal on Earth then your sadly mistaken."

Delaney pressed her head back against the door rolling her hips against his hand, "Oh god…"

Asher suddenly took his hand away and picked her up over his shoulder. She let out a squeal as he gently smacked her ass walking her further into the room towards the bed. She reached down grabbing a hold of his towel and loosening it from his waist.

"If I'm naked then so are you." She laughed as he sat her down on the bed.

She sucked in a shaky breath suddenly face to face with Asher and all his glory, "Holy shit."

A wide grin spread across his face, "Thank you. Now lay back beautiful."

She crawled up further on the bed shaking her head, "Honestly Asher you don't have to do that."

"Tell me is that because you genuinely don't like it or is it because you've never properly had a man go down on you?"

Delaney looked away from him, "I've never had… anyone go down on me before."

She glanced over at him to see his eyes wide and jaw slacked. Suddenly it seemed like a spotlight was on her and she curled in on herself.

"Hey, hey don't hide." Asher crawled onto the bed beside her.

"It's embarrassing." She mumbled into the mattress.

Asher rubbed her back, "What's embarrassing?"

She sighed, "I'm sure you've been with plenty of women and are well experienced in giving mind blowing orgasms. I'm not. I've only been with two guys. You were the first and then Ty. Being with him wasn't exactly wonderful. I… I just won't ever be able to compare."

Asher gently lifted her head enough for her to see his concern filled eyes. The few tears that escaped down her cheeks he caught and then kissed her.

"I won't lie and say I was some kind of monk. I definitely got around especially in college after I thought I lost you forever." He slipped his arm under her head cradling her to him, "I don't see your lack of experience as anything but a good thing. It means there are a few things we still get to experience together for the first time."

"I never thought of it like that." She sniffled, "When did you get so smart?"

He chuckled, "Comes with my old age. The fact that your ex didn't worship you from head to toe says more about him than you. If you're okay with it I would like to show you just what you've been missing out on."

Delaney's stomach tensed as she nodded her head. Asher rolled her onto her back leaning down and kissing her. His hand drifting up her side, over her stomach making it flutter and stopping beneath her breast.

"May I?" he asked against her cheek.

Delaney let out a breathless yes before arching her back into his touch. His lips were leaving a trail of kisses down her neck and chest. She let out a slow moan as his tongue circled around her nipple. His thumb rubbing against the other one.

"Ash-Asher…"

He continued his kisses down her stomach until reaching her hip bone, "You okay? Do you want me to stop?"

"Ke-Keep going."

The moment his lips pressed against her clit she closed her legs around his head. The vibration of his laugh send waves of pleasure through her.

"Damn, I forgot how powerful your legs are. Gonna have to hold them down. If you get uncomfortable then tug on my hair. Okay?"

Delaney couldn't remember how to breathe let alone speak so she nodded. His arms curled around her thighs spreading them wider.

"Shit!" She cried out as his broad tongue trailed up her pressing against her clit.

Asher repeated the slow motion over and over driving her crazy. She gripped the sheets beside her while the pressure deep in her belly tightened.

"M-More Asher… need more… of you." She moaned wanting nothing more than to grab onto his hair.

She felt him smile then one of his arms let go of her leg. His mouth covered her clit gently sucking on it before she felt one long finger push inside her.

The raw, satisfying moan that came from deep within her chest surprised her. She couldn't remember the last time she had felt pleasure coursing through her veins, but she never wanted it to end. She could feel the pressure building fast as Asher push a second finger inside her and sucked her clit harder.

"Cum for me baby. Let it all go and let me hear you."

His fingers picked up the pace, and she was so close that all she could hear was her heart pounding in her ears. Then the perfect storm happened all at once. Asher curled his fingers hitting a spot she didn't know existed in her while pressing his tongue against her clit. Suddenly, her hands were tangled into his hair as she rode out her orgasm against his face crying out his name.

"S-Shit… I'm s-sorry." She let go of his head as he crawled over her body.

"Don't you dare apologize. That was the hottest thing I've ever experienced. New bucket list item is having you sit on my face and ride it all night."

Delaney stared at him in complete shock, "Oh no. What if I broke your nose or you couldn't breathe?"

He leaned down nipping at her neck, "One hundred percent worth it."

"Not to me. I'm partial to your face." She placed her hands on either side of his face before running them down his chest to his hips, "Among other parts of you."

Asher groaned pressing his head into the crook of her neck, "Fuck me that feels amazing."

She wrapped her hand nervous around his cock slowly stroking him then whispered against his ear, "I need you."

Asher reached between them placing his hand on top of hers, "Fuck… I was not prepared for this."

She knew what he meant and a wave of sadness hit her. She guided him right to her entrance both sighing and whispering to one another as he pushed inside of her. She felt whole and complete all at once.

"I know you're going to have questions, but for this moment… right now trust me when I tell you that you don't need it. We're fine."

He stared deeply into her eyes before starting to move against her. Delaney had never felt more peace or happiness than being with Asher. The love and security wrapping around her had her choking on emotions. She wrapped her arms around his neck pulling him closer to her. This moment was all she had ever wanted in her life, and Asher was the only person in the world she ever wanted it with. A weight that had been weighing her down for as long as she could remember was lifted the moment they were both crying out each other's name in release.

When their breathing had returned to normal and Asher was lying beside her. Delaney feared she would never feel weightless freedom of being loved once she told him her secret.

Delaney didn't remember falling asleep, but when she woke up the bed was empty and flashes of the day Asher had left her filled her mind.

"Oh no, not again…"

"I'm right here."

She looked off to the side where Asher was sitting on a chair watching her. His shoulders were tense and his hands balled into fists on the armrests.

"What's wrong?" She pulled the sheet around her body walking around to him.

Asher pulled her down onto his lap, "You said I would have questions and I only have one."

The sadness from earlier returned with the force of a hurricane, "And that is?"

"Did he hurt you?" She cocked her side to the side confused as he continued, "Did your ex hurt or force you to…"

"What? No! Asher, I promise you it's nothing like that. Ty may be a dickhead, but he never forced me to do anything. Actually, quite the opposite."

Asher let out a long sigh of relief, "Good. Because I was ready to fly back to Evanston and make sure no one ever found his body. Wait, what do you mean quite the opposite?"

Delaney wrapped her arms around herself, "Soon after we were married, Ty wanted to have kids. We tried for years to do it naturally before finally going to a specialist. I found out that I can never have kids of my own. My body simply doesn't produce viable eggs to carry a pregnancy. I had always had abnormal and painful periods all my life."

"I remember sitting with you curled up with a hot pack. I felt helpless."

His admission warmed her heart, "I still go through that but not as often. After Ty found out I could never have kids he didn't want me anymore. Little did I know that he was already cheating on me and had a son with his mistress now wife. The last few months we were together he was hardly home and certain didn't touch me when he was."

"Nevermind, I think I'll still make sure no one finds his body." Asher growled, making her laugh.

"He's truly not worth it and not the point to why I'm telling you. I can't get pregnant. No matter how many times we have sex. So, you not being a good boy scout and being prepared is okay. I'll keep your secret."

A sly smirk appeared on his lips, "So we can have all the sex we want and no chance of you getting pregnant?"

"Yes, but it also means if you ever want kids that we'll have to find another way." The shame she felt was immense and she hadn't realized she curled into herself slightly.

Asher lifted her chin, "There are plenty of children in this world that have super shitty parents and need a pair of awesome people in their corner. When the time comes we'll cross that bridge." He kissed the tip of her nose.

"That sounds good to me." She laid her head on his shoulder as he wrapped his arms around her.

"In the meantime, I think I would love to put this have all the sex we want to the test."

She looked up as he wiggled his eyebrows at her, "Oh god… I've created a sex monster."

"A respectful sex monster." He carried her back to the bed where once again she lost herself into the depts of love and pleasure with the man who always held her heart.

DELANEY

Delaney felt something warm on the side of her face. Peeking her eyes open she found the sun shining in through the large window in Asher's room. She stretched her arm out only to find that his side of the bed was empty. Trying not to let her panic immediately take over she turned onto her other side and saw a note waiting for her on his pillow. On top of his note was a newly drawn bookmark of the New York City skyline. She flipped over the bookmark to see his handwriting on the back. She placed the bookmark on the table beside her then opened his note.

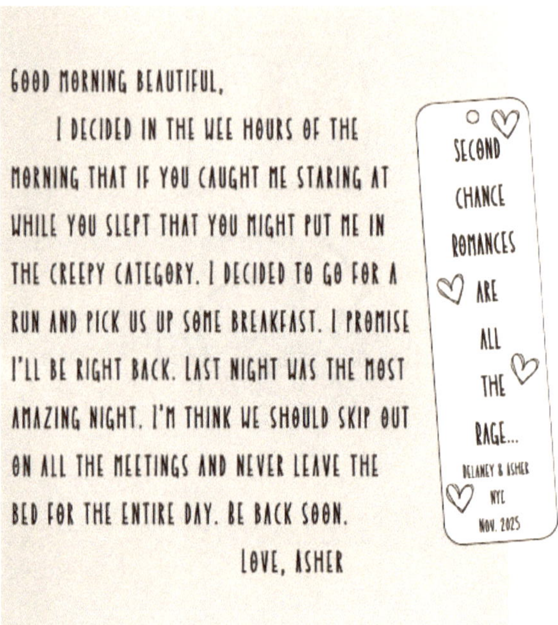

She couldn't help the small giggle that bubbled from within her chest. Not knowing what time, he had left or when he would be back she walked into the bathroom and started the shower. Either he would join her or she would be freshly showered and ready for their meetings today. She was hoping for the former of the two. Stepping beneath the hot stream, she clipped her long hair on top of her head. Letting the water beat down on her wonderfully aching muscles. Not to long after she heard the door close and Asher's voice fill the bathroom.

"Do you have room for one more?"

She stuck her hand out from behind the curtain and wiggled her finger for him to join her. Delaney didn't think Asher could get any sexy to her until he stepped beneath the steady stream of water. Suddenly, she couldn't keep her hands off his slick body. Reaching between them, she starting stroking his cock and was about to kneel down in front of him when he grab a hold of her waist.

"You'll have plenty of chances to do that when we're back in Wilmington. Right now, I need to be inside of you." He pressed her back against the tile wall lifting one leg around his waist.

She pretended to pout, "But I wanted to taste you now."

The low growl that came from him send shivers down her already overheating body. In one swift motion, he thrust into her while holding her steady. Unlike last night, when they went slow and rediscovered each other's bodies. This was raw need for a release. He snapped his hips hard against her making her cry out. It wasn't long before they were both holding onto each other through their releases. Now Delaney's legs felt like jello, and she wasn't sure she was any cleaner from before she got in the shower. After eating a cold breakfast and getting ready for their day of meetings, they headed out of the hotel hand in hand walking down the streets of New York City.

Walking into the monumental office building and heading up to the publishing house offices, Delaney stepped inside feeling like she found where she belonged. Books were displayed everywhere, people sitting in open areas or cubicles reading books. As they walked through the offices, she could hear conversations people were having about upcoming releases or new covers being announced. When she looked over at Asher, he looked down at her with a wide smile.

"I love it when you're like a kid in a candy store." He chuckled.

She squeezed his hand, "I'm pretty sure this is heaven. I've died and been a good girl who got to go to heaven."

His eyes darkened as he leaned down whispering, "You were definitely a good girl last night."

"Asher!" She whispered loudly hitting his arm.

He started laughing until Dom stepped out from behind a glass door. Asher's mood immediately changed and she dropped his hand putting on her professional mask. No reason to give Dom any more reasons not to like her.

"Asher. Delaney. Come on in." Dom held the door open for them.

She hadn't expected for her stomach to suddenly fill with raging butterflies as she stepped in front of a room full of people. Everyone looked formal and important. Looking down at her brown slacks and maroon button down, she began to wonder if she should have went out to buy something more formal. A woman with blonde hair cut into a stylish blunt bob and wearing the tallest heels she had ever seen walked right up to Asher smiling.

"Asher Graham, it's been too long." She kissed his cheek letting her hand slowly slide down his arm.

Delaney wanted to push the woman away especially when she saw his body tense up. She stepped behind him where no one could see her hand pressing into the small of his back. She felt him relax the moment she touched him and she smiled bright up at the woman.

"Hi, I'm Delaney Bishop and you are?"

The woman looked down at Delaney as if interrupting whatever she was imaging was going on between her and Asher.

"Moira Petersen, executive assistant to Mr. Browning." She turned to Asher smiling once more, "Ash, did you finally get an assistant? I told you I would leave if you ever needed one."

Delaney's eyes narrowed on her hand still gripping Asher's arm, "That's me alright, I'm assisting him by co-authoring a new book with him. That's why we're here to discuss our new book."

"Oh, I thought it was a joke when they said you were writing a book with a partner." Moira glared down at Delaney.

She stepped beside Asher leaning in closer to Moira, so she had to remove her hand from his arm, "Not a joke. Now, don't you have notes to take or coffee to get. I believe this meeting is about to start."

The look on her face was priceless and was worth the guilt Delaney would feel later for being a bitch. She didn't like anyone pawing at her man let alone a stuck up money chaser like Moira Petersen.

"Your jealous and protective side is sexy." Asher whispered as they all started to take their places.

"Well, no one touches my man without his or mine permission. Especially heel wearing, pretty blondes."

Once they sat down, Asher reached beneath the table squeezing her hand, "Your man, huh? I love the sound of that."

She smiled up at him, "So do I."

Delaney pulled out her notebook so she could take notes on topics discussed and decisions that were made with such an anticipated release. The editors already had their first nine chapters, and we were excited to read the rest. She noticed that one of the editors had said very little but keeping looking towards Delaney. She wrote the editors name in her notebook to go speak to after the meeting was done. She was shocked that Dom had kept quiet throughout most of the meeting. Every now and then she would catch him looking her way then looking back at his tablet. It was only when the cover designers started discussing their ideas is when Delaney spoke up.

"If I may, I had an idea for a cover that I create for inspirational purposes." She pulled out her tablet pulling up the mock cover design.

"You designed a cover?" Asher asked standing to go behind the cover designers to see her mockup.

"Before opening my bookshop and writing full time I was a social media coordinator for our local school district. I would create graphics and posts all the time for our schools. I picked up a few tricks and taught myself how to create book covers. Owning a bookshop helps me stay in know of cover trends in all genres."

The proud smile spreading across Asher's face took her breath away.

It was at that moment Dom decided to speak up, "I'm sure your little doodle is great for self-publishing, but this is the major leagues. Leave it to the professionals to decide the cover."

"Actually, this is an amazing design. I love how the bright colors are complimented with the shadows giving it the horror vibe we're looking for. From this cover you get what you'll be reading and that's important to readers. It's eye catching and a really great foundation to work off of. Do you mind if I email this to myself. I'll start working on some mockups right away."

"Absolutely. I'm glad you found inspiration from it." Delaney narrowed her eyes on Dom before looking back at Asher.

She could tell he was seething beneath the smile on his lips. His eyes were pinpointed onto his agent and his cheeks steadily turning red by the second. Except for the moment with Dom, the meeting had gone way better than she had expected. It seemed that everyone working with Asher truly cared about his passion for this project and wanted to see it succeed. Which is why she couldn't understand why his agent would be so against it.

"Miss Bishop?"

She turned to see the editor, Laura O'Brien, standing beside her, "Hi, please call me Delaney. Laura, right?"

She nodded, "May I have a moment of your time?"

Delaney looked up at Asher who was talking with the CEO of the publishing house, "Sure." She followed her out into the hallway where they stopped a few doors down from the conference room.

"I'm the editor-in-chief. All projects come through me once our editors have a pass at them. I wanted you to know that the only reason we were able to read your manuscript was because your agent, Miss Meyer, sent it to us."

A cold sense of dread washed over Delaney, "I was under the assumption that Dom Kincade was responsible for handing in our chapters since it was decided to publish under Asher's publishers."

She nodded, "You're correct. When Sam, my assistant editor, brought to my attention we were only receiving the chapters written by Mr. Graham, I personally reached out to your agent to see where your chapters were. To say she was beyond angry is an understatement."

"Oh, I bet. I wonder why she didn't tell either of us."

"You'll have to ask her, but I've set it up to where she'll email me your chapters in order for us to edit the manuscript properly." Laura finally smiled, "You're an excellent writer, Delaney. It's been quite some time since I've truly enjoyed reading a manuscript and this project is one I've thoroughly enjoyed."

Delaney returned her smile, "That's means everything to me. Thank you and thank you for going above and beyond to reach out to Leigh."

"You're welcome. I love seeing smart, talented women succeed. I won't take up any more of your time. It was lovely meeting you."

She shook Laura's hand as she continued to walk down the hall out of sight. Delaney took a moment to collect her emotions and ready herself to face everyone again. She made her way back towards the conference room when she saw Dom stepping out with one of the executive's offices. Neither of them saw her as they stood there talking.

"I don't know Dom. I think your first impression of Delaney Bishop might be wrong."

Dom scoffs, "Oh it's not wrong. She has this small town girl charm that bewitches everyone. I'm telling you her true colors will show it's self soon. She's talentless and only after Asher's big payday."

The other man looked skeptical, "Have you even read her work? I read her debut novel and some of her chapters from the manuscript. She's talented and compliments Asher's talents. If you keep pushing against Asher I'm afraid he's going to take his talents elsewhere. So get your shit together, Dom."

"I have my shit together. I just need Asher to get his dick sucked by little Miss Bishop so he can finally move on." Dom started to walk down the hall away from Delaney with the executive.

Tears were threatening to slip down her face. Anger and humiliation filled her chest making it hard to breathe. She wanted to leave, to go outside and let the cold wind cool her blistering face. She hadn't realized that she was staring off until Asher stepped in front of her.

"Are you okay?"

The concern filling his eyes helped calm her, "Y-Yes, I'm fine. I guess I'm a little overwhelmed from everyone loving our project."

His hand slid down her back, "Well I was going to show you around a little, but if you prefer to go back to hotel to rest we can do that."

She shook her head, "I'm sure I wouldn't get much rest back at the hotel."

"Well… eventually you would get rest," He leaned down, "After some blissful, sweaty, exhaustion."

"Keep it in your pants, Ash. Now show me around especially where they keep all the books." She slip her arm through his, feeling slightly better being by Asher's side.

Dear Diary,

June 2007

This has truly been the best month of my life. Asher is amazing and it's hard to even think about my life before he was in it. We went to a drive in movie about 30 minutes outside of Wilmington. They were playing the third Pirates of the Caribbean and Hostel II. During Hostel I nearly jumped on top of Asher during one of the scarier parts. He put his arm around my shoulders and shielded my eyes any time a scary or gory part was on screen. I would have happily hid my face into his chest during both movies. He smelt like the ocean from the day went spent at the beach.

I received a letter from Quinn telling me all about her California adventures. Apparently, she's been making out with any boy that looks her way. Sometimes I wish I had that kind of confidence. I keep wishing and dreaming of kissing Asher and I'm starting to think he may just not like me in that way. One thing Quinn said in her letter was she wants me to let loose and go wild while I'm out here. Again... if only I was confident like her. I miss my sis.

I'm going to tell her about Asher when I write back to her. About how he makes me feel and how badly I want to kiss him. I can almost hear her voice saying, "Don't wait for him to kiss you. Just do it yourself! Kiss the damn boy!"

I really think I'm falling for him in ways I never believe I would fall for a boy. Sure, I've read about kids my age falling in love and being with that person, but I never thought that was for me. Being with Asher makes me believe that I could have that... with him.

OMG... I think I'm in love with him

I ♥ Asher Graham

Until next time,

Smile¨ Laney

ASHER

Asher was sitting at his desk staring at a blank screen. He looked over to Delaney's empty chair and his heart sank. After an amazing time in New York City, as soon as they had returned to Wilmington things had changed. He thought that they would be sharing a bed and waking up with her in his arms. Instead, it had been two weeks of sleeping a part and hardly seeing each other. Delaney had been keeping herself in her room except for coming out to grab food or something to drink. He didn't know what he had done or what had changed but he wanted to fix it.

In the last week, Dom had called him nearly every day about their chapters being late. He could care less about pissing Dom off, but it wasn't like Delaney to not be submitting her chapters. He was genuinely worried and didn't know how to reach out to her. He pulled out his phone scrolling through his contacts and hitting Thomas Reed's number.

"This is Thomas."

Asher felt ridiculous calling him, "Hey Thomas, it's Asher. I need a favor."

"You need to talk to Leigh, don't you?"

"What the hell dude? Are you psychic or something?" Asher chuckled.

Thomas joined in laughing as well, "Leigh gave me a heads up that there was a possibility you would need to get a hold of her. However, I thought it was going to take you longer to call so now I'm out twenty bucks."

"I owe you then. How did Leigh know I would call?"

"Her and Delaney have been talking a lot." He could hear Thomas moving into a different room, "Hold on a second."

Asher chuckled as he heard Leigh celebrating in the background before getting on the phone, "Asher Graham, thank you good sir. This is by far the best twenty dollars I've ever had in my hands."

"You're welcome, I think."

"So, you're calling me to see what's going on with Delaney. Why she's keeping her distance from you and acting like a damsel locked away in a tower."

Asher opened his mouth to speak then a thought popped into his head. His muscles relaxing slightly as he realized part of what was going on.

"Yes, but the fact that you're talking to me and not flying out here to rip my balls off means I'm not the problem."

A soft chuckled came through the phone, "Delaney said you were smart. That's right, you're not the problem and honestly she's really torn up about not saying anything to you."

"What isn't she tell me? I know whatever it is that it happened in New York. She seemed fine during the whole trip…"

"Yes, after you two finally sexed it up."

Asher groaned hanging his head, "I like to say we reconnected, but yes. It was at the meeting, wasn't it?"

"You're getting warmer."

He started thinking about the meeting. Everyone seemed to love Delaney and vice versa. One editor was eying her throughout the meeting then snatched her away after it. Dom had been his normal asshole self and then Moira had been a complete bitch. Delaney had held her own against Moira and Dom.

"Was it the editor? Laura, I think was her name. I know she pulled Delaney out of the room to speak with her."

"No, actually Laura is fully in Delaney's corner. Think closer to you."

He hated playing guessing games, "Why can't you just tell me so I can figure out a way to fix it."

Leigh sighed, "Part of the reason Delaney doesn't want you to know is because she knows you'll do something rash and possible ruin your career."

"Dom. My asshole agent did something. Am I right?"

"Ding! Ding! Ding! Winner, winner. You'll have to cook your own chicken dinner." She paused for a moment before continuing, "Are you sure you want to know?"

Asher could feel the burning rage starting to flow down his body, "Tell me."

After Asher hung up with Leigh he was seeing red. He couldn't believe Dom would purposely try to ruin Delaney's career and their project. He stood to make a good chunk of money off it even if Asher didn't. He had made sure nothing of Dom's income would change. Ever since Asher told him about who Delaney was, Dom's whole attitude changed. Almost overnight he went from being Asher's friend to his sworn enemy. He needed to burn off the anger steadily building up inside him. Grabbing a piece of paper, he wrote Delaney a note and drew a little bookmark on it. He slipped it under her door before grabbing his keys and heading out.

When Asher had told Delaney he wasn't much of a cook he was being honest. However, there was one meal that he knew how to cook, and it was one his mom used to make him all the time. He sat in the grocery store parking lot typing out everything he would need on his phone. He also decided to stop by the local florist to pick up some flowers for Delaney. He was halfway through grocery shopping when his anger subsided and turned into heavy guilt.

He didn't know what he should do. He wanted to punch Dom in his fucking face, but he knew that would cause more problems than solve them. Honestly, he wanted to break his contract with him and never work with him again. That would take a lot of calls and a hefty payout. As he loaded the groceries into his car all he could think about was what Delaney wanted. He wanted her to be a part of this decision, and he couldn't do that with her hiding from him. He understood why she was doing it, but if they were truly going to be together then they needed to face this together.

Arriving home, he immediately began prepping dinner in the kitchen. Pulling out his dusty slow cooker, he washed it out then set it off to the side. It took him an hour, and one band-aid to get everything in the cooker and start the timer for four hours. Going back into the office, grabbed his notebook and a piece of card stock then headed into the living room. He started drawing a fireplace with books on the mantle above it. He wasn't a great artist but the few art classes he took in high school and college made it to where he didn't suck completely. Usually, he would use color pencils to color it in, but this time he decided to use shading techniques.

Once he was finished Asher wrote out a short note for Delaney to go with it. When there was a half-hour left for the slow cooker he went about setting the table. Making sure he used the good bowls and grabbing two soup spoons. He threw the dinner rolls on a cookie sheet and into the oven to warm them up. The final touch was lighting two taper candles on the table then placing the bouquet of blue violets and peonies in the center. Finally, his timer went off he turn the setting to warm and headed down to Delaney's room.

He slipped the note and bookmark beneath her door then gently knocked on it. He heard her get up walking towards the door. Asher nervously waited for his note to be returned and let out a long breath when he saw the piece of paper reappear.

MISS DELANEY BISHOP,

WILL YOU DO ME THE HONOR IN

JOINING ME FOR DINNER? PLEASE

CHECK THE CORRESPONDING BOX WITH

YOUR ANSWER.

☑ YES *I'll be up in a few minutes.*

☐ NO

LOVE,

MR. ASHER GRAHAM

Asher smiled folding the note and slipping it into his back pocket. He hurried back upstairs pouring them each a bowl of his mom's stew. It was one of his favorites meals and she would always make it whenever he was upset or sick. The smell alone always gave him comfort and reminded him how much he missed her.

Sitting at the table, he watched Delaney appear in her typical writing outfit. He did notice that the hoodie she was wearing was his and that sent his heart soaring.

"I hope you like beef stew." He stood, holding out a chair for her, "It's the one thing I know how to cook."

She sat down placing her hands around the bowl, "I love beef stew, but I especially like it now since it can warm my hands."

Asher place his hand palm up on the table, "How cold are they today?"

"Icicles." She placed her hand on top of his making him flinch.

"Shit Delaney, I didn't know it was that cold downstairs. I'll turn up the heat."

He went stand, but she grasp his hand, "You don't need to do that."

They sat there neither of them eating or talking. The silent tension slowly building with each minute that passed. Finally, Delaney picked up her spoon and took a bite of her dinner.

"Asher, this is amazing. You've been holding back." There was a small smile on her face that sadly didn't reach up into her eyes.

"So have you." The words were barely above a whisper, but he might has well screamed them at her as she flinched, "I don't mean that in an accusatory way. I just mean… well I spoke to-"

"Leigh, I know. She called me immediately after getting off the phone with you."

Asher took her spoon bringing her hand up to his cheek, "I wish you would have told me when we were there. I would have said something to him."

She scoffed, "I think you meant to say you would've punched his lights out."

"Tomato, tamato." He kissed her palm, "I understand why you didn't tell me. After talking to Leigh, I understand why you placed distance between us…"

"But." She said running her thumb over his cheek.

"But… I don't want anything or anyone to come between us again. We've lost too much time, and I don't want to lose another second with you." He pulled her up sitting her on his lap, "When I said I wanted to be with you forever that meant through the good, the bad and the ugly. I want to know when something is bothering you so we can decide how to handle it together. I only want to make the tough decisions with you."

Delaney wrapped her arms around his neck, "I'm sorry. I've been on my own for so long that my default is to isolate myself."

"You're not alone anymore. I like to think I'm a strong, strapping man that can assist you in carrying the heavy stuff."

This time when she smiled her eyes lit up and he couldn't help matching it.

She leaned in kissing his cheek, "I'm grateful for you being willing to help carry my crazy. Just be patient with me. Five years of isolation and insecurities isn't going to go away overnight."

"I know it's not. I just want you to remember that you have someone beside you whenever you need me. Okay?"

"Okay." She rested her head against his, "Do you want to talk about it now?"

"Only if you want to." He turned towards her smirking, "We could always go snuggle in bed and talk."

She chuckled, "Whenever we cuddle in bed the only talking going on is me being complete incoherent as waves of pleasure wreck my body."

"Is that such a bad thing?" Asher smirked, then noticed her eyes look away from him, "Hey, what is it?"

He watched as tears slowly rolled down her cheeks. She wiped them away before burying her face into the crook of his neck. He held her tighter rubbing slow circle on her back.

"Whatever you're feeling you can tell me."

"It's stupid." She mumbled against his neck, "It's so stupid."

He lifted her chin so she would look at him, "If you're feeling it then it's not stupid. It's not dumb. It's not invalid. You can feel all the feels you want rather happy, sad or mad. As long as you let me know so I can be there for you."

She pressed her forehead to his, "How did I get so lucky to have you in my life?"

"Well, you took a walk on a beach and said hello to a strange boy watching the ocean. So, really you only have yourself to blame for me being here." He smiled as she laughed through the tears still falling.

Delaney wiped away the tears again, "I feel stupid because once again Ty popped into my head."

"How so?" Right next to Dom was Ty on Asher's list of people getting punched in the face.

"Towards the end of our marriage we tried marriage counseling. We were in a session, and he told the therapist that I was a sex addict. That all I wanted to do was have sex all the time." She sniffled.

Asher tighten his arms around her as she continued, "I told the therapist that I did in fact love having sex with my husband. I told them that I thought it was normal for a wife to want to have sex with her husband. After that day, I never thought about sex the same way again. It wasn't long after that Ty moved out and we went through filing for divorce."

"You know, Dom was at the top of my punching list but your dumbass ex has taken back the top spot again." Asher couldn't believe any man would ever complain about having sex with Delaney.

She leaned in kissing his cheek, "My hero. Seriously, he's not worth it."

"You're right, he's not worth it. He's not worth your tears or pain you've put yourself through." Asher kissed her lips, "For the record, I love having sex with you. I love the way your body reacts to my touch. I love the little sighs and moans that come from your lips. I love that you worry about my pleasure more than your own. I love that you trust me to show you how sex is meant to be between two people."

"So… you wouldn't think I was a sex addict if I suggested we went upstairs right now?"

Asher scooped her up, carrying her towards his room, "Hell no!

Any time you wanna have sex I am game! You know unless it's illegal then we'll just have to be extra sneaky and quiet."

159

ASHER

Asher stretched his arm out expecting to feel Delaney beside him. His eyes snapped open when he felt the cold sheets where she had been sleeping. The sun was hidden behind gray clouds as waves were crashing against the beach. Sitting up on the bed, he could tell a storm was coming and hoped that it would only be outside. The previous night a lot of old wounds had been opened for Delaney, and he worried that he might have pushed her too far. If that was the case, he didn't want to face the possibility of her closing herself off again.

He pulled on a pair of dark sweatpants and an old Princeton hoodie that had seen better days but brought him a lot of comfort. Opening the bedroom door, he was instantly hit with the smell of bacon and coffee. The aroma was pulling him to the kitchen like a siren. He stopped at the entrance to see Delaney wearing one of his t-shirts and a pair of his boxers. Her earbuds were in and she was swaying her beautiful hips to whatever was playing in her ears. He stood mesmerized before sitting at the kitchen island.

"Shit!" Delaney yelled as she turned around seeing him there, "Scared the crap out of me."

"It's your own fault. I was under your spell watching you dance and cook." He smirked as her cheeks blossomed a rosy pink.

"Next time announce yourself so I don't almost pee my pants." She chuckled.

Asher walked towards her pulling on the waistband of his boxers, "I believe these would be mine." He watched as her nipples pebbled against the thin fabric of his shirt.

She let out a shaky breath, "I hate that you have such control over my body. I shouldn't turn into a whimpering mess with one simple touch or simply in the presence of your sleepy sexiness."

"Sleepy sexiness?" He laughed.

"Yes, your whole unruly-I-just-woke-up hair and your dark, sleepy sex eyes. It's not fair."

He picked her up sitting her on the island counter, "You know what's not fair?"

Delaney yelped as he pulled her against him, wrapping her legs around his hips, "W-What?"

"Having the sexiest woman in the world wearing my clothes, cooking breakfast and swaying her beautiful hips for all to see." He rolled his hips against her rubbing his hard cock against her, "Then expected me not to watch her and think about all the things I want to do other than eat her delicious breakfast." Her breath hitched as he snapped his hips against her.

"A-Asher…"

"What do you want Delaney?" He lifted her chin locking his eyes were hers.

"I… I…"

He could see she fighting with herself. The trauma her ex inflected had his blood boiling as he watched her struggle to tell him what she really wanted.

"Delaney?"

Her eyes shined with tears, and she bit her lower lip. He cradled her face gently kissing her. He swore if he ever saw her ex the first thing he was going to do was wreck his face then thank him for being a fucking idiot. He focused on her again whispering what he knew she needed to hear.

"Beautiful, it's not only normal but it's healthy for you to want sex. To want intimacy. To tease me and vice versa driving each other crazy."

"My brain and my body can't get on the same page. I feel like everything between us had been about sex and it has to be more than that or I really am what Ty said I was." She looked away from him.

"Hey, hey, hey," He moved to where he could see her again, "First, you are not a sex addict. You're a healthy woman with a healthy sexual desire to be with the person who gratefully, wholeheartedly and with pleasure wants to be with you. Do you think of me as a sex obsessed man like a lot of women think men are?"

She shook her head, "No, I still can't believe you actually want to be with me." Her half-hearted chuckle nearly killed him.

"I want to be with you in every possible way I can." Her eyes snapped up to his, "I want to be your everything because Delaney Bishop you are my everything. I told you in New York that I'm in this for the long haul and I meant that. No matter what, I'm going to be by your side."

She finally smiled, "Even though I completely ruined this moment with my stupid insecurities?"

"Your insecurities are never stupid. They give me a goal to help empower you to defeat them." He kissed the tip of her nose making her giggle, "You didn't ruin anything. This big, old house has many, many surfaces that I plan on christening with you. Including this very nice kitchen island."

She wrapped her arms around his neck, "Do you still want my pancakes and bacon, or would you be alright with just having me for breakfast?"

Asher couldn't get his boxers off her fast enough. She started giggling until her ass hit the cold garnet top. He didn't give her time to think about it before rubbing small circles against her clit.

"I mean this in the most respectful way but fuck the pancakes and bacon. I'll choose you every day and twice on Sundays." Delaney gasped against his lips as he pushed two fingers inside of her.

"A-Asher… oh god…" He was about to dive in when she stopped him, "Wait, I want something more before you have me."

He couldn't help to small growl that escaped his lips. He stepped back as she hopped off the island. She pulled his shirt off standing before him in all her gorgeous glory. She pushed him back against the island before lowering onto her knees. When he realized what she was doing he cupped her cheek while she pulled his sweatpants down.

"You want this before I have you?" He hissed as her hand wrapped around his shaft, "F-Fuck…"

He watched as she licked her hand then wrapped her slick fingers around him again, "You have tasted me many times. You have given me some of the most mind blowing orgasms I've ever had. I've wanted to taste you for a long time. May I?"

Asher looked down at this enchanted woman and could only nod as the brightest smile spread across her face. The moment her warm lips wrapped around him, and she slid him inside her mouth he knew that this woman was a goddess. She was too good for him, and he would spend the rest of his life worshiping her. It wasn't long before his hand was gripping her hair and he was coming in her mouth. Once the stars cleared from his eyes, Asher looked down to see her plump lips pulled into a grin and her rosy cheeks deepening in color. He pulled her up and placed her back on the island not giving her a chance to say or do anything. He dove between her legs and had the only breakfast he would ever want for the rest of his life.

Eventually, they ate Delaney's reheated breakfast and decided they would both work from their laptops in front of the fire in the living room. It was the perfect stormy day to be curled up on the couch. More than once, he caught himself staring out over the ocean as the waves crashed into the beach. Dark, ominous clouds were hovering over the raging waters. Lightning flashed off it the distance and the low rumble of thunder filled the room.

Asher decided to check his emails when he saw one marked urgent from Dom. He wanted to ignore it but knew he couldn't.

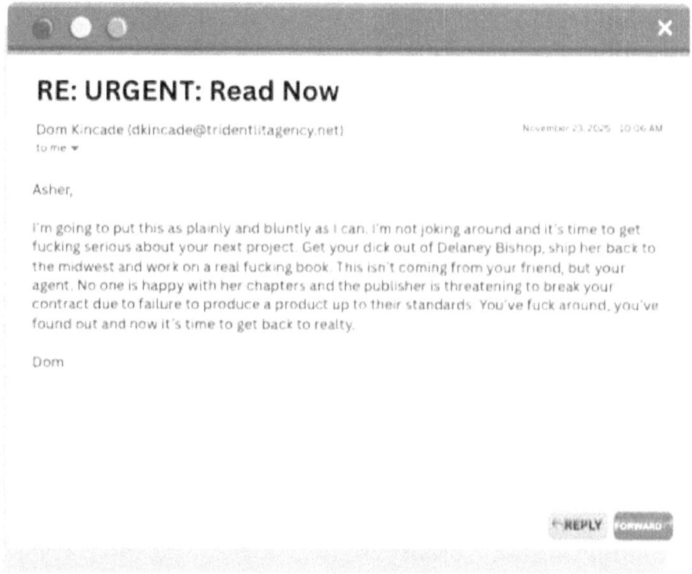

RE: URGENT: Read Now

Dom Kincade (dkincade@tridentlitagency.net)   November 23, 2025   10:06 AM
to me

Asher,

I'm going to put this as plainly and bluntly as I can. I'm not joking around and it's time to get fucking serious about your next project. Get your dick out of Delaney Bishop, ship her back to the midwest and work on a real fucking book. This isn't coming from your friend, but your agent. No one is happy with her chapters and the publisher is threatening to break your contract due to failure to produce a product up to their standards. You've fuck around, you've found out and now it's time to get back to realty.

Dom

"Ash, you okay?"

He looked over to Delaney who had a worried expression on her face then felt her hand on top of his. His knuckles were white as snow from the tight grip he had on his laptop.

"It's nothing. I need to go make a few phone calls in our office." He loosened his grip then leaned over kissing the top of her head, "I promise, everything will be fine."

"You're going to tell me what happened later."

It wasn't a question and yet he still answered, "Yes, I promise."

Asher headed up to their office, closing the door behind him. The first call he made was to his publishers. What Dom didn't know was he was really close with the CEO. His family and Asher's had grown up together. Asher knew he wouldn't bullshit him if he asked about being dropped because of his new project. As he had suspected Dom was blowing smoke up his ass. To cover all his bases, he spoke with the editor-in-chief and the main editor working on the project. They both loved the project and once he was off the phone he felt slightly better. The next call he needed to make would put into motion some big changes for him and stir a lot of shit. He knew a change was needed sooner rather than later.

After four rings, the other end answered with a big sigh, "Asher Graham this better be life or death." Leigh's frustrated groan made him flinch.

"Sorry for interrupting, I'll make this quick."

"You better. You have exactly one minute before Thomas begins making me make noises you'll never get out of your head."

Asher never spoke so fast in his life, but with five seconds to spare he let the silence fill the call praying Thomas wasn't doing his thing yet, "Leigh?"

She hummed, "Let me make some calls and I'll get back to you within the week. Now can I go back to my fiancé finger fuc-"

"Whoa! Hanging up now, thank you Leigh. Bye."

Asher ended the call and felt even better knowing Leigh was going to help him out. He headed back downstairs seeing Delaney completely focused on her laptop. Her fingers breezing over the keys as the words flowed out of her like water. He knew they needed to finish their chapters. Especially after his conversation with Leigh, she would be getting both their chapters now to submit to the editors. Seeing Delaney stretched out on the couch all he wanted to do was snuggle with her and watch a movie or TV or take a nap. He came up beside her gently grabbing her laptop off her lap.

"Hey! Asher, give me back my laptop." She reached for it but he stepped away from her quickly.

He made sure she wasn't in the middle of a sentence or thought then saved her work in both spots he knew she saved to. Shutting her laptop down he crawled over her laying his head on her stomach and wrapping his arms around her waist.

She let out a soft chuckle, "Asher, we have a deadline coming up rather quickly and neither of us are near hitting it."

"I know, I just…" He looked up at her seeing genuine concerning within those blue irises, "I really need snuggles right now. I'm man enough to admit it. I need snuggles and to take a nap with you. No funny business, I promise."

He felt her trying to wiggle down and he lifted himself enough for her to get comfort. Now his head was laying on the two best pillows god ever made and Delaney started stroking his hair.

"Who am I to turn down snuggles and naps with a handsome man." She kissed the top of his head before turning on the TV.

Asher closed his eyes hearing Austin Jameson's voice through the speakers. Her steady heartbeat lulled him into a peaceful sleep for the next couple of hours. When they woke up, they were both refreshed and decided to get some serious writing done in their office.

It was nearly four in the morning, and Asher was still lying awake. He couldn't shut his brain off even after making love to Delaney in their office this time. She was blissfully sleeping beside him. Looking down at her, he couldn't help to be utterly amazed that she was there. Something she had said earlier that day was playing on repeat in his mind.

…I feel like everything between us had been about sex and it has to be more than that…

He carefully got out of bed making sure not to wake her. Making his way back into the office, he sat at his desk pulling out a sheet of paper. She had been right. So far, their reuniting had been all about sex. Honestly, he felt no guilt about that since they were making up for decades of lost time. However, she was right to want more. He had kept telling her he was in this for the long haul but never said how madly in love with her he is. He had never asked her on a proper date or discussed if titles were important to her. He wanted to tell everyone that she was his girlfriend. Hell, if he thought it would be the right move he would have proposed to her right now, but he knew that would be rushing things. Saying I love you and asking her to be his girlfriend seemed childish, but it was important.

After twenty minutes of writing and drawing, Asher could finally feel his eyes getting heavy. Quietly returning to his room, he placed the note and bookmark on the table for her to find when she woke up. Laying down behind her, Asher slid his arm around her waist and buried his face into her soft hair falling asleep immediately.

DELANEY

"What do I do?" Quinn's laughter only fueled Delaney's panic, "Stop laughing at me!"

"I'm not laughing at you. I'm laughing at the fact that you're freaking out over a little note." Quinn's laugh faded into sigh, "Why are you panicking?"

Delaney stared down at the note and bookmark on her bed, "What am I supposed to do? What do I wear? How do I act? I haven't been on a date in years. I don't know what to do."

"First take a deep breath and calm the fuck down." Quinn took a deep breath with her, "You've slept with this man multiple times without a second thought, but he asks you out on a date and you freak out. Doesn't it seem like you're overreacting a little?"

She shook her head even though her best friend couldn't see her, "When you say it like that then I could see where I'm overreacting. I don't want to screw this up, Quinn. I'm really falling him again and it scares me."

"For once, I understanding completely what you mean."

"Everett?" Delaney asked, not exactly surprised.

Her friend let out a shaky breath, "I think I'm in love with him. I think I want to build a life with him. That's a scary thought after seeing everything you went through with Ty."

Delaney had never thought how her experiences would have affected Quinn, "Is that why you've never gotten serious with anyone before?"

"Partially. Seeing your heart completely shattered and you become a shell of the woman I knew. It scared me to ever get close to anyone emotionally."

She didn't know how to react or apologize for holding her friend back. She had seen her with so many men over the years. Some of them truly making her happy. Knowing Quinn never settled down because of her made her slowly slump over onto her bed.

"Quinn, I'm so sorry."

"There's no need to apologize. It was my choice and you didn't know that I was keeping all those guys at bay. Obviously, none of them were the ones so really I should thank you."

Delaney scoffed, "Thank me? For what?"

"If it wasn't for you I would have never met Everett and know without a doubt that he's the one for me. Maybe we could have a double wedding one day!" She heard Quinn clap excitedly.

"Double wedding? Can I make it through the first date before wedding planning?"

Quinn chuckled, "Killjoy. Okay, tell me what clothes you have with you, and I'll see if we can hobble something together."

For the next hour, Delaney and Quinn went through every piece of clothing she had with her. They decided she needed to go into town and buy something new. Planning on a Facetime call the next day, they spent another half-hour talking about the bookshop and covering a few orders coming in for events. By the time Delaney was off the phone it was lunchtime and she emerged from her room to the smell of peppers cooking.

Walking into the kitchen she found Asher standing in front of the stove. He was the picture perfect of a main character in a rom-com. He had on a backwards hat with littles curls sticking out beneath it. A black t-shirt stretched across his shoulders and back. It was his snug gray sweatpants showing off his perfect bubble butt that had Delaney curious how he looked from the front.

"Hi."

Asher jumped slightly making her laugh, "Fuck me! Let a guy know you're behind him."

"Would you rather I done this?"

Delaney stepped up behind him wrapping her arms around his waist and running her hands across his stomach. His large body relaxed against hers as she pressed forehead in the middle of his shoulders.

"Yes…" His answer came out breathless, "Delaney…"

Her hands drifted down over his hips slipping one of them over his hardening length, "Asher…"

His head rolled back with a long sigh as she stroked him, "Wait one second."

Delaney withdrew her hand immediately, watching as Asher turned off all the burns on the stove. He turned around taking her hand and placing it back on his cock.

"Now that the house won't burn down, please continue."

His dark green eyes were shining with desire as they watched her hand stroke him. His hips thrusting forward slightly as he leaned in boxing her in against the island. His head came to rest on her shoulder with a low moan coming from his lips.

"So, announcing myself this way is acceptable?" She asked, slipping her hand down the front of his pants.

"Y-Yes… fuck Delaney…" Suddenly he grasped her hand pulling it from his pants, "I think we have more surfaces to leave our marks on."

Scooping her up over his shoulder Delaney smacked his ass as he carried her downstairs passed her office and bedroom. Walking into a brightly lit room with a large sectional couch and TV in it. He gently placed her down next to the floor to ceiling windows looking out to the private beach. She looked back at him as he pulled his hat and shirt off. It was when he pushed his sweatpants down that she realized what he wanted to do.

"What if someone sees?"

He grinned walking towards her as naked as the day he was born, "Then we better give them a good show."

Her back pressed against the cool glass, "Are you serious?"

"Unless it makes you uncomfortable then I will take you to your room to continue this." He pulled her hoodie over her head grinning when he saw she had nothing on underneath, "I promise if I see anyone peeping in I will make sure they get full view of my ass and not yours."

Asher knelt in front of her pulling her pajama bottoms down around her ankles. She kicked them to the side running her fingers through his soft curls.

"I don't want anyone seeing your ass either. That's mine to see."

The smile spreading across his face melted her heart, "Yours, huh? I'm yours?"

She held her finger up for him to wait as she walked to room grabbing his note. He was leaning his back against the glass when she came back.

"You asked me a question…"

His crooked an eyebrow at her, "Yes I did."

She looked down at it one last time before handing it to him, "I've always been yours." She whispered.

Asher let go of the note letting it float to the ground before pulling her to him and kissing her. He picked her up wrapping her legs around his waist and pressing her back against the glass.

"And I've always been yours. You're okay with the title change?"

She smiled letting out a breathy sigh, "From friends with benefits to girlfriend? Yes, I'm very good with that."

"Good because I'm considering doing press junkets to tell the world you're mine and no one else's." He chuckled against her neck.

Asher rolled his hips against her, "Oh god… no press junkets for this."

He reached between them holding his cock at her entrance pushing inside of her slowly, "What about your boyfriend making love to you?"

"Now that you can definitely do." As Asher consumed her every thought, feeling and touch, Delaney forgot all about the possibility of people seeing them or their naked asses through the window.

When they finally returned upstairs, Asher finished cooking his shredded chicken for tacos and they settled in on the couch with their laptops. The next chapters they were writing were a second plot twist and their characters were reaching their breaking points to cross that final line into lovers. She was trying to decided how to reveal the killer while they were in the throes of passion that made sense. She looked over to Asher flashes of their first time together in New York was. It was passionate as they took their time discovering each other. Would the killer watch them?

"What are you over thinking?"

Delaney looked up to see Asher smirking at her, "What makes you think I'm over thinking?"

He leaned in kissing her lips, "Your teeth left a mark on your lip and I'm pretty sure your forehead is permanently furrowed. One of the best things about being co-authors is bouncing ideas off one another."

"There's a dirty comment in there somewhere but my brain hurts."

She sighed setting her laptop off to the side, "My next chapter is the smexy chapter and the killer reveal. I'm trying to think of a way that it would make sense for the killer to reveal themselves when her targets are having sex for the first time."

Asher sat his own laptop to the side, pulling Delaney's legs over his lap. She moaned when he started massaging her calves. She rolled her head back relishing his hands working over her tense muscles.

"Let's start with the tipping point. They've been flirting and tiptoeing crossing this line, so what is going to push them over the edge finally?"

"They're going to have a conversation about Daniel offering himself as bait. He's obviously been our killers main focus and he's going to finally give in to the killer's desire of them being together." Delaney closed her eyes imagine Daniel standing in front of Andie telling her his plan, "Obviously Andie is against this."

Asher's hands came to rest on her legs, "I imagine she would cause an argument, and it would get heated between them. Where is this going to happen? Last I remembered they were visiting some of Daniel's friends in the city. They are sharing a hotel room with only one bed."

Delaney chuckled, "It's one of my favorite tropes. Yes, which brings me to the first point of my hang up. Is it realistic that our killer would be able to access their room and hide within it without them knowing it?"

"Well, let's see." Asher picked up his laptop resting it on top of her legs warming them instantly, "I happen to know the manager of the Marriott downtown in Wilmington."

She cocked an eyebrow at him, "Is that where you would rendezvous with all your fangirls?" she chuckled.

His eyes narrowed at her, "Only fangirl I rendezvous with is you. I would go there for writing retreats whenever my office would become suffocating."

"Oh, so it was your version of the diner." An idea popped into her head, "Maybe we should book a room and…"

Asher held up his finger as he brought his phone up to his ear, "Hey Micah, I have a favor to ask you."

Within the hour, they were checking in at the Marriott into a single king size room. Micah was nice enough to sit with them and explain how security of the room and access in and out of the hotel worked. He told them stories of how fans would sneak in to catch glimpses of actors from a teen show being filmed there. Micah took them on a tour of the hotel including areas that would be restricted and be hard to access without a keycard.

"I mean, I guess they could always pay off an employee for they keycard, but I would like to think most people would not want to risk their job." Micah walked them back to their room, "Anyway, you have any more questions just text me. I'm on the graveyard shift so I'll be here all night."

Asher shook his hand, "I appreciate everything Micah."

"Yes, thank you. You've been a great help." Delaney also shook his hand.

Micah brought her hand up to his lips, "Whenever you're done with this loser come see me."

Her eyes immediately went to Asher who was rolling his eyes, "Alright, alright, get your mitts off my girlfriend."

Delaney felt her cheeks burning as Micah let go of her hand. Asher playfully pushed his friend out of the door shaking his head.

"He was joking, right?" she asked.

"No, he wasn't." He looked up at her and tilted his head slightly, "Why do you look confuse?"

She shrugged, "I don't know. Men don't usually hit on me or approach me. It just felt weird."

Asher walked up to her pulling Delaney into his arms, "I'm sure you've had men hitting on you and you paid them no attention. I'm sure after everything your ex put you through and me…"

Delaney placed her hands on his chest, "You were just doing what you though was right in the moment. At eighteen I think that was pretty mature of you."

"Maybe, but it cost me decades of being with you." He locked his hands at the small of her back, "Anyway, now that we have a little more research are you feeling better about your chapter?"

"Yes, I think I have a good idea however now onto my next problem at hand."

He sat down on the bed leaning back on his hands, "What's that?"

Delaney stared at him watching as her mind morphed him into Daniel sitting on the bed. She walked over straddling his lap and wrapping her arms around his neck.

"Whatever problem it is I'm liking it already." He chuckled.

She looked over his shoulder to the window and immediately got up going over and pulling the curtains back. She watched as Asher's reflection walked towards her.

"Delaney, have you've gone all beautiful mind on me?"

"I think I know how to write the scene, but I need your help for a moment." She turned around holding out her hand to him, "Pick me up and act like you're going to fuck me against the window."

Asher froze for a moment, "I'm sorry, say that again." A sly smirk curled onto his face.

She rolled her eyes, "You heard me. I think the moment of the killer's reveal won't be during round one of sex but probably in round two. I'm thinking that they could both see her at the same time."

Asher picked her up wrapping her legs around his waist and pressing her back against the window. She could see clearly if someone were to come out from the closet or bathroom.

"Could you see someone's reflection coming from the bathroom or closet?"

He leaned back slightly looking to the window, "Maybe if it were at night. Right now, it's too bright to see anything. Not to mention you're not factoring one important thing into this idea."

"What's that?" A small moan slipped through her lips as he thrust his hips against her.

"Daniel and Andie won't exactly be focused on catching someone behind them. At least I know I wouldn't be if I was fucking the girl I've been chasing for months."

Delaney bit her lip, "Hmm, you have a point."

"Wait…" Asher pressed his hips firmly against her, "What if Andie noticed her throughout the moment thinking it's her mind playing with her then they both notice her in the moments after?"

"I love it! I can totally write that!" She smacked her hands against his chest excitedly before kissing him, "I love you!"

They both froze for a moment staring at one another. Delaney slapped her hands over her mouth panic filling her chest making it hard to breathe.

"A-Asher… I'm sorry. It kind of slipped out in the moment. Please don't think you need to say anything back or even acknowledge it. I—"

His lips covered hers, "I love you too Delaney. God, I've been trying not to say it because I didn't want to freak you out."

"You… you love me?" Her mind wouldn't allow for her heart to believe it, but she could feel the walls crumbling as he held her tighter against him.

"Of course I do. Delaney, I've been in love with you since the moment we met on the beach and it's never gone away. Laid dormant, yes but never did it go away. I love you with all my heart."

Each word out of his mouth brought down another stone from the fortress around her heart, "So you're okay with me saying I love you?"

She needed reassurance from him to knock down the final layer of stone. Asher placed her feet on the floor and placed his hands around her face. Pressing his lips gently against hers again, she felt him smile.

"More than okay. I think we should tell each other we love one another every single minute of every day for the rest of our lives." He looked down at her with a fierce determination and admiration, "I'm never leaving your side again. I'm never going to let others make decisions for me that affect my relationship with you. You, Delaney Bishop, are the most important thing in my life and I will not lose you again."

Delaney hadn't realized that tears were falling down her cheeks until he kissed them away. She pushed herself up to kiss him again.

"I love you, Asher."

"I love you too, Delaney."

She smiled, "Say that again, except this time say it the other way."

The grin that appeared on his face as he realized what she was asking him to do was breathtaking. She felt a rush of relief as the final stone crumbled into pieces and her heart was allow to fully accept the man standing in front of her. As soon as he said it again, they both fell onto the bed together taking full advantage of their hotel room.

"I love you too, Laney."

Jun. '07

Dear Laney,

I've spent the last hour since coming home from hanging out with you thinking of all the things I love about you. Does that sound weird or creepy? I don't mean it that way. There's just so much to love about you and I know right now you're scowling at the paper. Let me run with this and then if you find this weird or creepy then I promise I will keep my thoughts to myself. I can't promise that I won't think about you because it seems I'm not capable of not thinking about you. Here are the things I love about you:

I love your eyes. They're a brilliant shade of blue that reminds me of the ocean. When you get excited they brighten and seem to sparkle.

I love your hair. In just the right light it shines like copper. I swear it's the softest thing I've ever touched, and I love how silky it feels between my fingers. What I really love is how there is always one strand that falls in front of your face and gives me an excuse to brush it behind your ear. Giving me the perfect opportunity to kiss you.

I love your love for books. I love that you would rather sit and read for hours than do any other activity. I love see the wide array of emotions on your face as you read and how you silently say every word you read.

I love your creativity. My favorite moments with you were when we've both been so focused on our writing projects. Going to the library when it first opens and not leaving until they close, spending the whole-time writing. I love how I can bounce ideas off you and makes me hope that one day we'll write a book together.

I love your compassion. You care about the happiness of other people. When you see someone in need you immediately help them no matter what. The love and compassion you have for others is awe-inspiring.

I love your joy. I know you don't always feel happy, but you never let it show. You greet everyone with your breathtaking smile and make anyone around you happy by being near them.

I love your body. Wait, wait... it's not what your think so don't judge me yet. I love how perfectly you fit within my arms and against my body. It was like God specifically made you for me. We're two pieces of a puzzle that fit perfectly. Also... your body is beautiful, but I can't go into details because then I will truly turn into a typically guy.

All that to say, I love you. I know it may be too soon to say those words, but I mean them. I love you, Laney.

Love,
Asher

ASHER

Standing in front of his closet, Asher stared at all of his dress shirts. Most of them were your standard causal white button downs or Oxford dress shirts. He had a few darker color ones that span from black to blue and even a purple one. He wasn't current on all the fashion trends but one thing he always appreciated when seeing couples out at events was how they matched. Anna popped into his mind for a moment from the last time they had gone to one of her work parties. She had dressed them in the same shades of dark teal and had wowed everyone they conversed with that night. He tried to think of what color Delaney would pick out to wear tonight. He knew Quinn had insisted they go shopping together via Facetime and was continuing that conversation in her room as she got ready.

Normally, he would have assumed Delaney to be in dark browns, olives, hints of ivory or cream. She would more than likely pick some dress pants or a skirt and boots or heels. The thought of Delaney in heels made Asher's knees wobble for a second. Maybe one day he would be brave enough to ask her to wear some around the house. He shook his head focusing again on the shirts in front of him.

"Why is this so fucking hard?" He mumbled to himself before

admitting defeat and text Quinn.

> What color should I wear?

Quinn Larson: OMG you too! You two are hopeless!

> Please Quinn I want everything to be perfect. I want to impress her. I'm begging.

Quinn Larson: Alright, no begging needed. I won't tell you what she's wearing but I would think green or olive, earthy tones would be best on you

> Will that match with her? I always found couples who matched looked best.

Quinn Larson: Okay Mr. Fashionista, you score bonus points from me for this. Black pants, off-white to cream button down and dark forest green or olive tie. I expect pictures.

> You got it and thank you

Asher pulled out everything Quinn specified and quickly got into the shower to get ready. Once he was dressed and his unruly hair tamed into place he looked at his watch.

"Damn, cutting it close." He grabbed his blazer making his way towards the front door.

He stopped when he heard Delaney's voice in coming from the stairs, "Seriously, I'm going to kill myself in these."

Asher desperately wanted to see her but didn't want to ruin his reaction to her so he headed for the door keeping her out of sight. He heard her sigh dramatically and tried to keep his chuckle quiet.

"You've enjoyed torturing me too much today. I didn't think it was possible for you to torture me over the phone, but your powers seem to even reach me from a thousand of miles away." She paused then laughed, "I'll make sure to get a picture of us to send to you. Now I need to get off here and find Asher."

He was about to head out the door when he heard her gasp, "Quinn Larson! I should have never told you about the night in the hotel…"

He grinned, heading out the door with a minute to spare. He watched his watch counting down in his head until it struck six o'clock on the dot.

5…4…3…2…1… He knocked on the door.

"Asher? Asher were you expecting someone?" He heard Delaney yell out before opening the door, "What the…"

Delaney Bishop was a goddess standing before him. He was so glad he decided not to sneak a peek at her. Her long copper hair was going down her back in waves of curls. She wore a beautiful navy dress that clung to her body like a second skin. The ended right above her knees where her long, bare legs went on forever into a pair of navy heels. Asher couldn't help to take a second look at her meeting her blue eyes that seemed to be brighter than ever before.

"You know if you take a picture it will last longer." She joked.

"Very true and I owe a photo to Quinn." He chuckled as Delaney's jaw dropped just slightly.

"You talked to her? About what? Did she tell you what I was wearing?"

He shook his head, "No. I asked her for help as to what I should wear. I told her I wanted to match you, but I think I see the theme she was going for."

Asher watched Delaney's eyes trail from his eyes down his body, "E-Eye color. She matched our eye colors." When her eyes met his again they were a darker ocean blue.

"If you keep looking at me like that," He slipped his arm around her pulling her to him, "We're going to be late to our reservation."

The mischievous smirk on her lips nearly took him out, "Would that be such a bad thing?"

He leaned down kissing her lips, "I haven't decided, but I'm going to go with yes because I fear Quinn will fly out here and kill us both."

Delaney's laughter warmed his cheeks, "I think you're absolutely right."

"Shall we?" Asher stepped back holding his hand out to her as she took walking beside him to the car.

The summer they had met there had always been one restaurant he wanted to take her to. It was the nicest date spot in Wilmington, and it was right on the ocean. In the summer it was nearly impossible to get a reservation especially for an eighteen year old boy. However, in the winter, it was incredibly easy to get the perfect table.

The hostess sat them at a private table next to a large window. The sun had long set but the moon and stars were shining brightly in the sky. The ocean waves were steady as creating ripples in the moon's reflection. They gave the waiter their drink orders then sat in silence looking out the window. Asher couldn't believe how nervous he felt sitting across from Delaney. Part of him feeling ridiculous since they practically lived together and had slept together. Yet, he found himself tongue tied in fear of making a fool of himself or scaring her off.

"Did you read Leigh's note on our latest chapters?" Delaney asked before taking a sip of her water.

"No, I didn't see an email from her." He pulled out his phone to check seeing an email from Delaney's agent.

No longer did he rely on Dom to send him anything nor had they spoken in a week or so. He had spent many hours on the phone with various members of his team talking about options to querying new agents. They had advised him to wait out the six months left in Dom's contract. Agreeing with them Asher had made a point of having as little contact with him as possible.

"The editors seem to love everything so far. A few tweaks here and there, but that's normal with any book."

Delaney nodded, "There was a comment made by Dom of the unrealistic plot reveal in the hotel scene. Leigh highlighted it and gave her own opinion."

Asher scanned the document hitting the scene where their killer was finally revealed while the two main characters were in the throes of passion. He immediately went to Dom's comment and frowned.

This would never happen in real life. No way someone could gain access to a room in a reputable hotel. Maybe Miss Bishop would remember that she's writing a thriller in the real world and not a fantasy.

"That son of a bitch…" He muttered, feeling his blood boiling.

Delaney chuckled, "Read Leigh's response."

I happen to know on good authority that our authors, who are above all else professional and smart, did their research for this scene. Not only is this realistic but after speaking to hotel manager they found it to have happened multiple times. Maybe instead of jumping to conclusions or uninformed opinions you trust that our authors know what they're doing. Also, productive criticism is what this space is for. Keep your personal opinions to yourself.

"Damn she put him in his place." Asher laughed noticing Delaney still staring out the window, "You know not to pay any mind to what Dom says, right?"

She smiled, "Yes, I know. However, his comment got me thinking."

"Okay, talk it out with me."

She reached across the table lacing their fingers together, "We're supposed to be out on a proper date and yet here we are having conversation that could have easily happened at home in our pajamas."

Asher brought her hand up to his lips kissing her knuckles, "True, but then you wouldn't be wearing that beautiful dress driving me absolutely crazy with your sexy legs and heels."

"Crazy huh?" Her cheeks deepened to a dark pink.

He leaned forward, "The only thing keeping me from having those legs wrapped around my head is the fact that we're out in public and even then I think it would be worth getting arrested."

"I have a feeling this date night is going to be a short one." The intense desire shining in her eyes took his breath away.

For a single moment he thought about getting the check and taking her back home, but he wanted her to know that this was more than just physical attraction or need. He valued every moment he spent with her and wanted her to feel that. To feel as special as he thought she was to him.

"As tempting as that would be, what kind of boyfriend would I be to not wine and dine my girl." He leaned back in his chair, "Now, tell me what you were thinking about for our book."

For the next hour over dinner, they talked out Delaney's idea to have a point-of-view from the killer. Asher thought it was a brilliant idea and knew everyone else would love the idea. It meant more work for her to write additional chapters, but the more she talked it out he could see how excited she was.

Asher decided to take her for a walk down the boardwalk. All the shops were decorated for Christmas that was only a couple of weeks away. As they walked he gently took her hand in his and swung it between them. She had his blazer over her shoulders to keep the sea breeze at bay. Walking inside a little trinket shop, Delaney had found a snow globe for a Christmas gift for Quinn.

"She had a whole collection of them."

Asher laughed as he handed the clerk his card, "Seriously? Of all things for her to collect it's snow globes?"

Delaney took the bag thanking the clerk, "It started when we were kids. Her family would take summer and winter vacations. Every time she would come back with a new snow globe. Majority of them are packed away in storage, but she has about ten to fifteen of them in our apartment."

They continued to walk down the boardwalk when Delaney stopped at the large Christmas tree in the center of the shops. She looked up at it with childlike wonder. The colorful lights reflecting off her glasses and creating a rainbow upon her face.

"I think this is the first holiday that I'm actually looking forward to in a long time."

He wrapped his arms around her, "Why is that?"

"You." She turned in his arms, "You broke down all the walls I had up and freed my heart."

He leaned down kissing her firmly. Her hands drifted down his sides coming to rest on his hips. When he opened his eyes staring into hers he knew it was time to go back home.

"Let's go home." He whispered.

She nodded then stopped him, "We need a picture for Quinn."

Asher pulled out his phone holding it up to get as much of the Christmas tree in the background as he could. Delaney wrapped her arms around his waist as his other arms wrapped around her shoulders. He took a couple of photos of them then leaned down kissing Delaney and taking another photo hoping they were in frame. He text them to Delaney so she could send them to Quinn.

She smiled up at him, "Now we can go home."

They were laughing and giggling as they stumbled through the garage door. Asher couldn't keep his hands off of her as they made it into the kitchen. He pressed her against the island pulling her hair away from her neck and kissing it. Her perfect ass pressing into his hard cock as she moaned when he nipped at her neck.

"A-Asher… bedroom." She turned towards him taking deep breaths.

"But we have so many more surfaces to explore." He towered over her and didn't realize until then that their height difference was a turn on to him.

Delaney giggled, "We have all the time in the world to explore them. Right now, I want my sexy, charming boyfriend to make love to me. The perfect ending for the perfect date."

He sighed smiling, "How can I argue with that." He picked her up carrying her into his bedroom.

He was kissing her and about the unzip her dress when her phone rang, "Leave it and call Quinn back tomorrow."

"It's Emerson. I better get this." She picked up the phone, "Hey Em, what's…"

Asher sat on the bed as Delaney faced away from him.

"Wait, wait, slow down. What happened?"

Her frightened tone had his immediate attention. She turned towards him the rosy color on her cheeks draining and he knew something bad had happened.

"Oh my god, are they alright? What hospital are they in?"

"Delaney, what happened?" He asked as she held her finger up to him.

He pulled her towards him watching as her hands began to shake. She sat on his lap, her free hand gripping his shoulder. Her eyes were frantically searching the floor as if the answers for life's mysteries were there.

"I'm booking the first flight I can and will text you the information. If there's any updates please let me know. Even when I'm on the plane just text me." She ended the call staring at the phone.

"Delaney, what happened?"

The devastation in her eyes broke his heart, "Quinn and Everett… th-they were driving from their little getaway weekend in Michigan. A…

a… oh god…"

A heart wrenching sob erupted from her as she crumbled into his arms, "Laney, are they okay?"

She shook her head, "A semi side swiped them into a median and they're both in critical condition. I-I have to get back to Chicago because it doesn't look good."

Asher hugged her tighter, "I'll get everything booked for us and we'll leave as soon as possible."

"I c-can't lose her, Asher. What will I do if I lose her?"

"You won't lose her. Quinn Larson is a fighter and she's gonna fight to get back to you." He kissed the top of her head before pulling out his own phone and calling his travel agent to book their tickets.

DELANEY

Delaney's leg was bouncing as she looked out the window beside her. Clouds were floating beneath her as the world continued to turn. Meanwhile, her world had come to immediate halt after Emerson's call. Being on a plane flying back to Chicago was not how she imagined her first official date with Asher ending. Hearing Emerson's frantic voice in her mind brought her back to a few hours earlier.

"Delaney, you need to get back to Chicago asap. They were in an accident and I'm trying to get a hold of Quinn's parents. Oh my god, I have no idea who they are."

"Wait, wait, slow down. What happened?"

Emerson took a deep breath, "I'm sorry Delaney everything is happening so fast. Everett and Quinn were coming home from their little romantic getaway in Michigan. A semi-truck side swiped them running their car into center median. Quinn was ejected from the windshield. From what little I've been told is that her seatbelt broke. It's bad Delaney... it's really bad."

"Oh my god, are they alright? What hospital are they in?" Quinn laying on the ground, bloody and broken immediately popped into her mind.

"Delaney, what happened?" Asher asked as she held her finger up to him trying to listen to Emerson.

"They airlifted Quinn to Chicago Memorial, and they took Everett in an ambulance. My dad is already there. Pacey and I are getting on a plane now. If you can book a flight, then we can wait for you to drive to hospital together."

Asher pulled her towards him sitting her on his lap. She gripped his shoulder to keep her from crumbling to the ground. Her eyes were frantically searching the floor as if the answers were there.

"I'm booking the first flight I can and will text you the information. If there's any updates, please let me know. Even when I'm on the plane just text me." She ended the call, staring at the phone not knowing what to do next.

"Delaney, what happened?"

The concern in his eyes broke the final string holding her together, "Quinn and Everett… th-they were driving from their little getaway weekend in Michigan. A… a… oh god…"

An agonizing sob erupted from her chest as she crumbled into his arms. She couldn't process what was happening, all she knew was that she needed to get back to Chicago. To get back home, but as Asher's arms wrapped around her, the sense of home wound around her tearing her heart in two different directions.

"Laney, are they okay?"

She shook her head, "A semi side swiped them into a median and they're both in critical condition. I-I have to get back to Chicago because it doesn't look good."

Asher hugged her tighter, "I'll get everything booked for us and we'll leave as soon as possible."

"I c-can't lose her, Asher. What will I do if I lose her?"

"You won't lose her. Quinn Larson is a fighter and she's gonna fight to get back to you." He kissed the top of her head as she buried her face into the crook of his neck letting her tears fall freely.

Delaney opened her eyes as she felt the plane descending watching the clouds wisp by her window. The ground was coated in powder white as the smoke from furnaces created their own clouds in the skies. An overwhelming sense of nostalgia and comfort spreading over her. Being consumed by the wonder and awe of being back in Wilmington with Asher had briefly masked how homesick she really was for Chicago. Even if her heart still longed to be with Asher in Wilmington right now.

Her plane landed and Delaney was able to quickly get off the plane with her carry on and head to her meeting point with Emerson and Pacey. She sent a quick text Asher that she made it to Chicago and would let him know what was going on when she arrived at the hospital. She spotted Pacey Tucker wearing his Explorers baseball hat holding two cups in his hands as Emerson stood beside him on the phone.

"Pacey…" she waved at him as he bumped his elbow against Emerson.

"Hey Delaney, she's talking with her dad at the hospital. Quinn's parents arrived a couple of hours ago. They've rushed Quinn into surgery for internal bleeding." He handed her a cup, "Em thought you might need some tea."

Delaney managed to smile briefly, "Thank you."

"She's here now so we'll be there within the hour." Emerson paused for a moment then smiled sadly, "I love you too daddy. Tell Everett I love him too."

Emerson turned to Delaney immediately pulling her into a hug, "Is Everett alright?"

"More or less. He has a concession and a broken leg. The biggest thing right now is that he's blaming himself for the crash when it was absolutely not his fault. Anyway, let's get out of here and hopefully Quinn will be out of surgery when we arrive."

Delaney followed them out to a car climbing into the backseat. As they were driving, Asher called her giving her an update on what was going on with Dom and their book.

"He's being a complete asshole. I'm one short step from saying fuck it and getting a new agent."

She couldn't help but smile, "Well, Leigh did you email you a bunch of names to consider. Never hurts to look and have a few conversations. May scare Dom straight."

"Enough about my idiot agent. Have you made it to the hospital yet?"

"We're about twenty minutes away. Traffic from O'Hara is a nightmare of course. Emerson's dad is keeping us updated on Quinn. She's still in surgery so no news is good news." She leaned her head against the window watching the snow covered buildings pass her by, "I miss you."

His soft sigh brought tears to her eyes, "I miss you more. You're sure you don't want me to come out there? I can be on the next flight out. Just say the word and I'm there."

"I know and I love you for that. It's important that you meet with Dom and get to the bottom of whatever his game is. I'll keep you updated and as you told me yesterday Quinn is a fighter. She's gonna be fine and I'll be back in Wilmington before you know it."

"I hope you are because this house is way too quiet and empty without you. Call me as soon as you have an update on Quinn. Delaney..." He paused as Pacey pulled off the highway, "I love you."

She couldn't help the wide smile spreading across her face, "I love you too."

Emerson turned around in her seat, "So..." she wiggled her eyebrows.

"I may or may not have to consider writing my own fangirl book."

"I knew it!" She smacked Pacey's arm, "I told you, didn't I Pacey? I told you Delaney was going to have her own fangirl experience."

Pacey winced, "Yes, yes you did. Please stop hitting me."

Delaney rolled her eyes, "To be fair, Asher and I knew each other when we were teenagers and had a fling. We reconnected as a fangirl and her favorite author.”

“Still counts. Laurel and Zepp were best friends since kids.” She grinned, “All of us will be there to help you write your fangirl love story when you’re ready.”

They pulled into the hospital parking lot and Delaney’s stomach immediately started to churn. All of sudden an overwhelming wave of dread washed over her. Emerson hooked her arm with Delaney’s as they all began walking up to the hospital entrance. As they got closer her and Emerson noticed Leigh standing outside with Thomas.

“L-Leigh? What happened?” Emerson asked letting go of her arm.

Leigh’s bottom lip trembled as she closed the distance to Delaney, “I-I’m so sorry…”

Delaney’s heart shattered knowing she was too late, “No… no…” she pleaded as the tears freely flowed down her cheeks.

“Quinn lost a lot of blood, and she went into cardiac arrest. They couldn’t… she’s gone.”

Everything around her stopped. She could barely hear Emerson crying beside her as a loud, piercing scream filled her ears. She recognized that scream. Was it Quinn? No… not Quinn. Not her best friend. Not her anchor in the storm. No, the vibration from this scream was shaking her from the inside. Ripping out of her very soul as the tether of her best friend severed.

The next thing she knew, Pacey and Thomas were on either side of her helping her inside the doors of the hospital as tears blurred her vision and she wished for the Earth to open up to consume her, taking her away from the hell she was in.

DELANEY

One Week Later

Delaney gripped the edge of the sink leaning against it. Trying to steel herself enough to put makeup on but the tears wouldn't stop slipping down her face. Gritting her teeth, she angrily wiped away the tears from her eyes and looked down at the eyeliner laying on the counter.

"Fuck…" She whispered.

"Baby, you okay?" Asher knocked on the bathroom door before peeking his head around it.

The wave of sadness hit her and a shaky sob she had been holding at bay escaped her lips. Asher immediately came to her side, pulling her into his arms. The last week that had been the only place she could find any peace. His hand ran down her back soothingly, allowing her to unload the next wave of tears over his dress shirt.

"I-I'm sorry." She muttered, taking a step back.

"It's just a shirt. I have another one I can wear. Is there anything I can help with?"

All he had done was help her. Thomas had called him immediately after getting her settled into the waiting room with Emerson and Quinn's family. Asher had taken the next flight from Wilmington to Chicago and was by her side by the end of the day. Unable to face her apartment or the bookshop, Asher had booked them a hotel room for her to wallow in while he helped with whatever he could for Quinn's funeral arrangements. He had also worked with Jay to have the bookshop closed for a few days.

Delaney wrapped her arms around his waist, "You've done so much already, and I haven't even said thank you." She looked up at him, seeing a small smile.

"You don't ever need to thank me for taking care of you. That's what you do when someone you love is in pain and dealing with a shit ton of... well shit."

She chuckled before pushing herself up to briefly kiss his lips, "I appreciate everything you've done. Could you do one more thing for me?"

His cocky smirk brought a smile on her face, "I mean I could but then we'll be late. Where I think Quinn would one hundred percent be okay with that, I don't think you would be."

Delaney playfully smacked his chest, "Not that. Do you mind getting one of the girls to come in here and help me?"

"Not at all." He kissed her forehead before leaving her alone in the bathroom.

Within a few minutes, she could hear Raelyn, Laurel, Emerson and Leigh all coming into her hotel room. After a brief moment of tears and some laughs. Raelyn and Emerson sat Delaney down on the edge of the tub to help apply some simple makeup to her face. She looked at herself in the mirror wearing the black dress Quinn had picked out for her when they had gone on a virtual shopping trip for her date with Asher. Standing in front of the mirror with the four ladies she considered friends, she couldn't help but feel like Quinn was also standing there with them.

Quinn's service had been beautiful inside the small church her family had attended when she was a kid. Quinn's mom had asked her to deliver a eulogy in which she had barely made it through without breaking down. She told one story that truly represented the kind of person Quinn was.

"When we were designing the interior of the Scattered Pages, Quinn had one area of the bookshop she insisted on having." Delaney smiled as the memory popped into her head.

Quinn stood near the back wall staring at it with a smile. Delaney stepped up next to her envisioning the tall, beautiful bookcases they had picked out a week earlier being placed there. Books filling the shelves and a sitting area being in front of them.

"The Writer's Nook." Quinn declared, grinning.

"What? No, bookshelves and a sitting area, remember? We decided on no writing nook."

Quinn shook her head, "You decided on no writing nook. If I remember correctly you said it would be completely selfish of you to have one."

Delaney rolled her eyes, "I stand by that statement. This is a bookshop not a coffee shop or diner. We're here to sell books not write them."

Her best friend wrapped her arm around her shoulders, "Why can't it be both? You don't think young writers, aspiring writers would find inspiration among books and like-minded people?"

"Quinn Larson, bringing logic into this. That's my job." Delaney laughed, "Why is having a writing nook so important to you? Seems like I would be one to argue for it."

"That's exactly why it's so important. You of all people should want to inspire writers to do what they're called to do. To have a place to feel inspired and comfortable to creatively express themselves. To create what you have at the diner. I want this spot to represent all of the Delaney Bishops of the world. I want to watch future bestselling authors write their books in this very spot."

Delaney felt the tears welling up beneath her eyes as she pulled her best friend into a hug, "I hope all the Delaney Bishops have a Quinn Larson by their side to inspire them. Okay, let's go design our Writers Nook."

"Of course, whenever Quinn would tell anyone about the Writers Nook, she would never take credit for it. She would tell everyone it was my idea for the writers nook when it was all her idea. She knew that having that nook would change the lives of many writers. She knew it would be a safe haven for so many young creatives. She knew…"

Delaney paused to collect her emotions, seeing all her friends, family and loved ones sitting in the front few rows. Then her eyes landed on Asher sitting in between Quinn's mom and Everett. His eyes were shining with love and pride watching her at the podium. She watched him mouth the words *'I love you'* followed *'by you got this'.*

"She knew as much as the writers, artists and creatives would need that space. She knew I needed it to. That as much as the ones who would use that space would be inspired that they would in return inspire me. Quinn could always read people and anticipate their needs. Her compassion and empathy knew no bounds. She loved with her whole heart, and my only hope is that I can take all the love she has given to me since we were kids and spread that to as many people as I can. That is the legacy we all can strive to pass along in the memory of Quinn. To be kind and to love one another as Quinn had done with all of us in this room."

As they sat at the burial site, Asher's hand gently gripped her shoulders. Looking up at him, a sad smile greeted her as the minister spoke about the peace of death. Delaney took a long, deep breath trying to push down the anger building up within her. For the last week, she had cried endlessly and wallowed in her grief. Now, sitting and watching her best friend being lowered into the ground for the final time all Delaney could feel was rage. Everett was sitting beside her as everyone began to leave the site. Asher had stepped away from her to talk with Emerson leaving her and Everett alone with Quinn's casket in the ground.

Everett held out his hand to her which she gratefully took, "What are you feeling right now?" she asked needing to know if she was the only one raging on the inside.

"I'm sure the same as you. Empty. Void. Nothingness. I'm pretty sure I can't cry anymore either."

She chuckled, "I'm definitely feeling all that and more. I think my tear ducts are permanently empty."

He squeezed her hand, "I'm… I'm grateful that you and Emerson met one another. I would have never met Quinn if two hadn't met and my life would have been worse off without Quinn in it."

"I'm glad you and Quinn were together. Even if I didn't get to threaten you like she threatened Asher." She chuckled turning into laughter as Everett laughed with her.

"She actually warned me the next I saw you to be prepared for a stern talking to." He paused a quiet sniffle coming from him, "Delaney, I'm so sorry. I should have been paying more attention while driving. I was joking with her and looked towards her for a split second when the semi-truck changed lanes hitting the front of our car."

Delaney turned towards him placing her hands on either side of his face, "Everett, look at me." His eyes slowly came up to meet hers, "This was not your fault."

He stubbornly shook his head averting his eyes again. This time she knelt down in front of him lifting his chin to meet her eyes again. Tears were threatening to fall from his warm brown eyes and she swiped her thumbs beneath his eyes encouraging him to let them go.

"Everett Holbrook, listen to me very clearly. This. Was. Not. Your. Fault. In no way was any of this your fault. I know if Quinn were here she would say the same thing." She smiled seeing the tears finally falling down his cheeks and she tried to do her best Quinn impression, "Why are you blaming yourself for something you had no control over you dummy. Stop being so dramatic. That's my job."

Everett started laughing through the steady stream of tears, "You almost sound just like her."

For a brief moment they both laughed before Everett pulled Delaney into a hug, "I miss her… so… much."

Their laughter turned into quiet sobs as she whispered, "I miss her too."

An hour later, they were all at the diner. Louisa had given Delaney the biggest mom hug she didn't know she needed until she was within the woman's embrace. Everyone was telling stories of Quinn as Delaney was sitting in her normal booth observing all the people who were in Quinn's life. Her eyes searched out for Asher who was in a conversation with Emerson's dad and Pacey. She walked up to him touching his arm to catch his attention.

"I'm going to get some air outside. I'll be right back."

He pulled her to him, "Do you want me to come with you?"

She shook her head kissing him quickly, "I'll be fine. I promise to be right back."

Delaney pulled on her coat stepping out into the bitter cold stinging her cheeks. She walked down to the corner and found herself continuing to walk down the street. She was thinking about all the things she would never get to experience with her best friend. Double dates with Asher and Everett. Book releases and author events. Proposals. Celebrations. Weddings. Their kids growing up to be best friends. The rage from all the stolen moments she would never have pushed her feet further and further until she found herself standing in from of the Scattered Pages.

Opening the front door, she stepped inside the warm store front and immediately shed her coat breaking into a sweat. The only light was from the overcast sky and reflection of the snow on the ground. Delaney walked around the first display table towards the counter. Events for the month written in Quinn's handwriting sparked the rage that had been building all day. The next thing she knew, she picked up the sign and threw it across the room. Looking towards the display of her debut book, Delaney started throwing and knocking them all down to the ground. Then her eyes landed on the Writer's Nook.

All the memories of Quinn and her building the tables, painting the walls, watching the first writers to use the table and her saying 'I told you so'. A moment of stillness placed her in front of the tables then she erupted like a volcano. She started pushing the tables into other displays and shelves knocking over books and pictures. She grabbed the neon sign saying, *'The Writers Nook'* and ripped it from the wall. She swiped all the books from the shelves on the wall onto the floor before slamming her fists against them.

"WHY?! WHY DID YOU LEAVE ME?! I STILL NEEDED YOU HERE! I STILL NEED YOU TO TELL ME WHAT TO WEAR AND HOW TO DO MY MAKEUP! I NEED YOU TO TELL ME WHEN I'M BEING DUMB AND TO KICK ME IN THE BUTT! DAMN IT QUINN WE WERE SUPPOSED TO GET MARRIED AND HAVE KIDS TOGETHER SO THEY CAN BE BEST FRIENDS!"

She tore off one of the shelves from the wall and slammed it against the wall. She let out an agonizing scream before she felt her legs about to give out on her unable to hold all the rage and sadness inside of her. Suddenly, two arms wrapped around her waist holding her up.

"I got you, Laney. I got you." Asher's calm voice pierced through the buzzing inside of her head, "Laney, it's okay. Let it out. I've got you."

Resting her body against his as she began to tremble, Delaney looked at the ruin writers nook breathing heavily. The burning anger in her chest cooled and her body began to shake as sobs wrecked through her. Turning in Asher's arms she clung to him freely giving herself over to her grief. He picked her up cradling her to his body then sat them down on one of the chairs in the front of the store. Gently running his fingers through her hair and pressing gently kisses against her temple.

She had no idea how long they sat there the only noise coming from her crying or sniffling. The room was growing darker, and she finally lifted her head to look up at him. His eyes were on her filled with concern and sorrow for all the pain she was having. Delaney opened her mouth, but his lips sealed over hers.

"No need to thank me or apologize. I love you and there's nothing I wouldn't do to help you through this no matter what it is. I told you, I've got you."

She kissed him back, "I don't think I would have made it through this without you. I'm grateful that we reconnected and that Quinn encouraged me to go out to Wilmington with you. I really don't want to imagine my life without you."

His smile washed away the last embers of anger she had burning in her chest. His lips pressed against hers igniting something new in her. Delaney pulled back smiling knowing Quinn would be cheering her on for what she was about to do. Standing up, she held her hand out to Asher and leading him up to her office.

"Delaney? What are you doing?" He asked amusingly as she shut her door behind them.

"It's not the most comfortable spot but it's one spot I've always fantasized about."

His eyes widened before quickly closing the distance between them, "Who am I to deny the love of my life to fulfill one of her fantasizes."

Even in her grief and anger of losing one of the most important people in her life. Delaney could push everything aside to focus on the man she was madly in love with to keep her sadness at bay even for a little while.

DEAR DIARY,

July 2007

I can't believe how fast the summer is going. I wish I could slow time and spend more time in Wilmington... and with Asher. It's amazing how much has changed in the last couple of months since being with him. I feel like a completely new person and I'm kind of worried about when summer does end. Dillon and I will be heading back to Chicago in just a few weeks. Asher will be heading to college rather in New Jersey or if he can convince his parents to take a semester off to come to Northwestern in Chicago.

Speaking of which, Asher is traveling with his parents today and he was going to convince them to let him come to Northwestern. I've never been the praying type but I've been praying to any higher being that will listen that he can come to Chicago. I'm scared if he goes to Princeton then our relationship may not survive.

Why did I have to fall in love with Asher Graham?!?

<u>OMG!!!</u> I'm in love with Asher Graham.

What am I going to do if he goes to Princeton? I could always be the third wheel with Quinn to dances because there's no way Asher could fly to come to any of them. I definitely don't think my parents would allow me to visit him by myself.

Then there's Ty? What the hell am I supposed to do about Ty and his crush on me?! He has been persistent about us dating and he'll never believe I'm dating a freshman in college. Man... everything is so complicated and all I want to do is be with Asher on the beach.

I'm going to go back to reading my book and staring at my new bookmark from Asher.

Until next time,

Smile :) Laney

ASHER

It had been two weeks since Quinn's funeral and it was the first day the Scattered Pages was reopening. Asher had spent most of his time helping Delaney and her staff with repairs. They spent one whole night repairing and painting the writer's nook adding a memorial plague with Quinn's photo dedicating the space to her. Ever since they finished the area, Delaney had not stepped near it nor had she looked towards it. With each passing day, Asher's concern for her slowly consumed every fiber of his being. Only doubling with the reopening of the bookshop.

Asher stood on the second floor looking down at the full store below. Delaney was running from one corner of the store to the other helping customers. Many customers offering their condolences to her and other staff. Anyone else around her would never know that she hadn't slept more than three hours a night since Quinn's death. If she wasn't working within the shop then she was writing throughout the night until the sun started to rise.

Grabbing his laptop from her office, Asher headed down to the Writer's Nook to work on one of the final chapters of their book. There were a couple of people sitting in the nook with their laptops and headphones on. Opening his own laptop, Asher groaned as his chat app popped up filled with messages from Dom.

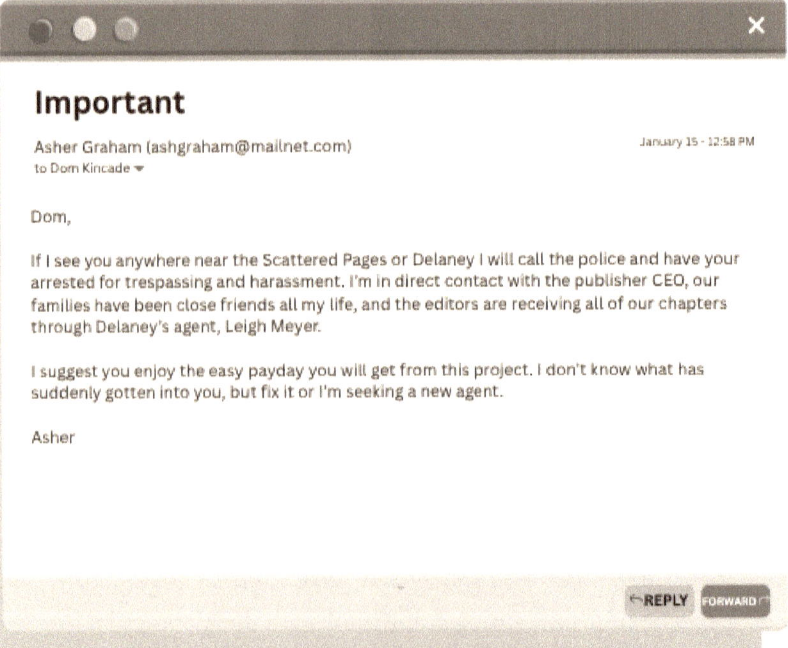

Asher shook his head quickly typing a response and emailing it to Dom after replying to his messages.

He clicked send and pulled up his manuscript to work on his next chapter. Without his earbuds, Asher was having a hard time focusing as he would hear Delaney talking with customers or see her out of the corner of his eye grabbing a book or two off shelves. He caught a moment when Delaney was looking for a book and took a moment to shut her eyes taking a deep breath. The exhaustion laying heavily on her eyelids as she slowly opened them.

"She's working too hard." He looked up to see Gen, one of the clerks, watching Delaney moving books to a display, "I'm worried."

He nodded, "I am too. I wish Quinn was here to talk to her or to tell me how to help her."

"Quinn would have shut the bookshop early, sent everyone home and dragged Delaney home for dinner and movie night. Quinn told me she would have to do that whenever Delaney was pushing herself hard to meet a deadline."

Asher smiled, "Well, I think we should do as Quinn did and close the shop a little early today."

Gen nodded with a smile, "I'll let everyone know."

When he saw Delaney walk towards the stairs to her office, he shut his laptop and headed towards her.

"Hey Superwoman."

A tired smile spread across her face, "Hi. I just needed a little break before updating another display."

"Baby, I think you need more than a little break. Gen is going to close the shop early while you and I head back to the hotel for dinner and a movie."

She shook her, "No, we shouldn't close early after being closed for so long after…"

He watched as tears immediately welled up within her blue eyes, "Delaney, you and your staff need some rest. You haven't stopped working for even a moment between the remodel, the opening and writing. Take the night, eat some take out and let's watch a terrible movie or Red Moon." Asher placed his hands on either side of her face, "Please."

Delaney sighed, leaning into hand, "Okay, but could we go to the diner instead of take out? No writing, but maybe just talking about our project."

"Deal. Let's go get our stuff and head to the diner."

After thirty minutes of Delaney telling Gen and Jay things to get done before closing, Asher finally got Delaney out of the bookshop and into the car. The shops along the main street were still decorated for Christmas and New Years. Both had past quietly as Delaney was grieving and Asher focused on how best to support her.

"Miss Delaney! How are you, my dear."

Asher watched as Delaney was enveloped into a big hug as they walked into the diner. She relaxed into the woman's embraced mumbling something to her that he couldn't hear.

"Has this guy been on his best behavior? Not bothering you?" Louisa pointed to him as he mocked offense to her comment.

For the first time since Quinn had passed, he watched as a genuine smile spread across Delaney's face, "I wouldn't have made it through these last few weeks without him. He's been an incredibly supportive boyfriend."

"Good, because if not a plate of fresh fries would make it onto his lap."

Delaney slid into her side of their booth while Asher slid into his as Louisa went to check on her other customers before getting them their usual order. Asher was getting ready to reach over to grab Delaney's hand when he was surprised to see her getting up and moving to his side of the booth. He placed his arm around her shoulders, pulling her into his side.

"I don't think I'll ever not love hearing you call me your boyfriend."

He kissed her temple as she leaned into him.

"Well, I love being able to tell people you're my boyfriend." Delaney looked up at him, "Speaking of, I've been thinking…"

"If you're about to propose then I'm going to be really upset that you beat me to it." He joked as her jaw dropped, "I mean I'm just getting used to boyfriend, but fiancé has a nice ring to it."

Delaney smacked his chest before reaching into her bag and pulling out her notebook, "That honor is all on you, Ash. I wouldn't dream of stealing away the panic and fear that will come from picking out the ring, planning the moment and wondering what my answer will be."

He swallowed the large lump lodged in his throat, "Thanks… I think. To take my mind off of that terrifying realization, tell me what have you been thinking about?"

"With our book's first draft almost done, I've been thinking about my next project. I want to know what you think about it." She opened her notebook in front of them.

Asher read the first couple of bullet points then looked up to her, "Genre jumping? Are you sure you want to write this?"

She nodded, "As long as you're okay with it. I feel like it's a worthy story to tell and…" Delancy looked down with a soft smile, "I think Quinn would encourage me to write it as well."

He lifted her chin, "Then I think we need to start plotting."

With a basket of fries and milkshakes, Asher and Delaney sat in the dinner plotting and outlined the first few chapters of her new project.

During the following weeks, Asher began to help Delaney to pack up Quinn's things. For a couple of days, Delaney and Everett sat in Quinn's room reminiscing, crying and laughing. Asher found himself shutting down his emotions unable to keep them under control as he watch the woman he loved hurting. Asher volunteered to organize everything to be shipped to Quinn's parents as Delaney headed into the bookshop for the day. Sitting in her apartment, he pulled up his email to see if the realtor he contacted had gotten back to him when his phone started ringing.

Seeing an all to familiar name, he let out a long sigh before answering, "What do you want, Dom?"

"I'm breaking the contract and book deal with Delaney. She is in breach for noncompliance of submitting her chapters on time and to me. I wanted you to know."

Hot, red, rage flashed over Asher's body, "I swear to god Dom, I'm not even joking, I will end your entire career if you do that. The editors and publisher is happy with our work. They're excited about our project, so I know it's not them. So, tell me, the truth and not your normal bullshit, tell me why you hate me working with Delaney so much."

"She's beneath you."

His agents words sounded so far away, "W-What?"

"She is beneath you. You want the truth then here it is. Delaney Bishop is a tumor spreading and corrupting your successful career. She is hitching a ride on your fame, on your hard work for an easy way to make herself famous. She is talentless, a loser, a Midwest bumpkin trying to make it the big leagues by riding your tails. You either can't see it or won't see it because your dick is doing all the thinking for your head."

Asher's hands were shaking with every vile word coming from his agent until the silence filled his ears and a wave of calm came over him. His racing heart slowing to a steady beat and his body relaxing back into the couch.

"You're fired."

Dom chuckled, "No, I'm not. You can't fire me."

Asher pulled up a saved email he had drafted several weeks earlier in Wilmington to his lawyers, agency and publishers. He blinded copied

Leigh to let her know the plan they had discussed when she had reached out to other agents in her agency on his behalf was now in motion. He also included Dom on his email before blocking his email address.

"You will see an email in your inbox clearly stating all the reasons why I'm dropping you and your agency as my representatives. My lawyers are also included in this email along with your boss and the publisher. I suggest you start thinking of other career opportunities because I will make sure you never represent another author again. Goodbye Dom."

He heard Dom take in a sharp breath, "You son of a bit-"

Asher ended the call and went back to looking through the listings the realtor sent him. For the first time in a long time, he felt a weight lifted off his shoulders.

DELANEY

Sitting in her office, Delaney stared at her laptop trying to decide where to start on her to-do list. Saying that she was overwhelmed was an understatement. The mere thought of staying in her and Quinn's apartment without Quinn was heartbreaking. However, the thought of packing and moving without Quinn filled her chest with dread. The last few days packing Quinn's things with Asher and Everett had taken a toll on her emotionally and she couldn't even think about finding a new place to live. It wasn't only finding a new place and leaving behind all the memories she had with her best friend in their place.

Delaney had allowed herself to start thinking about a future with Asher. Starting a life together with him. However, his life was in Wilmington. She loved it there, but it wasn't home. Evanston and the Scattered Pages was home to her, but so was Asher. She couldn't imagine her life without him, but how she could tell him that she didn't want to leave Evanston after he had uprooted his own life for her after losing Quinn.

"Hey Delaney?" She looked up to see Jay standing at her door, "Gen and Shep could use some help downstairs."

She nodded, "I'll be right down."

Walking down to the sale floor she saw a line nearly to the door. With only two registers, they could only go so fast when checking customers out. For a Wednesday, there were a ton of people in the shop. Delaney walked around talking with people in line about the books they were buying. A few people asked her to sign her book and asking about what was next for her. Once the line was under control Delaney decided to give Gen and Shep a well-earned break.

Walking around, she stopped near the Writer's Nook and tears filled her eyes. There were no spots for anyone to sit at the tables, but what amazed her more was the collaborations happening between them. Ideas were being shared, projects trading hands to read, edit and comment on. She was getting ready to go over and talk to few writers when Gen came up to her holding out her phone.

"It's been ringing nonstop."

Delaney looked down to see many missed calls and texts from Leigh and quickly made her way up to her office.

"Delaney, I'm so sorry to call you during bookshop hours." Leigh sounded panicked and that worried her.

"It's okay, what's going on? Everything okay?"

Leigh's sigh told her that it wasn't, "Asher's agent is being a complete asshole and in case he hadn't had a chance to tell you about it I wanted to."

She looked back down at her phone placing Leigh on speaker to see if there was anything from Asher. She was surprised to see there wasn't and that worried her even more.

"What happened?"

"Dom tried to break our contract claiming to you were in breach of it for not completing your chapters and submitting them to him. I'm sending you the email that Asher sent to his agency, the publishers and his lawyers. Read over it, talk to him about everything and know that everything is going to be okay."

Delaney saw the email pop up, opening it immediately and scanned over it, "What. The. Hell."

"I know, I know. Read it over carefully and send me anything you may want to add to it. I'm going to do everything on my end to make sure none of this reflects on you. Everything will be okay, I promise." Leigh was not reassuring her at all.

"I need to talk to Asher. Please send me any updates." She started shutting down everything and packing up.

Delaney could hear Leigh typing as she spoke, "I promise to update you with any new information I get."

She ended the call, grabbing her phone and bag rushing downstairs. Letting Jay know she needed to leave and if they needed to they could close the shop early. She was never so thankful to live close by and rushed up to her apartment. She walked inside to see Asher packing his bag.

"Delaney? What are you… I was going to come see you at the bookshop." Asher dropped his bag and pulled her into his arms.

"Leigh called me and sent me your email. What is happening?"

"I'm flying to New York to handle this Dom situation once and for all. There's nothing for you to worry about. Ever since our first trip to New York, I've had my lawyers involved sending them any correspondence with him. The publishers have my back, so I'm not worried about any of it."

Delaney clutched his shirt at his sides, "I'm glad everyone else is not worried, but I am."

Asher wrapped his arms around her holding her tight, "Honestly, if I thought this was going to be a fight then I would have both you and Leigh at my side. My lawyers and the publishers have assured me that they are in our corner. My agency is trying to do everything in their power to keep me but I've already decided to seek other representation."

He kissed the top of her head as she rested it against his chest, "I trust you, but I can't promise I'm not going to worry."

"Just one of the many reasons why I love you." He leaned down, kissing her long enough to make Delaney almost forget about everything going on, "Will you be okay while I'm gone? Would you prefer to stay at hotel?"

She shook her head, "I need to pack and look for a new place."

A brilliant smile spread across Asher's face, "I may have something to help with that. After I leave, check your email and let me know what your thoughts are." He looked down at his phone, "Shit I have to get going. My Uber should be downstairs for me."

Suddenly, Delaney felt panic seize her chest and she gripped his arm. Asher pulled her to him once again holding her for a moment and whispering into her ear.

"I promise I won't be gone for long and if you need me then call or text me."

"I-I know… I'm used to having you here and the thought of you not being here feels weird." Delaney took a deep breath, "Maybe I'll see if Emerson is in town. I know she's been spending a lot of time with Everett."

"That sounds like a good idea." He kissed her once more, "I love you."

"I love you too. Be careful please." She kissed him quickly as he headed out the door.

As soon as the door shut, the silence enveloped her making her ears ring slightly. Delaney sent a text to Emerson to see if she was in town and was overjoyed to find that she was in Elmhurst for the next few weeks before spring training started in March. They made plans to meet up for lunch tomorrow and much like Asher, her friend made sure to know she could call or text her any time if being alone become to be too much.

Deciding to distract herself by packing her own things, she spent most of the last afternoon and evening going through her closet and shelves in her room. Many times, she would stop to laugh at a gift from Quinn or cry from reading a note from her. When she stopped to order dinner, she remembered that Asher had wanted her to check her email.

Five listing links were in the body of the email. She was surprised to see they were all within a mile or two of the Scattered Pages. Delaney's shoulders immediately relaxed as she went through each house listing. She had figured that Asher would try to convince her to move back to Wilmington. She couldn't help the doubt seeping into her mind that maybe he didn't want her to come with him.

Trying to push that thought out of her head, Delaney looking through the listings one more time and picking her top two choices. She contacted her friend at the bank they used for the Scattered Pages to help her work the financial side of buying a house. Once she had all the numbers and a budget figured out she felt confident in the choice she made and only hoped Asher would like it as well.

MAY '07

DEAR LANEY,

I THOUGHT ABOUT SENDING YOU A TEXT BUT THEN I REMEMBERED YOU TELLING ME THAT YOU LOVE GETTING NOTES OR LETTERS FROM YOUR FRIENDS. I CAN'T REMEMBER THE LAST TIME I WROTE A LETTER LET ALONE TO A BEAUTIFUL GIRL. THAT'S RIGHT I CALLED YOU BEAUTIFUL BECAUSE YOU ARE. I THOUGHT YOU WERE BEAUTIFUL FROM THE FIRST MOMENT I SAW YOU WALKING ON THE BEACH. NORMALLY, I DON'T CALL OUT TO GIRLS, BUT WHEN I SAW YOU LOOKING NOT AT ME BUT MY BOOK I KNEW I HAD TO TALK TO YOU.

I WON'T LIE WHEN I FOUND OUT YOU WERE BOBBY AND MARY'S GRANDDAUGHTER I ALMOST LOST MY NERVE TO HANG OUT WITH YOU AGAIN. I LIKE TO THINK OF MYSELF AS A GOOD GUY BUT I'VE DEFINITELY HAD MY FAIR SHARE OF BEACH PARTIES AND DRINKING WHERE BOBBY CAME OUT TO BREAK THE PARTY UP. I DIDN'T WANT THEM THINKING I WAS GOING TO CORRUPT THEIR GRANDDAUGHTER. I ALSO DIDN'T WANT YOUR BROTHER TO TRY AND PICK A FIGHT WITH ME AFTER HE CONFRONTED ME AFTER WE HANG OUT AT YOUR GRANDPARENTS' HOUSE.

I REALLY WANT TO MAKE A GOOD IMPRESSION WITH YOUR FAMILY BECAUSE I REALLY LIKE YOU. I'VE HAD A FEW GIRLFRIENDS IN THE PAST BUT THEY'VE NEVER MADE ME FEEL THE WAY I DO WHEN I'M AROUND YOU. THAT SOUNDS KIND OF CREEPY, BUT I SWEAR I'M NOT. MOST GIRLS ARE INTO SHOPPING, MYSPACE OR THE LATEST BOYBAND. NOT YOU... YOU LOVE BOOKS AND WRITING LIKE I DO. THE MORE WE HANG OUT TOGETHER THE MORE I WANT TO BE WITH YOU.

I'M SCARED THAT IF I TELL YOU EXACTLY WHAT I'M THINKING OR FEELING THAT I MIGHT SCARE YOU AWAY. HONESTLY, IT KIND OF SCARES ME BECAUSE INSTEAD OF THINKING ABOUT GOING TO PRINCETON IN THE FALL. ALL I'M THINKING ABOUT IS IF I CAN FIND AN UNIVERSITY CLOSEST TO YOU TO BE WITH YOU. ONE OF THE SCHOOLS I ADMITTED TO WAS NORTHWESTERN IN CHICAGO AND I COULD TRANSFER THERE IN THE SPRING SEMESTER...

SEE WHAT I MEAN YOU'RE PROBABLY THINKING I'M A CREEPY, OBSESSIVE DUDE SO I'M GOING TO END THIS LETTER BEFORE I SAY ANYTHING ELSE THAT WILL SCARE YOU OFF.

ASHER

PS: I REALLY HOPE YOU LIKE THE BOOKMARK. THE SONG REMINDS ME OF YOU

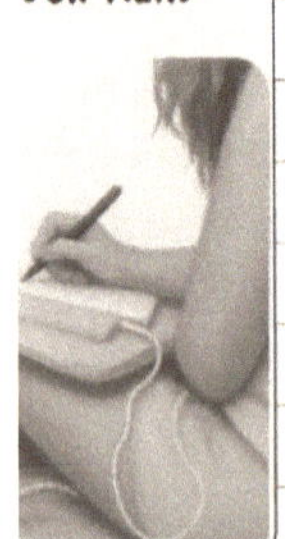

ASHER

Andie stared down into the eyes of Miranda Bennett. She seemed normal on paper and her social media. She worked as an administrative assistant for the police department. She regularly attended social gathering with friends and co-workers. She would go on dates and vacations. Her social media was a complete timeline of her seemingly perfect life. Little did the people around her know that a little fender bender would introduce her to Officer Daniel Marshall who she would become obsessed with and dedicate her life to being with him. That was until he had met Andie and threw Miranda's fantasy into a spiral.

Now Miranda was in the wind and Daniel taken by her. That left Andie to find the man she loved on her own…

Asher looked up from his laptop to see the clouds soaring beneath him. He only had another hour before landing in New York. The only way he kept himself from swan diving into his rage was reading Delaney's latest chapter. It was hard to believe they were writing the last few chapters of their thriller. He made a few notes for his chapter coming up before shutting down his computer. Looking down at his phone, Asher switched from his project playlist to one that Delaney had surprised him with.

***

"May I see your phone?"

Asher looked up at her suspiciously, "Why?"

A sweet and innocent smile spread across her face, "I made something for you and want to share it to your phone. May I?" She held out her hand.

"That smile doesn't fool me, but lucky for you I'm sucker for it." He handed over his phone, laughing as she practically skipped to her desk.

About thirty minutes later, Delaney returned his phone and headed down to the kitchen to start lunch. His music app was open and on a new playlist.

***

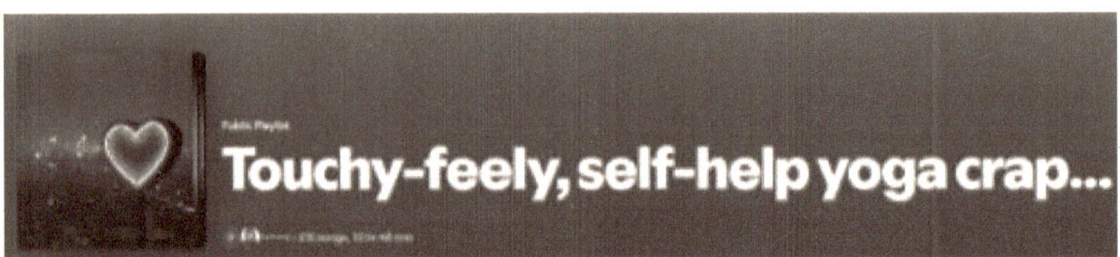

Asher looked down at the playlist and immediately went to the one song that always reminded him of Delaney. His body relaxed against his seat as soon as the first few notes played. He closed his eyes for what only seemed like a second before he heard the pilot announce they were descending for landing. Thankfully all he had was his backpack with two sets of clothes, his laptop, notebook and all his chargers. As soon as he was off the plane Asher headed to his normal hotel. His phone chimed in the taxi and his mood soured.

He rolled his eyes, ignoring Dom's text and placed it back into his pocket. Watching the city flash past him a small smile crossed his face. A lot of his weekends at Princeton were spent in the city seeing plays or concerts. He would walk around Times Square and people watch. Some weekends he would book a cheap hotel and write without his roommate to interrupt him or his friends to drag him out to a party. He always thought he would end up in a place in SoHo or the Upper East Side once his career took off.

They passed by the bookstore he took Delaney to and a distant ache began to bloom over his heart. Nights of them working in their office with the ocean breeze coming in through the window or watching a movie in the living room with the fire going flooded his mind. Pulling out his phone again, Asher looked down at his lockscreen. He was kissing Delaney's cheek and her giggle echoed in his ear seeing her bright smile. No matter how much he may love Wilmington or New York City, Asher knew for a fact that his home was wherever Delaney was.

He pulled up Leigh's number sending her text.

> Hey, since I'm currently agentless do you mind helping me with something?

Leigh Meyer: Really? I have four beautiful and talented ladies plus a large man child to take care. Now I have you too?

> Please *pouts*

Leigh Meyer: Oh. My. God. What is it?

Asher texted her exactly what he needed, and her response was one word in confirmation. He made a note in his calendar to send Leigh a thank you note and gift. He then added to ask Thomas what he should get her.

Arriving at his hotel, he checked in and settled into his room. Once he had room service ordered, he called Delaney. He started to get a little nervous when she didn't immediately pick up the phone. Finally, she answered slightly out of breath.

"Sor-sorry, I was…" She took a deep breath, "I was on the floor in my room and forgot my phone in the kitchen."

Asher chuckled, "You gonna make it or do I need to fly back to give you mouth to mouth?"

The low hum coming from her sent warm vibrations over his body. Now, he was wondering if he could have done this whole meeting by email and go back home to her.

"I'll be fine. You're trip there was okay? Have you heard from Dom or anyone else?"

"Dom text me to meet him for dinner to talk, but I'm done playing into his game. I want all this to be hashed out once and for all so I can move on. He dug his own grave and now he can lie in it."

There was a long pause before Delaney spoke, "Ash, are you…" she stopped.

He could imagine her biting her lip nervously, "Am I…what?"

"Are you sure you want to do this? I mean, Dom has been an asshole more so than his reputation says. You two have worked together for a long time. Are you sure it's worth burning that bridge and starting with a whole new agent?"

"Delaney, the way he has treated you and what he has said about you are unforgivable. He had no right to act that way towards you especially knowing how much you meant to me. Not only did he disrespect you but me to. People like him shouldn't be rewarded for bad behavior." He paused for a moment, "Plus, what kind of man and boyfriend would I be if I didn't stand up for the woman I love."

"Asher Graham, one day I'm going to write a super cheesy romance novel and the MMC is going to be based off of you." She laughed.

He joined in with her laughter, "You're writing down what I just said, aren't you?"

"You better believe it. Pure gold. So, are you in for the rest of the night then?"

There was slight edge in her tone that caught his attention immediately, "That's the plan. Room service is on its way, and I need to finish writing my next chapter. Why?"

He could hear her shutting a door, "Oh I don't know. I thought maybe you could help me with a scene. I have this idea…"

Asher's jaw dropped, "I'm assuming this research would be for a new project and not our current one? I don't remember us outlining a phone sex scene."

"You're right, we didn't. However, I may be able to use it in another project later down the road." Her voice dropped to a sultry tone, "What do you say handsome? We could even kick it up a notch and go on Facetime."

He immediately ended their call without another word and called her back on Facetime. When she answered the first thing he heard was her beautiful laugh and then he saw her pulling off one of his shirts.

"I'll take that as a yes."

"Oh yes… we can research like this any time you want to." He propped his phone up on the side table while he took off his own shirt.

By the time he and Delaney said goodnight to one another, his food was waiting for him in the hall. A cold hamburger and fries was worth it for what he experienced with Delaney for the last hour. Eating and working on his project for a little while, Asher fell into the best night of sleep he could have without Delaney being there.

Asher's meeting wasn't until ten o'clock and he woke up with plenty of time to get his head in the game. Leigh had emailed him all the information he needed, and he thanked her repeatedly for doing him a favor. Delaney called him as he was stepping out of the shower from a run down in the fitness room.

"Good morning beautiful,"

"I know you said you were sure last night, but are you really? That is a big player on your team to get rid of especially with you starting a new era of your career. I don't want to be the reason your career flops suddenly and then you would resent-"

"Whoa, slow your roll Laney. Take a breath." She did as he said, "Right now is the perfect time for me to make changes. You're right, Dom and his team have played a huge part in my success. However, I'm wanting to branch out and see what else is out there for me as an author. I have ideas that Dom would never let the publishers see and now I can find someone who will go to bat for me."

She took another deep breath, "You're right."

"Said that again so I can record it." He laughed

"Not a chance. Okay, I just need to get that off my chest. I know no matter what your success as an author will only soar higher. I had to make sure this decision wasn't all about me because I would feel horrible if your career tanked."

He couldn't help the wide smile on his face, "That's one of the billion reasons why I love you. You're always looking out for me. I promise you, I feel deep in my heart that this is the right move for me. Honestly, I'm excited to take this leap into the unknown and see what comes from it."

There was a soft sigh from Delaney, "I'm proud of you Ash. Now, go get ready for this meeting and kick it in the ass."

Asher had walked into the bathroom looking at his reflection, "Yes ma'am. I love you."

"I love you more. Oh! I almost forgot. Whenever you have a moment, check your email. I send something to you."

"Is it more research in the form of sexy pictures?" He asked, hearing her giggle.

"No, but maybe if you're a good boy I will send you some later tonight. Now go get ready. Love you."

His cheeks hurt from smiling so much, "Love you too, Laney. I'll call you when everything is over."

It didn't take him long to get ready. He had packed his best suit jacket and one of his dress shirts. He decided on a pair of dark jeans and black boots to complete his business meeting attire. He was getting ready to leave when his phone started buzzing in his pocket. Seeing Leigh's name on the screen his heart seized with panic.

"Leigh? Is everything okay? Did something happen to Delaney?" His words were frantically coming out of his mouth.

"Calm down, she's fine Asher. Jeez…"

He took in a shaky breath, "Thank god. Wait, why are you calling me then?"

"You shouldn't be going into this meeting without proper representation from your new agency. Since your brand new agent is handling a family matter I decided I would come represent you."

"Really? You're in New York?" He asked completely baffled by this revelation.

She chuckled, "Yes really. Madison will be sending over the final contract to your lawyer during the meeting. She wanted to come herself, but something happened to one of her brothers and she needs to stay in Nebraska. You just had to pick the cowgirl to be your agent."

"I like her. I think she's going to be open to some of my new ideas and she's good at convincing people to do shit." The tension in Asher's shoulders released as he let out a sigh, "I won't lie, I'm a little more at ease now knowing you'll be there in my corner."

Leigh started laughing, "There was no way in hell I was going to miss the opportunity to rub it in Dom's smug face that my agency swooped in and nabbed his best client. I know it really wasn't like that but I'm choosing to believe it happened that way. That way I don't think too hard on the real reason and end up going to jail."

"Don't worry, I would bail you out or be right beside you in the cell." They both laughed, "I guess I will see you in a few minutes then."

"I'll be outside waiting for you. Oh, and make sure you check out Delaney's email. She wanted me to remind you. Maybe check it after the meeting though."

Asher grabbed his bag heading towards the door, "Will do."

True to her word, Leigh was waiting for him along with his lawyer. Dom and the agency's lawyer were already seated when they walked in. Asher could sense a shift in the air as they sat down, and Dom wouldn't meet his eyes. His arms were crossed over his chest like a pouting child. Before his lawyer started talking, Asher knew that Dom had loss and for a moment he felt bad for the man he once called his friend.

His previous agency suspended Dom for the time being making him attend seminars on hostile workplaces and anger management in high stress jobs. He was going to be closely monitored by higher agents in the company before he could resume his client list. Asher knew it was a big blow to Dom's career but also hoped that it would be a new start for him.

Asher insisted that Dom still received the payout agreed upon for his next published work with Delaney. One thing his dad had impressed upon him was that good men keep their promises. Asher intended to keep his. When the meeting was over, Asher stood holding out his hand to Dom.

"This isn't how I wanted things to go between us. You were a great colleague and friend to me throughout the first part of my career. I wish nothing but the best for you."

Dom looked down at his hand before grasping it, "I hope she was worth it."

Dom went to let go of his hand, but Asher pulled him in closer, "She is."

"You'll regret this. In the end, you'll regret choosing her."

Asher let go of his hand shoving him lightly, "I doubt that. Not get out."

Dom narrow his eyes on him before storming out of the meeting room. Asher turned towards Leigh who had her phone pointed at him.

"For Delaney. You'll thank me later when this little show of testosterone gets you laid." She started typing on her phone then turned to his lawyer, "Contract is in your inbox for review and to be signed. Assholes have been punished. My work here is done."

He chuckled as Leigh took a small bow, "Seriously, thank you for everything. Not just the whole mess with Dom and suggesting Madison as my new agent. Thank you for always being there for Delaney and the other girls. You're one hell of a woman, Leigh Meyer."

"I appreciate you saying that. I'm truly happy that you and Delaney found each other again. I can't imagine her being with anyone else." He was taken back when Leigh hugged him, "However, it still stands if you break her heart then all of us are coming after you to break your face or hands since you need those more."

"Duly noted." He walked out with her saying goodbye and decided to walk back to his hotel.

Asher stopped at a little coffee shop to people watch and remembered Delaney's email. He opened it on his phone and saw the subject line then smiled.

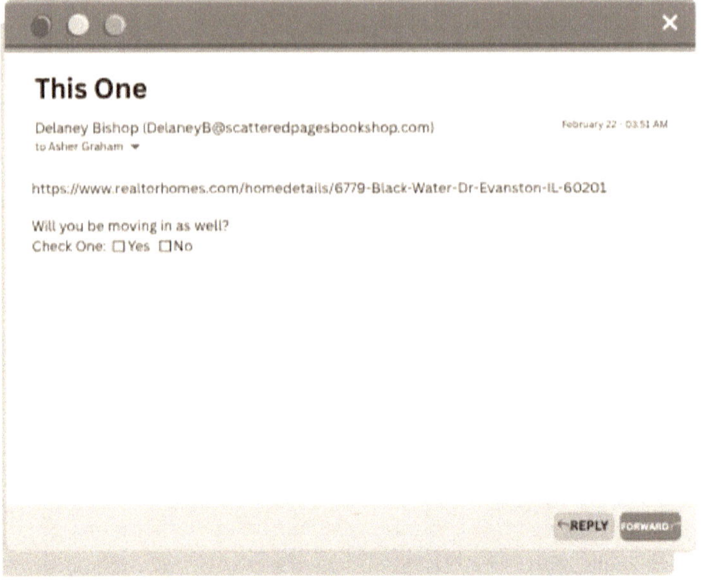

He already knew his answer, but he needed some time to do things the right way. He tapped out of Delaney's email and went to the one Leigh had sent him. Confirmation of car rental and moving trucks. The next thing he had to do was going to be difficult but in the long run he knew the ending would be the best happily-ever-after he could ever dream of. He hit Delaney's number and her sweet voice was caressing his ears immediately.

"How did it go?" She asked.

He told her everything and then he gave her his answer about moving into the new house. There were tears from both of them, but at the end of their call they both murmured I love you and the next chapter of Asher Graham's life began.

DELANEY

Three Months Later

Laying in the middle of an empty bedroom, Delaney had her eyes closed taking in a slow, deep breath. Today had been a whirlwind with the bookshop being closed and her amazing clerks helping her move into her new house. They had celebrated at the Scattered Pages with pizza and beer once every box was placed somewhere inside the house. Now she was only a ten minute walk from the bookshop. She had stood at the end of her driveway staring up at her new home.

It was a cute split level home with three bedrooms and two bathrooms. The lower level was around the same size as her and Asher's office in Wilmington. She had big plans to make it into a joint office for them and a library with a reading nook. However, right now Delaney needed to find the strength to get off the floor and at least find a space to sleep for the night. She felt her phone vibrating next to her.

"How's it goin-" Asher paused seeing her on the floor, "Laney, what's wrong?"

A loud cackle escaped her lips, "There's stuff… everywhere. I don't know where to start or what to do with it all. How I want to decorate anything. Furniture I want in each room. I can't... I just can't."

Delaney sat up feeling the tears ready to spill down her face. She needed him here to help make decisions. It was as much his house as it was hers. Yet he was in Wilmington, looking cozy on the deck with the ocean behind him.

"Where's your notebook? I know we made a whole bunch of notes before I left last time. We can find a good starting point in there."

She deflated, "It's packed away in a box somewhere in this big ole house. I have no idea where it is or remember what was in there."

"Delaney, look at me." He brought the phone closer to his face, "You got this. Start with one box in one room. Organize them into the room they belong in and then you can take on emptying one box at a time. There's no rush or deadline for this project. Our book is with the editors and cover designers. You're taking a break from writing for the next couple of months. Jay and Gen have the bookshop covered with the newly hired clerks. Take your time, beautiful."

She couldn't believe how soothing Asher's deep voice was to her. Suddenly, all her worries were wiped away and only his words of wisdom rang clearly in her mind. She nodded, letting out a breath slowly.

"Thank you. Do you know when your next trip to Chicago might be?"

She was anxious to see him again. In the last few months, they had only seen one another three times. Asher decided to stay in Wilmington to focus on the last few chapters of their book. He didn't want to rush into anything, and he had answered her email with a yes, but not right now. Delaney knew he was right, but she missed him. She wanted to wake up next to him every morning and work in their office until the wee hours of the night.

"Actually, that's partially why I called you. I was hoping to come out at the end of next week. I know we'll have some edits to work on, and I want to working on them together in person."

She sighed, "Ten days? I think I can handle ten days. I don't know if the house will be put together, but I'll make sure the office is."

Asher's smile put her at ease, "First put together the bedroom then the office. It's important you have somewhere to sleep. Did the bed arrive yet?"

Delaney stood walking across the hall into the master bedroom. In the middle was a brand new king size bed set into a beautiful wooden frame with the headboard having a bookcase and storage drawers beneath the frame. She flopped down onto it.

"You seriously didn't have to buy me a bed. I would have been fine with my old one until we were ready to pick one out together."

Asher chuckled, "Your old one would have never survived the move. I'm sure I'll love it because you'll be lying next to me."

She couldn't help the smile on her face, "I miss you."

"I miss you too. Ten days, then I'll be there for an extended period of time. I promise."

Soon they were saying their goodbyes and Delaney lay in her new bed listening to the subtle noises only a new house would make. She walked into the empty spare bedroom thinking of Quinn.

"This definitely would have been your room. We would have gone out to pick everything you wanted in it. Hell, you would probably be living here with or without Asher living here."

She walked over to the window that looked out over the small front yard. Her house was at the end of cul-de-sac where kids were playing in the center of. She watched a little girl chasing a boy that had a ball in his arms. When she caught up to her they tumbled into the grass laughing. Delaney let out a soft laugh then turned back around looking at the empty room.

"You know what Quinn, I think I'll still decorate it to your liking. This can be a guest room that highlights how important friendship and chosen sisters are."

Delaney headed to the living room where she had cleaned out a spot on her couch for a folding table and her laptop. Pulling up Pinterest, she went to Quinn's dream room board and started looking for different items to purchase. When her stomach started to growl, she ordered pizza and settled in for the night watching Red Moon.

Slowly over the next several days Delaney, with some help from her dad and twin brother, was able to get her house in some kind of order. Spending time with two of her favorite men made the house seem more like a home. There was still a missing piece with Asher being in Wilmington and Quinn gone. After her dad and brother went back home, Delaney found herself in Quinn's room. She was putting some of the finishing touches in it with a gallery wall of pictures and some of Quinn's favorite items her parents had given to Delaney.

She grabbed her old shoe box that kept all of her treasured letters and trinkets from her high school and college days. The first letter she saw was the last one she had received from Asher the summer they fell in love.

Dear Laney,

This is the hardest letter I've ever had to write. Right now, you're lying beside me in the very spot we first met. Last night was the most amazing night I've ever had. Being with you, falling asleep next to you, I can't imagine life any other way. I want nothing more than to stay with you forever. To go to school in Chicago to be close to you, go to your prom and watch you walk across the stage when your graduate. Both of us going to the same college, living in an apartment together and building our life together. I want you to have the very best life because you more than deserve it.

She continued to search through the box then noticed a bundle of letters she didn't recognize. They were tied together with twine and in envelopes. That's when she realized these were all the letters and bookmarks he had tried to mail to her, but his dad intercepted. She opened one randomly and read it out loud.

OCT. '07

DEAR LANEY,

I SWORE I SAW YOU TODAY. I THOUGHT MY MIND WAS PLAYING TRICKS ON ME AND I STILL KIND OF DO. I SAW A YOUNG WOMAN WITH SHINING RED HAIR, BLACK RIMMED GLASSES AND A PRINCETON TIGERS T-SHIRT ON. SHE WAS TALKING TO ONE OF THE ADMISSION REPS WITH WHOM I ASSUME WAS HER DAD. I WAS ALREADY RUNNING LATE TO MY CLASS BUT I HAD TO KNOW IF IT WAS YOU OR NOT. I RAN TOWARDS THEM HOPING TO WALK PASS BEFORE THEY WENT INSIDE THE ADMINISTRATIVE BUILDING. AS THE DOOR SHUT I COULD HAVE SWORN I HEARD HER BEAUTIFUL VOICE. I SKIPPED CLASS AND WALKED AROUND CAMPUS TO ALL THE SPOTS I KNOW THEY TAKE PROSPECTIVE STUDENTS, BUT I NEVER SAW THE GROUP AGAIN.

NOT HEARING FROM YOU IS DRIVING ME CRAZY. I HAVE A BREAK COMING UP AND I'M TEMPTED TO FLY OUT TO CHICAGO TO SEE YOU. I DON'T WANT TO SHOW UP UNANNOUNCED BECAUSE, WELL FRANKLY, I THINK YOUR DAD AND BROTHER WOULD KILL ME. NOT HEARING FROM YOU HAS ME WORRIED THAT MAYBE YOUR DAD FORBIDS YOU TO TALK TO ME. MY ONLY HOPE IS THAT I CAN PROVE TO HIM THAT I'M ENSURING THE BEST FUTURE FOR MYSELF IN ORDER TO BECOME THE MAN YOU DESERVE. THE ONLY THING THAT KEEPS ME GOING EVERYDAY IS KNOWING IN THE END I WILL BE WITH YOU.

I MISS YOU SO MUCH LANEY. NOW I GET WHY POETS WRITE ABOUT TRAGEDIES AND HEARTACHE. PLEASE, PLEASE WRITE BACK TO ME. I WILL SEND AN ENVELOPE ALREADY STAMPED AND ADDRESSED FOR YOU TO USE. I NEED TO HEAR FROM YOU. I LOVE YOU.

LOVE,
ASHER

Delaney ran her fingers over his handwriting. She couldn't believe he saw the day she visited Princeton. She had looked for him around every corner they had visited that day. Hardly listening to the admissions rep as they show her and her dad around. When they returned to their hotel her dad had asked her the real reason why they had visited. All Delaney would tell him was she had a friend who went there that she met over summer and was hoping to see them. She knew her dad saw right through her, but he never pushed the subject any further.

Reading a few more letters from the stack, she reached Asher's final letter. There was no bookmark enclosed which she found strange. It was a year and half after the first letter his dad had kept from her. Opening it, a chill ran down her body as she read her full name instead of her nickname. There was a finality to this letter that made her heart ache.

FEB. '09

DELANEY,

THIS WILL BE MY LAST LETTER. I'M SO SORRY I WASN'T STRONG ENOUGH TO STAND UP TO MY DAD WHEN HE FIRST CONFRONTED ME ABOUT YOU. HE WAS THERE THE MORNING AFTER OUR FIRST TIME TOGETHER. HE SAW US IN MY ROOM WHICH IS SUPER EMBARRASSING, BUT DOESN'T MATTER NOW. HE CONVINCED ME TO BECOME A BETTER MAN... A MAN YOU DESERVED. NOW, I'M THINKING ALL HE WAS TRYING TO DO WAS KEEP US APART. AFTER NOT HEARING FROM YOU FOR OVER A YEAR NOW, I KNOW THE REASON MUST BE YOU HATE ME FOR THE WAY I LEFT YOU. ALL I CAN SAY IS I'M SO SORRY. I NEVER MEANT TO HURT YOU. I LOVED YOU AND WANTED TO BE WITH YOU FOREVER. NOW, YOU MUST HAVE MOVED ON AND I HOPE YOU FIND ALL THE HAPPINESS YOU DESERVE.

I... I MET SOMEONE AT THE BEGINNING OF THIS SEMESTER. HER NAME IS ANNA AND WE HAVE A LOT IN COMMON. SHE THE ONLY OTHER GIRL TO CAPTURE MY ATTENTION LIKE YOU DID. I THINK... I DON'T KNOW. MAYBE IT'S TIME FOR ME TO MOVE ON AS WELL. I'LL NEVER STOP LOVING YOU DELANEY BISHOP. I'LL NEVER FORGET YOU AND OUR SUMMER TOGETHER. MAYBE ONE DAY THE UNIVERSE WILL PUT US ON THE SAME PATH ONCE MORE. PLEASE BE HAPPY AND NEVER SETTLE FOR ANYONE WHO WON'T PUT YOU FIRST. YOU DESERVE THE BEST FROM ANYONE AND THEY SHOULD BE HONORED TO HAVE YOU IN THEIR LIFE. I KNOW I AM.

LOVE,
ASHER

Tears slowly slipped down Delaney's cheeks. She folded the letter placing it back into the envelope. How would their lives have been if they had fought a little harder for each other or for themselves back then. She leaned back against the wall looking up through the window to the twilight sky.

"I wish you were here Quinn. You would have some words of wisdom or words of rage for what Asher's dad did."

She paused, picking up the frame photo next to the bed. It was from the opening day of the Scattered Pages. Their arms wrapped around one another, smiling with tears of happiness running down their faces. The familiar ache that was constant in her chest throbbed as more tears flowed from her eyes.

"I'm scared Quinn. Asher left for New York to put his asshole agent in his place then ended up back in Wilmington. I'm scared he's figured out that I'm not worth all the hassle. That his dad was right and he deserves better." She wiped the tears from her face, "What if he doesn't want to move to Evanston to be with me? I can't leave the bookshop or you to move to Wilmington. What if we were never truly meant to be together?"

The ache in her chest started pierce into her heart. Suddenly, she was having trouble breathing. A loud sob ripped out of her mouth as she slowly lay on the floor.

"I can't lose you and him. I won't…" she hiccupped, "My heart can't take that."

Delaney tried to take in a deep breath closing her eyes as she did. She could almost hear Quinn's voice in her ears.

Breath in, one, two and three. Hold it, one, two and three. Let it out, one, two and three. Great job Delaney! Once more…

She repeated the exercise again, feeling her the panic loosen its grip from her.

"Jay and Gen have really stepped up since you've been gone." She took in a slow breath once more, "The bookshop is running amazingly with them in charge when I'm not there."

Pushing herself back up, she pressed the picture to her chest, "I miss you so much. The bookshop isn't the same without you there. I find myself sitting in your office just to feel close to you. With Asher not here, I feel all alone and it scares me. I don't want to be alone. I wish you were here to give me insight on how Asher is feeling about us. I wish you were here to train Shep on social media and event planning."

Another wave of tears rushed down her face, "I wish you were here to hug and tell me everything is going to be okay."

Delaney's head snapped up when she heard a knock on it. She wasn't expecting anyone tonight and for a moment she was hopeful it would be Quinn. That the last few months have all been a terrible dream. She stood up looking out the window and saw a large moving truck backing into her driveway. Suddenly, she was rushing down the stairs with a renewed hope that maybe she wouldn't have to be alone after all. Flinging opening the door, a wide smile spread across her face seeing Asher standing on the porch. He held out a sheet of paper with a bookmark attached to it.

She grabbed a pen from her bag near the door and checked the box next to Yes handing it back to Asher.

LANEY,

NEVER AGAIN WILL THOUSANDS OF MILES STAND IN OUR WAY. NEVER AGAIN WILL YOU WAKE UP ALONE OR GO TO BED WITHOUT ME TO HOLD YOU TIGHT. NEVER AGAIN WILL YOU EVER QUESTION IF YOU ARE LOVED OR WORTHY TO BE LOVED. I'M HERE TO TELL YOU HOW LOVED YOUR ARE. I'M HERE TO HOLD YOU AND TAKE CARE OF YOU. I'M HERE TO STAY IF YOU WILL HAVE ME.

LANEY, CAN I STAY FOREVER?

☑ YES

☐ NO

I LOVE YOU,
ASHER

His smile was beaming as he picked her up in his arms and spun her around. Delaney brought her lips to his sealing her answer and to mark the rest of their life to begin now.

Dear Diary,

AUGUST 2007

Still no letters from Asher and I'm starting to wonder if he even meant what he said. Maybe he realized that having a long distance girlfriend wasn't worth the trouble when he can be with college girls. That doesn't sound like the Asher I know and fell in love with, but who knows. I hear you change a lot when you go away for college. Maybe the Asher I once knew is no more and now he's like every other guy.

It still hurts that I didn't even get a proper goodbye. He could at least let me know that he's not interested anymore. Speaking of guys being interested... Ty has asked me out repeatedly since I've come back home. It's weird that the most popular guy in the school wants to be with me of all people. Quinn says I have a glow about me since coming back home. I haven't told her about Asher and I... well, you know.

I'm not sure how I feel about Ty now. Before summer, I would have maybe given him a chance but now... I'm just different. I feel different since being with Asher. Maybe I'll tell Ty I just want to be friends for now. Maybe I'll hear from Asher in the meantime.

Boys are so confusing. 

Until next time,

Smile Laney

OCTOBER 2007

Dear Diary,

That's it! I'm tired of not hearing from Asher. If he truly wanted to be with me or loved me then he would have tried to contact me somehow. It's not like I'm hard to find. After a long night of crying and a borrowed bottle of whiskey from Quinn's dad's liquor cabinet, I'm finally done waiting.

In other news, I'm going to homecoming with Ty. He's still been persistent on asking me out and I kept telling him I needed a friend right now. However, he came into the library yesterday in a full tux with some flowers (not my favorite but it's the thought that counts) and poster asking me to homecoming. How could I say no and embarrass him in front of everyone. I said yes and it was really nice to see someone so excited to be with me.

Quinn and I are going shopping for dresses tomorrow. I've decided to give Ty a real chance and try to move on from Asher. It will be super hard because I fell for him. He was everything I ever wanted in guy and he was the first one I trusted my body with. He will always hold a special place in my heart as my first love, but I can't wait around anymore. After dress shopping and buying homecoming shoes, I'm going to put all my letters and bookmarks into the shoe box. I will keep it in my closet where I won't see it and will kind of forget about it.

It makes me really sad to move on, but I'm kind of excited to see how things work out between Ty and me. As always, I'll let you know.

Until next time,
Delaney

PS: I decided when I came back this summer that I wouldn't be going by Laney anymore. Reminds me too much of him. So from now on it's Delaney.

LEIGH

One Year Later

Leigh Meyer was standing off in a corner by herself watching all of her favorite people mingling. In the distance she could hear the crowd gathering to their seats within the Scattered Pages. This event was officially the largest one they ever had and that didn't include the fact they were live streaming it on YouTube.

"Why are you standing over here being a creeper Meyer?"

She looked over to see Madison Callaway approaching her. She was finishing his first year as Asher Graham's agent. They were working closely together with Asher and Delaney Bishop's first book coming out in the upcoming weeks. She liked Madison even if she was a little green and a cowgirl which she lovingly called her.

"I'm not being a creeper, Cowgirl. I'm merely observing everyone gathering together. If you would believe it this actually makes me incredibly happy."

Madison let out a gasp, "You? Happy? Good lord mark this day on the calendar."

She playfully smacked her on the shoulder, "Don't you have something, anything else to do other than bother me."

"Yes, I'm going to go get my seat before someone tries to steal it. Break a leg, Meyer."

"Thanks Madison." She smiled when his jaw dropped.

The manager of the Scattered Pages, Jay, walked up with a microphone in his hand, "You ready?"

Leigh nodded, "Let's do this."

She walked out to the stage amazed by the sea of people in front of her. Taking her spot in front of the only single chair on stage. Leigh let out a breath then began to introduce her amazing friends.

"Hello everyone! On behalf of everyone at the Scattered Pages, we would love to thank you for spending your evening with all of our fangirls."

There was wave of applause as she continued, "Tonight is not only special because all four of our fangirls will be up here, but also the men that captured their hearts will be on stage to answer questions as well."

Now there was a roar of cheers that vibrated within Leigh's chest. She didn't know how Raelyn Burton-Jameson and Austin Jameson did this all the time.

"More importantly, this panel is in memory of a special woman. There was nothing more that Quinn Larson wanted than to have the fangirl authors have an event in the bookshop she built from the ground up with her best friend, Delaney Bishop. A little over a year ago, we sadly lost Quinn in a tragic accident, and we wanted to fulfill one of her wishes. Also, all proceeds will be going to a local non-for-profit organization that helps under privilege people of all ages, races, sexual identities to have tutors for reading and writing."

A long round of applause sounded as the Assistant Manager, Gen, revealed a new memorial plague naming the event area of the bookshop in Quinn's honor. Leigh looked off to the side to see Delaney standing next to Asher wiping tears from her face.

"Now, a few items of business before we bring out our guests. Please do not yell out a question or comment while our guests are answering someone else's question. We love polite and respectful fans. Make sure your question is related to their books or projects they may be working on. We all know you want the juicy gossip, again, please respect our guests privacy. If they want to share something then they will. Finally, there will be a signing line after our panel where all of them will sign your books or an item you have brought with you."

Leigh paused for a moment before giving the last bit of rules for a particular rockstar. Honestly, she never thought these words would ever have to come out of her mouth.

"Please, for the love of everything good, do not… I repeat. Do. Not." She looked from one side of the room to the other with her meanest glare, "Ask any of our guests to sign body parts of any kind. If you want them to sign a piece of paper to go get etch-a-sketch on your skin then by all means. There will be absolutely no signing of skin. Okay?"

There was laughter, claps and a few groans.

"Perfect now let's bring out our guests. Please welcome, Raelyn Burton-Jameson and Austin Jameson."

They walked out chuckling and waving to everyone. Austin whispered something to Raelyn that made her burst out into laughter then smack his arm.

"Laurel Ad-" Leigh stopped herself, "Sorry still getting used to this. Laurel and Zeppelin Foster."

Laurel hugged her as she walked out and whispered, "I'm still getting used to it."

"Emerson Holbrook and number 24, first baseman Pac-cey Tuck-ker!" Leigh gave her best announcer impression enjoying that Pacey was a deep shade of red.

"Last, but certainly not least. Owners of the Scattered Pages, Delaney Bishop and Asher Graham."

Leigh noticed the death grip Delaney had on Asher's arm and reached out to gently squeeze her shoulder. Delaney turned towards her and she whispered, "You got this."

As they all took their seats, Zeppelin remained standing, "Can everyone give it up for Leigh Meyer."

Everyone cheered and clapped as Zeppelin hyped them up, "Leigh, I think we're missing someone."

"Oh really? Whoever could you be talking about?"

She looked to the side of the stage to see her husband looking pointedly at his best friend on stage. She crooked her finger at him and his eyes narrowed on her. She knew she would pay for this, but the punishment was always the best part.

"Please give it up for our," Zeppelin pointed to himself and Laurel, "best friend and Leigh's sidekick, Thomas Reed!"

The events coordinator brought up another chair beside Leigh's, and she patted it as Thomas stepped up on stage. He took a mic pointing at Zeppelin.

"You'll pay for this." He looked nervously out into the crowd, "Hello everyone, I'll probably be the responsible adult of this motley crew."

The crowd laughed as he settled into his seat still glaring at Zeppelin. Leigh placed her hand on top of his knee before turning her attention to their friends.

"We're going to start with some basic questions for everyone then have a Q&A with questions from the audience and ones that were submitted by our online viewers. Y'all ready?"

They all nodded. Leigh leaned over showing Thomas the one and only she had for them to answer.

"Let's start with an update from each of you. New projects, any news or events coming up."

Raelyn picked up her mic, "I'll go first. I've been working on a new Red Moon series that follows a whole new generation of the wolf pack. The first book is in final stages and looking to release soon-ish. I'm currently drafting the second book while hanging around on set."

"Yeah, so we're still filming the Red Moon movie." Austin paused for the fans cheering, "I love being back in Rhys's boots and being back with everyone from the show. I also love that my family is able to be with me in Montana while I'm filming. Raelyn working on her book and our daughter, Bernadette, is shadowing various crew to get a feel of what it's like to work on a set."

"It's crazy to think that she's in college and majoring in creative writing. She really wants to write TV scripts or her fall back is writing a book." Raelyn shook her head, "Because writing a book is so easy."

"As someone who went to college to become an author, I'd be more than happy to give her some insights of how glamorous it is." Asher said as Austin gave him the thumbs up.

Emerson went next. "Currently, I have no plans to write a book. I've been working with Raelyn on some of her Red Moon books. I have a few ideas percolating but nothing solid. I'm now running everyone's social media accounts." She motioned to the whole group.

"That keeps me busy along with planning a wedding." Emerson looked over to Pacey, who was looking anywhere but at his fiancée, "Maybe by winter we'll finally get down the aisle."

Pacey shrugged, "Whenever and wherever, you know I'm there. I'm finishing up another season with the Explorers. Starting to think a little more seriously at what the future may hold for my career as I'm not getting any younger. Looking forward to finally making an honest woman out of Fangirl here."

Emerson punched his shoulder, "Honest woman my…" She stopped herself as everyone laughed with them.

Laurel was still laughing as she spoke, "As you may have guessed, I finally made an honest man out of the rockstar."

"Say what, now?" Zeppelin said as Laurel cocked an eyebrow at him, "Okay, she's right."

"She's always right." Thomas coughed making everyone laugh.

Laurel cleared her throat, "Anyway, we recently had a beautiful ceremony with all of our closest family and friends. We are enjoying newlywed life right now. I'm working on a new paranormal romance series that is cozy, small town vibes."

"So far it's really good." Zeppelin beamed, "Right now, Heartstrings is taking a little breather while I'm releasing my first ever solo album. We're in the early stages of planning out a summer tour in small venues. Getting back to my roots. I'm excited for everyone to hear the new music. It's pop punk meets rockabilly."

Laurel smiled, "It's amazing and I'm not just saying that. It's truly some of his best songs."

Leigh looked over to Delaney, "What about you guys? I know there is a lot going on for you both right now."

"Um, we have our new book coming out next month." Delaney said timidly, "Line of Sight is book one in our Officers of Bridgeway series. We're excited for everyone to read it or listening to it. I recently listened to the audiobook which has duet narrators and I absolutely loved it."

"We also are working on our own books that will be coming out next year." Asher was nearly bouncing out of his seat, "Thanks to my awesome agent for going to back for me. I'm getting way out of my comfort zone and writing a sci-fi western. I'm about three quarters the way through writing the first draft and absolutely loving it."

Leigh watched as Delaney relaxed as Asher spoke about his next Graham A. Jacob book, "I'm also in final edits for the first book in a new detective series. We will be following Detective Finn Blackburn as he works alongside a psychic who may or may not be seeing people's deaths beforehand. There will be a lot of paranormal and horror elements to this series."

"Delaney, I know you have a book you're working on that I'm personally excited to read." Raelyn said, leaning forward in her chair.

"Yes, yes. I'm also in final edits with my addition to the fangirl book series."

The applause and cheering was nearly deafening. Delaney truly looked stunned from the reaction of the audience. Asher ran his hand down her back.

"Leigh, do you think I can tell them?" She nodded, as Delaney smiled, "Project Bookmarks will be coming out this fall. There's small town romance, fall and summer love, and second chances."

She would never tell any of them, but Delaney's book for by far Leigh's favorite. She loved all of their love stories especially since her own love story was weaved into each of their stories.

Thomas looked over to her, "I have a question for you Leigh?"

"For me? Okay, ask away."

"Who's going to write our story? I mean I know I'm no fangirl, but I think our story would be equally as interesting." He smiled, leaning over to kiss her temple.

The crowd swooned as Leigh laughed, "I don't know. Maybe one day, I'll take off my agent hat and put on a writer hat. I know I'd have lots of support and help if I ever did."

"Damn right you would!" Emerson cheered as the other fangirls joined in with her.

"Who knows, but for now, let's get to some of our audience and those watching at home questions."

Nearly two hours later, all of them were sitting around a large table covered in pizza boxes. Everyone was exhausted but still riding the high of an amazing night. Leigh was leaning into Thomas's side as he spoke with Emerson's brother Everett, who came not only in support of his sister but also to honor Quinn. Delaney pulled a chair up next to her and handed her a sheet of paper.

"What's this?"

"A little something Raelyn and I brainstormed." It was rare to see Delaney smiling like the Cheshire Cat.

> *Title: Project Managers*
>
> *Tropes: Rivals to lovers (kind of), friends to lovers, roommates*
>
> *Leigh and Thomas's story*

She read over the scene notes they had written down and laughed, "You guys aren't serious?"

Now Raelyn was joining them as Delaney nodded, "We are. We were thinking that one of us could ghostwrite with you or co-write it. The way you and Thomas got together is pretty interesting."

"And from what I hear pretty hot as well." Raelyn chimed in.

"What?! Who…" Leigh looked over to see Zeppelin staring at them and quickly looked away, "I'm going to kill the punk before he gets the chance to tour this summer."

Delaney placed her hand on Leigh's shoulder, "You really encouraged me when I started writing Project Bookmarks. I don't think I would have ever finished it without you. Now, I want to return the favor."

"You really think…" Before she could finish all four fangirl authors were in front of her.

"Yes!" They all said at once.

Leigh laughed, "Okay, okay. I will give it some serious thought. For now, I'm going to focus on the four of you and making sure your books are the best they can be."

The five women huddled into a group hug with their men quickly joining the group as well. In the few short years that had brought them all together, Leigh couldn't imagine a better fan group… a better family to be a part of.

TOP 10

1. Still Into You – Paramore
2. Bad At Love – Halsey
3. So High School – Taylor Swift
4. Falling – Harry Styles
5. Ghost of You – 5 Seconds of Summer
6. The Only Exception – Paramore
7. Hey – Backstreet Boys
8. Just In Case – Morgan Wallen
9. You and Me – Lifehouse
10. Home Is Such A Lonely Place – Blink 182

Check out the full playlist by scanning the QR below!

ACKNOWLEDGEMENTS

I want to thank my friends for always putting up with my crazy writer ways. You all have provided me with endless support and love. I'm forever grateful to have you all in my life.

To J.A. the man who inspires me. The constant joy and light you give to the world through the roles you play and the music you create is immeasurable. Thank you for sharing your many talents with all of us fangirls.

Finally, I want to thank the woman whose unconditional love and support drives me every day. Thank you Mumsie for making me into the woman I am today. My silly little love stories wouldn't be here without you. I love you!

SNEAK PEEK

PROJECT PCA BOOK 1
COMING FALL 2026

"Why in the good god fuck are you shaking me?"

Ellie Adams peeked out from beneath her pillow. Her handsome, but extremely annoying roommate was urgently shaking her shoulder. Even in her sleepy stupor she noticed he was still wearing his clothes from yesterday.

"You're late. Whenever you start your day late you become one cranky ass bitch."

Immediately panic surged through her body springing her up from the bed and grabbing her phone. Staring at her screen anger burned over her body. She grabbed her pillow and started smacking her roommate repeatedly.

"I. Still. Had. A. Half-hour. To Sleep." He yelped with each whack, "For fuck's sake, Dawson!"

"Oh…" He smiled sheepishly, "Sorry El. If it's any consolation I have coffee and bagels ready for you in the kitchen."

She pointed towards the door, "Out. Now. Before I smother you."

He retreated through the door shutting it behind him. Ellie flopped back against her bed groaning. Deep down she truly loved Dawson Callaway like a brother. He was a great friend and overall, a wonderful man which was rare nowadays. Their physical age difference was balanced by their mental age difference making them perfect roommates and best friends.

Deciding to go ahead and get ready for the day. Grabbing her favorite worn out jeans, black tank top and bright green plaid overshirt. She walked out to the kitchen finding Dawson pouring himself a cup of coffee then leaning against the counter. Ellie could see more clearly now that his dress shirt was obviously slept in and his hair was somewhere between messy and hair pulling sex messy.

"Fun night?"

She sat down at their kitchen island taking the cup he had waiting for her. Taking that first sip of caffeine was what she needed to jump start her exhausted brain. Of course he had made her coffee perfectly. Taking another sip, she sighed and smiled up at Dawson.

"Now, I forgive you."

Dawson chuckled, looking down at his clothes. "Yeah, it was a good night. Did you end up with my brothers at The Horseshoe?"

Ellie shook her head, "Hell no, I know better than to go out with Grayson and Mason on a work night. Plus, I stayed with Hudson to help finish with inventory of supplies."

"Ohh… romantic late night with Hudson counting supplies." Dawson teased.

"Shut your mouth. There's nothing romantic about counting tools, mechanic parts and vet meds."

Ellie thought back on Hudson leaning against the worktable writing in his notebook. How attentive he was to double checking his numbers. Making her wonder if he was as attentive in other areas of his life as he was with inventory.

"El, you're drooling." Dawson laughed.

She shook her head getting the eldest Callaway brother out of her head, "Am not. As I've told you a million times before. I had a schoolgirl crush on Hudson a long time ago. He's my manager, my employer and there are absolutely no feelings or attraction there. None."

Dawson walked towards her, patting her shoulder. "You keep telling yourself that. Have a good day at the ranch. I'm going to bed."

"I hate you." She called out.

"Love you too!" She heard his door close and Ellie groaned burying her head in her hands.

It was no surprise Dawson could see through her denial. Of course, her feelings for Hudson only got worse as she started working for him. Four years of yearning for the man who risked his relationship with his best friend to show her the ropes of working on a ranch. Fantasizing about the man who held her as a child as she watched her mom being loaded up into an ambulance.

Hudson Callaway had been there for her on the worst day of her life, helped her pick up the pieces after being disowned by her father and celebrated every success with her since coming to the Callaway Ranch. However, she was pretty sure he thought of her as a daughter and not the young woman who wanted nothing more than be with him in every way possible. His partner. His confidant. Just his.

Looking up at the clock on the stove, Ellie figured getting a head start on her morning chores wouldn't be a bad thing. Getting her well-worn brown cowboy boots on and grabbing her baseball cap pulling her hair through the back of it. She headed out to Ruby, her bright red 1992 Chevy S10 pickup truck, she headed down to the barn to begin her day.

ABOUT THE AUTHOR

Nikki Rae resides in St. Louis, Missouri. She spends her days as a high school secretary working in the school library. She loves to read, play Dungeons and Dragons, attend concerts, fan conventions, and snuggle with any of her cats that deem her worthy of their time.